Th

The Deal

Detective Inspector Strong [illegible] a plan to use Andy Austin, a wanted murderer, to help him deliver justice to serious criminals the police aren't able to convict by conventional means. As Strong gets more and more confident with his scheme, he begins to make mistakes and leave himself exposed to a greater risk of being caught and ruining his career. This is the second great book in the DI Strong crime thriller series, following on from The Anniversary.

Other books by Ian Anderson:

Jack's Lottery Plan

This is the funny and moving story of Jack Burns. One day he finds out that a friend has secretly won the lottery and he embarks on a clandestine plan to get a share. But his plan goes hopelessly wrong impacting Jack and his friends in ways he would never have imagined.

Jack's Big Surprise

Jack Burns is planning a surprise proposal for his girlfriend Hannah. But as is usually the way with Jack, his plan doesn't quite go the way he was hoping it would. Instead he finds himself hopelessly involved in a series of hilariously funny, and sometimes, unfortunate incidents. This is the sequel to Jack's Lottery Plan and finds Jack just as chaotic as he always is.

The Anniversary

In the first book of the DI Strong crime thriller series, Andy Austin's family are killed in a road accident. With a sense of injustice, he becomes obsessed on seeking revenge. He befriends DI Strong and uses him to help carry out his plan. As the police get closer to catching him it becomes clear that not everyone is without a guilty secret.

For more information, please visit my website at:
www.ianandersonhome.wixsite.com/ianandersonauthor

Or find me on Facebook at:
www.facebook.com/IanAndersonAuthor

The Deal

By

Ian Anderson

Author website:
www.iananadersonhome.wixsite.com/iananadersonauthor

Facebook:
www.facebook.com/IanAndersonAuthor

Chapter 1

Detective Inspector Strong was sitting alone in his office. As was often the case. He liked his own space. Strong was leaning back in his black leather chair, official DI level approved furniture, his long legs stretched out under the desk with his ankles interlocked, a pair of size ten black brogues pointing skywards. It had been a quiet few weeks. Thankfully. Just the usual collection of drunks, addicts, petty thieves and domestic violence. Often all interlinked in some way or other. And, on top of that, some people who were just angry for no obvious reason. There's nowt as queer as folk. He knew he should be pleased that these were the only crimes happening on his patch. In today's society they were just seen as "normal" crimes. They were somehow acceptable. This is what today's world had become. Strong knew it wasn't unusual to walk through any city or town across the country and see people sleeping in shop doorways underneath a makeshift combination of clothing and cardboard, many of them with a drug or alcohol dependency. Yet they'd all started out the same when they were born, how had they come to this? This was the sort of mess that the police were now expected to clean up.

Still that wasn't really Strong's concern, not in his capacity as a DI anyhow. He was glad to leave all that to the politicians to debate. Thankfully it wasn't one of the many statistics he or his team were measured on, and that was what seemed to matter in the job of a policeman now. Strangely, as head of the Serious Crime Squad, DI Strong's job was to minimise serious crimes and so, in theory, to do himself and his team out of a job. On that basis they had been very successful over the last few weeks with hardly any new "serious crime" reported. Strong knew It wouldn't be long before the accountants came around and started cutting their budgets again. Short-termism - another modern day life problem.

But DI Strong knew that this relatively quiet period wouldn't last, and knowing that was what kept him going. He hadn't joined the police force all those years ago, more than he cared to remember, to sit around in an office and answer emails. If he'd wanted to do that he could have been an office worker or the accountant that his mother had hoped he would become when he was at school. Not that there was anything wrong with that, it just wasn't him. He needed action, risk, uncertainty.

He could still remember the two of them meeting the school careers advisor on a rainy February morning, many years ago. They were both sat on plastic school chairs, both of them damp from the walk to school in the drizzle. His mother asking about accounting and law careers and him keen to ask about the army and police force, but too shy to speak up. Like any mother, she had wanted her son to be safe and the thought of him having to deal with violent people had always scared her, but in the end he had got his way and he joined the police as soon as he left school.

Even now, after all this time, Strong still craved the excitement of being a policeman and he knew that soon there would be another significant crime case for him, and his team, to work on and resolve. A dispute that had got out of hand, someone carrying a knife, maybe combined with too much drugs or booze…then a point of no return. Once you'd crossed that line, there was no way out. No way back. He'd seen it many times and he could feel it in his bones now. No-one was born a criminal but he was old enough, and he had seen enough, to understand how easily it happened and how it would always continue to be that way, no matter what the politicians said or did.

He was looking out of his office window at the grey overcast sky, hoping that the sun might break through. It had threatened to a couple of times, but after a quick peek it had rushed back into hiding behind the clouds again. It was that time of year, with winter approaching, where any sunshine was welcome. Somehow it seemed to lift everyone's spirits, but it wasn't playing ball today.

Strong was about to walk down to the main office where his team worked, just to stretch his legs and remind them that he was in the office today, when there was a soft knock on his office door and one of his support team, Marsha, stepped inside. She wasn't a regular visitor to Strong's office and he smiled and welcomed her in, beckoning her to sit on the grey plastic seat in front of his desk. Bigger, but similar in style to those old school chairs he'd sat in many years before. Strong had asked about getting better chairs in his office but apparently these were the standard offerings for his grade and the only way to get any others was through some sort of medical evaluation, based on how often they were used and whether any of the regular users had back problems. Strong couldn't be bothered going through the process and so stuck with the grey plastic visitors chairs. Marsha sat down, upright, with her back straight and knees locked together. Excellent posture, she shouldn't have any back problems. Strong pulled his legs back towards him, sitting up, whilst dragging his chair nearer to his desk, unconsciously mimicking her position. Strong had known Marsha since the early days of his police career and had found her to be a very quiet, but diligent member of the team. You needed all sorts of personalities in a successful team and Marsha played her part. He guessed she was now in her late-forties or maybe slightly older. He never liked guessing women's ages, experience had shown him he wasn't very good at it. Other than the fact she was a good worker, he was slightly embarrassed that he knew very little else about Marsha. In fact, he couldn't even recall her surname. He must have known it sometime and seen it on emails, but he couldn't remember. He had heard once that she had been married with a child but her husband had died while the child was still a baby. But maybe that was someone else.

However, despite not knowing much of her personal details, Marsha had become very useful to Strong. Over the years he had found that he could ask her to do things confidentially for him. Things that he didn't want any of the rest of the team to know about, and he had complete confidence that Marsha would keep their secret. It was the nature of his work, sometimes Strong needed to get some information on the quiet, just to get things done. There were too many rules and regulations trying to stop you doing what needed to be done. Marsha was great for that and never questioned why he needed the detail he was asking her to find for him. He suspected that she might have a bit of a crush on him, he noticed she often blushed when he spoke to her, but that might have just been Strong's superior status. Either way, Strong was just happy that she seemed to be able to do anything he asked of her, without anyone else knowing. Over the years, she had been invaluable to him on a number of occasions.

Strong looked across the desk at his colleague. Marsha was always smartly dressed, usually a perfectly ironed white blouse and dark skirt, black tights and shoes. Standard office dress. Her hair was always cut neatly, dark and shoulder length with a few grey ones now poking through, which somehow gave her an air of simple elegance. Maybe she was older than he'd thought? In some ways she looked perfect, but you could also pass her in the street without even noticing her. Maybe not a bad thing, Strong thought. He realised, as always, she was respecting his seniority and so waiting for him to speak first.

'Hi Marsha, how are you?' Strong started with a smile.

'Oh, I'm fine sir,' she replied and Strong noticed her cheeks beginning to redden. 'I've got something I think you probably want to know. Is this a convenient time?'

'Sure, carry on,' Strong nodded his head, intrigued at what Marsha had for him.

'Well you remember last year you gave me a few names of people, and asked me to find out if any of them had popped up anywhere, and we found one of them had gone to Spain?'

'Yes, I remember,' Strong replied, leaning forward in his chair. His thoughts going back to the previous year when they'd been trying to catch a double murderer, Andy Austin, who he knew was using a number of alternative identities. He'd given the names to Marsha and she'd reported back a few days later that one of them had turned up in a remote town in Spain. Strong had hoped that he could use that information to stop Austin, who the Press had dubbed "The Anniversary Killer" but that hadn't happened and Strong knew Austin was still out there, somewhere. Thankfully murders were still quite rare, Strong could count on one hand the number he'd had to deal with since becoming the head of Serious Crime. So the fact that Andy Austin had done it twice had been big news, and there had been a lot of pressure on Strong's team to catch him which so far they had been unable to do.

'Well one of them, a James Gilmour, arrived into Southend Airport on a flight from Barcelona two days ago. I'm sorry it's been two days but my contact in the Border Force didn't tell me until today. Apparently he wasn't working yesterday,' Marsha said, her cheeks turning redder as she spoke.

'Mmm…' Strong replied and he picked up his pen and started turning it round and round in his hands. Marsha didn't know if he was pleased or upset. She hoped he didn't think it was her fault that he was only getting the information now, she knew she couldn't have told him any sooner and wondered if she should make that doubly clear to him. She didn't want him to feel that she'd failed him in any way. Before she could decide what to do, Strong stopped twiddling and spoke.

'Thank you for that Marsha, that's really helpful,' he said and he smiled at her making her blush even more deeply. Marsha was just relieved that he didn't seem to be upset with her for the delay. She'd no idea who this James Gilmour was or why Strong wanted to know his whereabouts. It was just one of the little things he asked her to do for him every now and again.

'Do you have anything else on this James Gilmour? Any idea where he went from Southend, did he hire a car or is there any CCTV of him at the airport?' Strong asked.

'Nothing has come up yet,' Marsha replied, 'I only got the information an hour ago so I'm still checking. I've contacted the car hire companies based at the airport but I'm not sure how extensive the CCTV is there. I can let you know later today.'

'Thank you Marsha, please do. For now let's continue to keep this to ourselves but as soon as you hear anything else please come and see me or call me on my mobile. Don't worry about disturbing me, this is important,' Strong said and he turned to look at his laptop.

Marsha took this as a sign that the conversation was over and she got up from her chair and left Strong's office, closing the door quietly behind her and allowing herself a little smile.

Strong was looking at the calendar on his laptop. It was early November, around six weeks away from the anniversary of the accident two years ago. The accident which had kicked all this off, resulting in the deaths of two innocent people last year. The accident which meant he had six weeks to find Andy Austin, or James Gilmour as he might now be known, before he restarted his mission to kill even more innocent people.

Strong could remember all the details as clearly as if it had happened yesterday. Two years ago, a young man called Jack Wilson had been driving home with three of his friends after a Friday night out. Lads out on the town. The date was the fifteenth of December. Wilson seemingly lost control of his car and ploughed into Andy Austin and four of his family who were walking home after a night out at a local restaurant. Tragically, Austin had been the only survivor, with apparently only minor injuries. Wilson was banned from driving for a year, and after the case Strong had built up an unlikely friendship of sorts with Austin. They'd both felt strongly that justice hadn't been done in this case and Strong helped Austin develop a plan to make amends for this apparent injustice. Strong had helped him with tips on how to avoid being caught by the police and given him a contact to help him change his identity. He had thought that Austin would perhaps take out some retribution on the driver, Jack Wilson. Maybe a bit of a beating, and that would be the end of it. Just what he deserved. What Strong hadn't realised was that Austin was suffering from a form of PTSD and his plans for delivering justice were much more severe than Strong had ever imagined. Austin's condition meant that he *needed* all of the occupants of the car that night to suffer in exactly the same way that he had suffered, which in his eyes meant that they each had to experience the loss of a close relative. Austin had already killed two innocent people, both relatives of the men in the car, and he was preparing to kill two more when the police finally tracked him down to a remote farmhouse. Although he managed to escape and flee the country, at least the other two intended victims were found safe and largely unharmed. However, Austin had left a message which left the police in no doubt that he would be back the following year to try and finish, what he saw as, his mission. He'd also given Strong information that suggested that Wilson may have been deliberately trying to run Austin down that night, that it hadn't really been the simple accident everyone had assumed, but there was no way to prove that.

With the help of Marsha, Strong had tracked Austin down to a remote town somewhere in Spain and he had tried to blackmail Jack Wilson, the car driver, into finishing him off, but he knew it was a long shot and that Wilson wasn't really a killer. Still it would have been a neat outcome for Strong, tying off several loose ends in the process. What Strong didn't know was that Wilson had secretly recorded their meeting and had kept it in case he needed to use it as a future safeguard. After Strong realised Wilson wasn't going to do anything, they'd lost track of Austin again and Strong assumed that he was probably using another identity. But as none of the false identities he knew about had surfaced anywhere he guessed that Austin had been clever and not relied solely on the contact Strong had given him. Austin must have also used a second forger for new identity papers and up until now Austin had been off radar again.

But now it seemed Austin was back and he'd used one of the identities that Strong had known about to re-enter the country. Was that a deliberate sign for Strong, he wondered? Another message? When he'd escaped the year before, he had left a message, scrawled in red paint on the farm wall, saying he'd be back next year. According to Doctor Collins, the police psychologist, the type of PTSD Austin had apparently meant that the date of the accident, the fifteenth of December, was of significant importance to him and he needed to carry out his retribution around that same date, exactly reflecting the timescales of his own relatives' deaths. Strong couldn't help thinking that Austin had deliberately used this James Gilmour identity as a challenge to Strong to let him know that he was back. A challenge he would have to accept.

As far as Strong was concerned, the gloves were off now. Austin had gone way beyond Strong's idea of the sense of justice he felt they had discussed, and it was his duty to stop him before he did anything else. Of course he hadn't known about the PTSD at the time and if he had he wouldn't have been so helpful to Austin. A lesson learned, he wouldn't make that mistake again. He realised he'd got too involved partly because of the similar circumstances of his own parents death. He picked up his phone and punched a few buttons.

'Gillian, can you tell DS Campbell I want to see him in my office as soon as possible and can you also get a hold of Doctor Sam Collins from the Police Psychology section and see if she is available also.'

'Yes sir, will do,' Gillian replied and Strong disconnected the call and sat back in his chair with a sigh. Six weeks and the clock had just started ticking.

Chapter 2

Andy Austin slowly opened his eyes and immediately closed them again. Too bright. The sun was already up and the morning light was shining through the thin, light-blue bedroom curtains. His head was aching. He reached across to the bedside table and felt for his bottle of painkillers. He opened it up and shook out two of the small, white tablets into the palm of his hand before throwing them into his mouth and swallowing them as one. He put the bottle back on the cabinet and reached for the glass of water he knew was also there. He took a long gulp before pulling himself up on the headboard and opening his eyes again. It was still very bright. He should buy a blackout blind, but then he wasn't planning to be here for too long. Two months maximum. He rubbed both hands over his face, feeling the bristle of his beard, and then up through his hair before scratching the top of his head and yawning. He extended his back and legs, flattening them on the bed, his toes pointing out over the end of the mattress. He lay like that for a few moments then let himself relax, exhaling fully.

Turning his head to one side, he looked at the clock. It was seven a.m. on another cold, bright

November morning. He hadn't slept well again, he just couldn't get comfortable, no matter what position he tried, and then sometime during the night the headache had come back. He'd taken some pills and must have snoozed for a bit, but it didn't feel like it. His headaches were getting more frequent and lasting longer and he knew he was taking more of the pills than he was supposed to. But what else could he do? At least they had some effect, even if it was only for a few hours. Maybe he could get stronger painkillers, but he doubted it. He knew these ones were already pretty strong and they gave him mood swings as a side effect. All the doctors had advised him on having an operation but he didn't want to do that. At least not before he'd finished what he had to do. And after that he didn't really care what happened.

In the periods when he had managed to sleep, he'd dreamt about Lucy, his ex-girlfriend. That was also something that was happening more frequently. Always Lucy. Lately the dreams had also been more vivid and he'd sometimes wake up thinking they were actually happening, surprised to find that he was on his own with no Lucy. In this latest one, the two of them were on holiday together, somewhere hot, on the beach. Maybe a Mediterranean island. It was one of those small, horseshoe shaped bays you see in holiday adverts and there were only a few people on the beach. The golden sandy beach merging into the clear blue water. Andy and Lucy were sunbathing, Lucy was reading a book, and Andy had got up and walked into the sea. It was warm and cool at the same time.

Perfect. He swam out about thirty metres and then turned around to wave back at Lucy, but he couldn't see her. The beach had suddenly got crowded and he stood there scanning all the faces. They all seemed to be looking at him, but none of the faces belonged to Lucy. He started to swim back in to the shore but, even though he felt himself going forward, he didn't seem to be getting any closer to the beach. He was definitely moving but the shoreline also seemed to be moving too, getting further away. He felt himself tiring and slipping under the water. He tried to get to the surface but he couldn't. A shoal of tiny fish had gathered around him, above him, and they seemed to be multiplying in numbers blocking out the light until everything turned dark blue. Then he woke up, sweating and gasping for breath.

He so wanted to see Lucy again, just to talk to her, even if only for a few minutes. Just to see that she was okay. He wanted her to be okay. She hadn't deserved the hurt he'd put her through and it was the one thing he'd always regret. He didn't regret the killings, but he did feel guilty about what he had done to Lucy. It had never been his intention to hurt her, but in hindsight there was never going to be any other outcome, no matter what happened. He knew he'd deceived her. They'd been living together when she found out who he really was and what he'd been doing. He'd left her a letter trying to explain why, why he *had* to do it. But he knew that wasn't enough for her, she deserved more. It wasn't something you could properly get across in a simple letter. She deserved the truth and he could only give her that if he could spend enough time with her to explain. But that was impossible.

He had seen her once since he'd had to leave. Not long after he'd escaped the country, he was hiding out in Spain and he'd spotted her sitting across the street in a café with a friend. It's a small world. She must have been there on holiday. He couldn't believe it at first, but it was definitely Lucy, he couldn't mistake that face. Lucy's face. She looked so beautiful and, although he had changed his appearance, he was pretty sure she'd recognised him too. He knew it was too soon to approach her, to try and talk to her and maybe she had felt the same. They'd exchanged a brief half smile and then she'd driven off with her friend. He hadn't seen her again since. Maybe it was a sign? But a sign of what, Andy didn't know.

He knew she still lived in the same flat they'd once shared, and he desperately wanted to see her again, to talk to her, but he knew that such a meeting would put her in an impossible situation. Knowing Lucy as well as he did, he believed she would feel that she had no choice but to do the right thing and tell the police if he contacted her. Despite what they had once had, he wouldn't expect her to do anything else. Her honesty was one of the things he loved about her. If it had just impacted him then maybe he would have taken the risk, but he knew it could only bring more pain and hurt to Lucy again and that was the last thing he wanted to do. Maybe it was better that he just forgot about her and let her get on with her life, but….

He eased himself slowly out of bed and stepped into the shower. He turned the tap and let the steaming, hot water soak his hair and run slowly down his face and body. Ah, that was nice. After a few minutes he began to feel a bit better and ready to get on with the day. Some days, these two minutes in the shower, under the hot water, were the best he felt all day. He left the bathroom and slowly towelled himself dry. As he got dressed he began to think about DI Strong and wondered if he knew that he was back in the country. He guessed he did, he knew Strong was clever, but also careful, and he'd have been surprised if he hadn't been keeping track of his movements under the various aliases he had used. Strong would know about some of them. But now he was living under another alias, from his second source, and there was a chance Strong wouldn't know about that, but even then Andy couldn't be certain. Strong seemed to know many people, a lot of them in the criminal underworld, and so there was every chance he could easily know the second forger he had used too. He knew Strong had been a policeman for a long time and he seemed to have a wide network of contacts so he wasn't taking anything for granted, being as careful as he could.

The risk now was that he knew Strong would try and catch him before anyone else got hurt. Although Andy didn't agree with him, he knew Strong thought things had gone too far and he would do all he could to stop him killing anyone else. He didn't have the detective "on his side" any more. Andy realised it wasn't going to be as easy this time, they'd be ready for him. Last year Strong had indirectly helped by not using all the information he had on him, but he knew Strong hadn't expected him to kill anyone and so it would be different this time. He was probably trying to find him already and he had to be very wary of that.

But Andy felt he had an advantage. He guessed that Strong and the police would be assuming he would try and do things exactly the same again, as he had last year. They'd know who his targets were and they would know that he planned to strike on the fifteenth of December, the date of the anniversary of the accident. The accident that had wiped out his family. And that was where he felt he had one up on them. In reality, Andy knew it would be practically impossible to do anything on that day, the police would be everywhere, waiting for him, and so he had already decided to do it before then. And with different targets this time. He knew that was his only chance of getting any deserved retribution for the suffering of his family. Maybe it wasn't what he hoped he could do initially, not his perfect plan, but needs must and it was good enough. The police wouldn't be able to watch all of the two remaining men's friends and relatives over a long period and so he knew that would be the best way of completing his mission. And they'd still experience the suffering he had when their relatives died, which was all that this was about. He'd finally get justice.

In truth he was also beginning to feel weary about the whole thing and he just wanted to get it finished. He had to do it. He'd had another year to think about things and he'd convinced himself that it didn't really matter who he killed, or when he killed them, as long as the outcome was that the four men who had murdered his family went through the same kind of suffering that he had endured. It never went away. He had achieved that for two of them last year and now he just needed to finish the job with the remaining two.

He switched on his laptop and, after making himself a mug of hot, black coffee, he sat down at the table and typed in his password. He'd virtually completed his research and felt pretty confident that he'd identified the two best alternative victims to ensure the two remaining car killers, as he thought of them, suffered as much as he had. He opened a document on his laptop and read their two names out aloud,

'Dan Sears and Jason Reynolds.'

Last year he had planned to kill one of Dan Sears' cousins, a man called Kevin Green - along with Bill Reynolds, who was Jason Reynolds' father. He had kidnapped them both and was holding the two of them in a rented farmhouse, waiting for the exact days to kill them to equate to the dates when his father and cousin had died. It was all going to plan. But before that day had arrived, Strong had called him warning that the police were on their way and he'd had to leave them in the old barn. He smiled when he thought of Bill Reynolds. He was a fighter and at one point he'd almost escaped from Austin but luckily he'd managed to recapture him. He couldn't help feeling a bit of admiration for the old boy. In another life maybe things would have been different but not this one with him being Jason Reynold's father. This year though he'd decided to switch the targets around, choosing Dan Sears' father and one of Jason Reynolds' cousins. Hopefully they would be as easy to get, and he had no intention of holding them captive this time around. That was what had gone wrong last year. His plan now was that they would just be simple, straight killings. In and out, quick as you like, just as he had done with the first two. That was much easier. He'd also found out that Kevin Green was now working away from home, somewhere in the Middle East, according to his social media, so that had also helped him justify his changed plan.

Another reason he had decided to try and carry out his revenge quicker, and in a less complicated way, was his deteriorating health. He knew he was getting worse and he didn't know how much longer he would be able to physically carry on. He was struggling and it was only his determination and the adrenalin that kept him going. He'd seen a doctor when he'd been living in Spain and the doctor had talked about a year or so before…well he didn't go into detail, but Austin knew the implied meaning. That meant he only had a couple of months left to finish his mission. Probably ideal timing. He was definitely getting worse, apart from the increased headaches he was also getting more irritable, sometimes more aggressive and certainly less predictable. He didn't really care about anyone or anything anymore, except for two things. Getting the job finished and seeing Lucy one more time. Those two things occupied his thoughts day and night.

Chapter 3

The meeting with Detective Sergeant Campbell and Doctor Collins in Strong's office had been fairly brief and confirmed most of what DI Strong had already thought. He liked those sort of meetings, no surprises and no one trying to prove a point. The three of them worked well together. DS Campbell was Strong's trusted right hand man. They had worked on many cases over the last few years, including the Austin case the previous year, the case that became known as the anniversary murders. Campbell was a good policeman, very structured and hardworking with some good ideas and Strong had also found him a useful sounding board. He had a stocky build and always reminded Strong of a middle-weight boxer. Campbell wasn't as politically aware as Strong, which was one of the reasons he hadn't made DI yet, but Strong knew that was probably just a matter of time. He was getting there, but Strong was happy to have him as his DS for now, they made a good team and Strong knew he could manage Campbell.

Doctor Sam Collins was in her late twenties, long blond hair and attractive, but at the same time very professional. She was smart and extremely dedicated to her work. She had aspirations to become an expert in a particular area of crime psychology, someone that people would go to for advice on a specific subject. Doctor Collins had been called into the anniversary murders case last year, to come up with a profile of Andy Austin so that the police had a better idea of who he was, why he was murdering people and, most critically, what he might do next. Strong had been impressed by her analysis and so he was keen to keep her in the loop. It was the first time she'd worked with DI Strong and she'd been pleasantly surprised by his attitude. He listened to what she had to say and took her seriously, unlike other senior policemen she'd worked with in the past who'd regarded her field of psychology as "airy-fairy" nonsense. One detective had even said that out loud at a team meeting and the rest of the team had laughed along with him. They didn't know Sam Collins though. She'd lived with prejudices all her life and every time something like that happened, it just made her more determined to succeed. She hoped that when they finally caught Andy Austin, Strong would let her have some time with him so that she could get an even deeper understanding of his illness. She had ambitions of writing a research paper on his condition and become one of the world's experts in that field.

Strong told his two colleagues that he had a tip-off that Austin was back in the country, apparently using the name James Gilmour, although he could now be using a different alias. After some discussion, both Campbell and, more significantly, Doctor Collins had concluded that Austin would probably attack the same two people in the same way that he'd done last year. Doctor Collins explained that the form of PTSD she believed Austin was suffering from meant that those people, and the date, were extremely significant factors to Austin and that he would feel a compulsion to finish the job, as he saw it, according to those rules. She had done a lot of research on the subject and although there were only a few documented cases, she felt pretty confident in her analysis. She'd learnt in her short career so far that you had to appear confident, even if you had some underlying doubts. Senior police officers didn't want "might-be's" or "maybes" – they wanted facts and definites, no flim-flam. Doctor Collins knew that in all of the other cases she'd looked at, the perpetrator had been caught within a few weeks of becoming violent and so had not suffered with this condition for as long as Austin had. She knew that meant she didn't know for certain what the longer term effects were. Did it change in any way, for better or worse, as time went on? She wouldn't know until they caught Austin and she was able to spend some time with him. At this point though she felt reasonably comfortable, in the absence of any contradictory evidence, that Austin would carry on with his violent activities until he'd achieved his overwhelming objective of ensuring equal suffering for the four men in the car.

'As you may remember, the specific condition Austin has is called PTED, post traumatic embitterment disorder. He's suffering a severe pathological reaction to the accident that killed his family which means he needs revenge. It's what he lives for. He needs someone to blame, and for them to suffer in the same way that he has, so that they understand. In his case it's the four young men who were in the car that night,' Doctor Collins explained. 'He sees them all as being equally responsible for what happened and they all need to pay for that.'

DI Strong listened closely. Although he still had some reservations about the benefit of using a police psychologist, he had been surprisingly impressed by Doctor Collins' input during the investigation previously and so he was keen to get her views again now that Austin had re-appeared. As always, he wanted to be prepared and fully in control.

'Is there any chance he might vary it this time?' DS Campbell asked. 'He'll know we will be watching Bill Reynolds and Kevin Green and that we'll be ready for him, especially in the period around the fifteenth of December. Might he try another relative of one of the men, or even try and get them at a different time?'

'Of course that might be possible, but I would say unlikely,' Doctor Collins replied confidently. 'I think, because of his PTED, the detail of the date and the victims will be key to him and he won't necessarily know that the police are aware of that, so I think he'll stick to that plan. The fact that he's come back into the country now would also appear to back that up.'

'Okay, agreed. But we may need to be flexible, just in case,' Campbell replied.

'Of course,' Doctor Collins replied, 'nothing is definite, these are our best assumptions, based on what we know about Austin and his condition.'

'One other thing I'd like your opinion on Doctor Collins,' Strong said looking directly at the woman across the desk from him. 'It was pretty easy for my source to find out that Austin was back in the country, I can't go into details, but do you think he was careless or he actually wanted us to know that he was back?'

'Yeh, remember he left that painted message on the wall at the farm, "see you next year" wasn't it? It's like he's taunting us,' Campbell added.

Doctor Collins thought about this for a minute, it wasn't something she'd come across before and there had been nothing like that in the other PTED cases she'd looked at, at least nothing had been documented like that. She didn't want to jump to a conclusion and get it wrong, perhaps destroying the credibility she felt she'd already built up with DI Strong.

'I don't know, is the honest answer. Let me think about it. He hasn't made too many mistakes so far, although you did manage to track him down to that farm. I'm not sure why he'd want to send you a message. It's not like he knows you personally..., oh wait, you did meet him once didn't you? I remember you saying. Did anything happen then that would lead him to think this was something more personal?' Doctor Collins asked Strong.

'No, I don't think so. It was only once after the original accident and I was only sitting in on an interview on behalf of a colleague. I doubt he would even remember me,' Strong replied, keen to shut that avenue of conversation down. The less talk there was about him and Austin knowing each other, no matter how slight, the better. He needed to keep a lid on that.

The three of them had gone on to discuss what they should do next and DI Strong impressed upon his colleagues that it was imperative to keep Austin's return as quiet as possible for now. The fewer people that knew the better, and that included within their own team. The three of them needed to work on this a bit further before they involved anyone else. They also didn't want word getting out to any of the families, especially since the car occupants had tried to take matters into their own hands the last time and that had caused them to miss the chance of capturing Austin at the farm. The car driver, Jack Wilson, had got there first and scared Austin off before the police arrived. Strong also stated that they needed to make sure it didn't hit the press. There must be no leaks. Strong could imagine the tabloid headlines,

"Return of the Anniversary Killer"

And he knew that his boss, the Chief Constable, would be especially keen that none of this leaked out. The Chief hated it when the press sensationalised any of the cases they were working on and he'd come down hard on some of Strong's colleagues in the past when they had been found to be a source of any unauthorised news story. At this point Strong wanted to remain in control and he knew he could trust Campbell and Collins. The DI was hopeful that, with the help of Marsha, he might be able to track Austin down on his own in the next week or two and if he did then he could manage things from there. Stay in control.

With them just finding out that Austin was back in the country, there was still a possibility that he might not be planning to return to his killing spree, even though they all thought that was pretty unlikely. The three of them knew they still had a few weeks to try and find Austin before the anniversary date of the accident, and silently Strong hoped *he'd* be able to do that himself, but, as a group, they decided it would be prudent to start preparing now by informing his potential victims. The two men he'd likely be targeting. DS Campbell was given the task of going to see Bill Reynolds and Kevin Green and discretely arranging appropriate security measures for them, but also stressing that they shouldn't tell any of the original four car occupants. The last thing they wanted was Jack Wilson and his friends messing things up again.

They also decided that both Strong and Campbell would go and visit Lucy Morris, who had been Austin's girlfriend at the time of the murders. She needed to be aware that he was back in the country too and there was also the chance that she might have heard from him, or that he would try to contact her. Austin had been living with Lucy at the time of the murders, under the false name of Paul Smith, but Lucy hadn't known anything about his real identity. When she did find out she had reported it to the police and that led to them finding Austin's farmhouse hideaway. Doctor Collins was keen to come along and meet her too, but Strong decided otherwise.

'I'd like to keep this under the radar as much as possible,' he explained. 'DS Campbell and I have both met her before and so we can position it as a friendly follow up call, keep it informal. I think if we brought you along too, it would look too official. Might scare her off, especially if she has heard from Austin. Of course if anything significant comes out of it, we'll let you know. You've been a great help so far and I'd like to keep you involved, if that's okay with you?'

'Of course, I understand. I'm happy to help in any way and would love to stay involved,' Doctor Collins replied. She was partly disappointed by his response, meeting the girlfriend might have given her some great insights into Austin, but in truth this was by far the most interesting case she'd worked on since joining the police, and she had ambitions to see it through to the end. She needed to keep on-side with DI Strong and by doing so she hoped she'd be able to interview both Austin and his girlfriend at some point as input for her planned, ground-breaking medical paper on PTED. She knew that would be great publicity for her and the key to potentially open up all sorts of career options.

Strong was keen to get things moving and so he wrapped up the meeting fairly quickly and Campbell and Collins both departed, leaving him sitting alone in his office. So far, Marsha had not found any further trace of James Gilmour since he had entered the country at Southend airport. Nor had there been any hint of Austin using any of the other names on the list Strong had previously given Marsha. The most likely conclusion was that Austin must be using another false ID and that he must have got that from another source. Another underworld forger. He opened his briefcase and took out a small mobile phone. He scanned his contact list, selected a name and hit dial. After a few rings someone answered.

'Hello stranger,' the voice said.

'I need a favour,' Strong replied.

'I guessed it wasn't a social call,' the voice said. 'What do you need?'

'The guy I put in contact with you last year, Andy Austin, I think he's using someone else too. I need to know who. Can you find out?' Strong said.

'I can ask around, there's not that many can do what I do,' the voice replied.

'Can you get on it now? I need to know pretty quickly,' Strong said.

'Okay, I get the message, I'll call you when I find anything out,' the voice replied.

'I'll be waiting,' Strong said and hung up.

He slipped the phone back into his briefcase and turned to resume work on his laptop, happy that he had things reasonably under control and confident that he would find Austin soon.

Chapter 4

DS Campbell had made contact with Austin's two potential targets, Bill Reynolds and Kevin Green. Both had been challenging, but in different ways. People were always different, never quite what you expected. Bill Reynolds had seemed almost pleased to hear that Austin was back in the country.

'Let him come. I'll be ready for him this time. He won't know what's hit him. Thinks I'm an easy target does he? Let him try.' The old fighter in him was still alive and raring to go.

They'd met at Bill Reynold's house, a well-maintained, Victorian style, semi-detached house on a quiet street, all with small front gardens. Lawns bordered by flower beds, although there weren't many flowers out at this time of year, but Campbell could imagine it looking a pretty street come springtime. It took Campbell some time, and the help of Bill's wife Vera, a small but determined woman, to calm him down enough for him to agree to listen, and work with the police to help bring Austin to justice. Campbell guessed this wasn't the first time Mrs Reynolds had needed to talk her husband out of doing something she didn't think was right. Even then, Campbell wasn't wholly convinced that, given the chance, Bill wouldn't try and get Austin on his own to deal out his own form of punishment. He was old school and wanted his own revenge, not some namby-pamby jail term where he got three meals a day, a gym, watched TV and perhaps did a degree. That wasn't proper punishment in Bill's eyes. This Austin needed a touch of his own medicine. A good kicking. Bill had tried it once before, but it hadn't been a level playing field then. In fact it had been a muddy field and Bill had lost a shoe and Austin hit him with a golf club. Not a fair fight. He'd like to get Austin in a boxing ring, just the two of them and see who came out on top then. He'd teach him a thing or two.

DS Campbell knew about the previous time when Bill had tried to escape from Austin's farm and guessed that he wanted revenge for that. Campbell, and again Bill's wife, had to remind him that they couldn't accept any vigilante type of action and he should let the police do their work. It was the best way. It wouldn't do Bill any good landing up with an assault charge would it?

Campbell assigned a police officer to watch the house, and more specifically to keep an eye on Bill whenever he went out. Even though he was in his mid-sixties, Campbell guessed the policeman would have his hands full trying to keep tabs on him. He could imagine Bill doing all sorts of trickery to avoid being followed. In one door and out another. Hopefully it wouldn't come to that though, and they'd get Austin before he, or Bill, could do any further damage.

Kevin Green was a different matter. There was no chance of him looking to exact his revenge. It turned out he was now working for an oil company in Dubai. Nice work if you can get it, Campbell thought. A life in the sun with no taxes to pay. When he'd reported this back to DI Strong they'd agreed that Green should still be told to continue to take precautions, although from what Green had said when Campbell had phoned him, it seemed security was pretty tight there anyhow. Better than the police would be able to offer him. All of the oil company's non-resident employees lived, and worked, in a secure compound which apparently had everything they needed. Green had said it was like their own little village with a pub, restaurant, gym, cinema and even a snooker hall. It sounded like a good set up to Campbell, maybe they needed some extra security staff? Then he remembered he was married and they were trying to start a family. Oh well, maybe in a different life, he thought. Green also told Campbell that it was very rare that he ever left the compound. In fact the last time he had come out had been three months previously, when he had left to go to the airport for a flight home. He reassured Campbell that he had no plans to repeat that journey in the foreseeable future.

'Why would I want to do that?' he said laughing. 'Last time I was home it was actually snowing. And bloody freezing! Can you believe it?' (Campbell could) 'I was glad to get back out here where the sun shines all day and it's got everything I need. I definitely won't be back in the UK for a while, I hope you catch that Austin though, he deserves to be locked up for life for what he did.'

Campbell and Strong had discussed what this might mean with regard to Austin's plans and agreed that it was now likely he would also find that Kevin Green was out of the country and his most likely course of action would be to pick another of Dan Sears' cousins as his next victim. They couldn't imagine that Austin would go all the way to Dubai to find Kevin Green, and even if he did, the likelihood of him getting to Green in the timescale he needed to was very remote. The police had previously identified that Green actually had sixteen cousins and so they dug out last year's files to see if they could identify who might be the most likely alternative victim. They knew they would have to make assumptions and that was a risk, but there was no way they could protect fifteen more people over a period of several weeks. There just wasn't the manpower or budget. They knew they'd have to identify the one or two most likely and focus on them until they knew any different.

'We're making a lot of assumptions here,' Campbell began to voice his concerns. 'One; we're assuming he'll pick on the same sort of people as he did last year. Two; we're having to guess who he might pick as another of Green's cousins. Three; we're assuming he'll do it in the same timescale to fit the anniversary date. That's a lot of unverified assumptions. Despite what Doctor Collins thinks, he just needs to do something slightly different, vary his approach or timing a bit and we could be stuffed.

We really need to find him before he can do anything.'

'I know,' Strong replied, 'and finding him should stay as our main focus, but we also have a duty to identify and make every effort to protect his potential victims. Don't forget, doing that may also lead us to catching him before he does any further damage.'

A little while later and Strong and Campbell were now on their way to see Austin's ex-partner, Lucy Morris. Campbell was driving an unmarked police car with Strong sitting alongside him in the passenger seat reading through some notes. There were smatterings of rain and Campbell had to keep putting the windscreen wipers on and then cancelling them a few seconds later as the screen cleared and the wipers started screeching against the glass. Wish it would make its mind up.

'So there are a couple of things we need to check out with Miss Morris,' Strong said to his colleague. 'Firstly we need to see if she has had any contact at all from Austin in the last year, since he disappeared. Secondly we need to tell her that Austin is probably back in town and see how she reacts to that. That will be interesting. I don't think we need to say he is definitely back, just possibly.'

'Yeh, although my impression of her is that she's very honest.' Campbell replied. 'Remember it was her that came to us in the first place when she realised who he was. I think if he contacted her again now, she'd tell us. He did do her wrong and from what I can remember she wanted him caught.'

'Yes I think you're right, but you never know,' Strong replied as he put his notes back into his briefcase and sat back in the seat thinking.

A short time later, they arrived at Lucy's flat and Campbell pulled the car up outside. The rain had gone off for a bit and there was a patch of blue sky above. It was a welcome sight, but they knew it probably wouldn't hang around for long, the forecast was for more rain. The two men approached the entrance to the flat and Strong stepped forward and knocked loudly on the white front door. They could hear someone coming and a few seconds later the door was opened by a young woman. Campbell and Strong both recognised her as being Lucy Morris but she didn't look anything like how they remembered her from a year ago. Her hair was different, it was now short and blonde, but the main change was just in her appearance generally. When they had met her last year she had just found out her boyfriend had been living a secret life and that he was really a murderer. Understandably, that must have affected her physically. The policemen remembered her as being small, stooped and with long brown, unkempt hair, her face puffed up from crying. Now she looked about ten years younger, the real Lucy, with a beautiful complexion and bright, sparkling eyes. The two policemen were delighted to see her looking so well.

'Hi Lucy, it's DI Strong and DS Campbell, you might remember us?' Strong said, smiling. 'Have you got a minute? Can we come in?'

'Oh, emm, yes, sure, of course,' Lucy replied and she could feel her cheeks reddening. She hadn't expected to see these two again and she had a sense of foreboding. It could only be something to do with Paul, or Andy Austin as they knew him. Maybe they'd caught him, …or something worse had happened? She wasn't sure what she wanted it to be.

She led them down a short hallway into a lounge where she quickly moved some clothes and toys off the sofa to let them sit down. Lucy stayed standing.

'Can I get you anything, tea or coffee?' she asked.

Although Campbell and Strong would normally have both accepted her offer, they didn't want to let her out of their sight. They didn't want to give her time to think in case she had something to hide. The element of surprise was going to be key, if there was anything to find out.

'No thanks,' Strong replied. 'Please have a seat,' he said nodding towards another matching sofa opposite to them. 'We were just in the area and thought we'd call in and see how you were doing. You're looking well. It's almost a year since we last met.'

'Yes, it must be I guess. I haven't really thought about it much to be honest, had, emm, other stuff on my mind,' Lucy replied as she sat down on the sofa.

'I take it you haven't heard anything at all from Andy Austin?' Strong asked her directly, trying to catch her off guard.

'Who….Paul? Sorry, Andy…I only knew him as Paul really. No, nothing. I don't expect to. I think we've moved on from that. Why, do you think he's back?' Lucy asked, blushing, hoping it wasn't too obvious.

'What do you mean…back?' Strong asked.

'What? Well I mean… from wherever he went. Didn't you say that you thought he'd gone abroad or something?' Lucy replied, conscious that she was now fully blushing and the two policemen must be able to see that. Lucy knew that Austin had gone to Spain because she'd seen him there when she had been on a break with her friend Jane, but it was a secret she'd kept to herself, and she had no intention of telling anyone now.

'Yes, he might have gone abroad,' Strong replied. 'We don't know for sure, but if he did, we think he may come back to the U.K. soon. Maybe in the next few weeks.'

'Oh, I see,' Lucy replied and the policemen could see her thinking, it was all a bit confusing. 'Of course, didn't you say the date of the accident was important to him. You don't think he's going to try and do it again do you? I mean, like, attack those people again this year?' She still couldn't fully believe he had done it the first time, although of course she knew he had. Surely he wouldn't do it again? She still couldn't reconcile this killer to the man she had lived with. It didn't make sense, in her head they were like two different people.

'No, we don't think so. We think we scared him off last year, but obviously if you hear anything about him, or if he tries to contact you in any way….' Strong was interrupted by the sound of a baby crying.

'Oh, sorry, excuse me a minute,' Lucy said as she got up and left the room. She returned a minute later holding a small baby in a white shawl. The child was crying softly.

'Sorry, he's just woken up from his afternoon nap, he'll usually settle down in a bit now that I've picked him up.' Lucy said as she gently rocked the baby in her arms.

'Ah, he's beautiful,' Campbell said, standing up to get a better look at the baby.

'Thanks, do you have any….kids?' Lucy replied, smiling.

'Not yet,' Campbell replied, 'but hopefully sometime soon.'

The baby started crying more loudly again and Lucy stood up, continuing to rock him, lowering her face towards him and making soothing noises, but the baby continued to cry, with the sobs becoming more continuous.

'I'm sorry,' she said, looking at DS Campbell 'he's usually okay after his sleep. I don't know what's up with him today. He might be teething.'

'That's okay, we won't keep you. As DI Strong said, we were just passing, but if you do hear anything from Austin please let us know. It's important that we get him and get justice for the people he murdered. Here's my card with my mobile number on it, please call me anytime if you hear anything.' Campbell said, handing her a small white card.

'Of course, no problem,' Lucy said as she showed them out the door.

It had started to rain again and Strong and Campbell walked quickly to their car and set off back to the station.

'What do you think?' Strong asked his colleague.

'Well, I don't think she's seen him and I honestly don't think she wants to hear anything from him. To me it didn't look like she was any sort of heartbroken girlfriend. It looks like she's well over him,' Campbell replied as he drove the car.

'I agree,' Strong replied, 'there was nothing there, except….how old would you say that baby was?' Strong asked his colleague.

'Mmm…I would say a few months, maybe three,' Campbell replied, glancing sideways at his boss.

'Yep, that's what I thought,' Strong replied, 'so that would mean she conceived about a year ago.'

'Yep,' Campbell replied, slowly nodding his head, 'when she was living with Andy Austin. So maybe we need to keep a close eye on our Miss Morris. She could be our best chance of finding him, especially if he finds out that he has a son. I'll get someone on it right away.'

'Yes, get someone we can trust though, I don't want too many people knowing at this point,' Strong instructed his detective sergeant.

Back in the flat, Lucy had managed to get the baby settled and she was sitting on the sofa with her little boy cradled on her lap. Her perfect bundle of love. She was on edge herself now though, the visit from the two policemen had brought back memories she had been hiding away, somewhere in her brain. Things she'd tried to forget.

It was towards the end of her holiday in Spain when Lucy had begun to feel a bit strange. Initially, she'd just put it down to the heat and maybe something she'd eaten. All that Spanish food, maybe too much fish. Surely not the alcohol! She had been drinking a bit more, maybe a bottle of wine a night, but that wasn't too bad for being on holiday was it? Not when you were with Jane.

Then about a week after they'd got back, Jane had come round to Lucy's flat for dinner. They spent the evening reliving the stories and some of the photos they'd taken on their holiday. Lucy had cooked them both a Spanish risotto, but she didn't seem to have any appetite and could only pick at it with her fork.

'Are you okay?' Jane asked her friend.

'Yeh, just been feeling a bit off lately, kind of lost my appetite,' Lucy replied. 'Probably just on a downer after the holiday. We did eat and drink a bit over there,' she laughed.

It was a few weeks later, and still feeling a bit funny, that she realised she'd not had a period that month. On her way home from work she stopped off at the pharmacy and bought a pregnancy test. As soon as she'd got in the door, she went straight to the bathroom and tried it. But even before the time had passed to look at the result, she knew what it was going to say. She was pregnant and the father was a man wanted for double murder, Andy Austin. Wasn't that just great!

She wondered if the two policemen had worked it out, she guessed they might have, but with it being a kind of social visit maybe they hadn't. Lucy hadn't told anyone who the father was. How could she when he was wanted for murder? She was too ashamed to admit it. She hadn't even told her mum, although she was pretty sure she had worked it out. It wasn't that difficult really, just a bit of simple arithmetic. But, being her mum, she hadn't pressed her and Lucy was grateful for that. She'd tell her when the time was right, of course. But not yet. Probably a few of her friends knew as well, or at least had their suspicions, but she'd never discussed it with anyone and they all seemed to understand, and just let her get on with her life. Being a single parent wasn't the most unusual thing in today's society. It probably suited everyone to just avoid the awful reality that the baby's father was a wanted killer. She'd named the baby Carl, James. Carl because she liked the name and James after her dad. She'd taken care not to call it any name that might give a clue as to who the real father was. As far as she was concerned she was happy that he didn't know and she didn't feel he had any right to know either. Not when he was a wanted man.

But the visit from the police had unsettled her again. If Andy Austin, she'd decided that was his real name, not the Paul Smith she had lived with, if he was back in the country and he was the father of her child, then maybe he did have a right to know

now? Would he want to see his son? And if he did, she couldn't really deny him that, could she? But, on the other hand, did he have any rights after what he'd done? He was on the run for murder, but then again, what was the phrase? Innocent until proven guilty. Wasn't that the way? And even if he was guilty, which seemed beyond doubt, that didn't stop him being the baby's father. What if he tried to contact her like the police had said he might? Was it her duty to tell him? Or just keep quiet? All these questions were running around in her head and Lucy didn't know the answers. There wasn't even anyone she could discuss it with, without having to confess, what she thought of as, her shameful secret. She placed the sleeping baby back in his cot and returned to the lounge, sitting down with a long sigh.

Chapter 5

There was a soft tap on Strong's office door and he called out,

'Come in.'

The door opened slowly and Marsha stepped quietly into the room. As always she was smartly dressed in standard office wear, white blouse, dark skirt and shoes. Strong couldn't imagine her dressed any other way. Maybe she slept like that?

'You wanted to see me sir?' Marsha asked from just inside the office door.

'Yes, yes, come in, sit down a minute,' Strong beckoned her towards the empty chair by his desk.

Marsha walked across the room and sat down, waiting. Strong continued typing on his computer for a few minutes before finally hitting the print button and turning around to take hold of a sheet of paper as it appeared from his office printer. He looked at it briefly before handing it across the desk to Marsha. As he did so, he caught the aroma of her perfume. A sweet smell he couldn't quite place.

'Here's another list of names for you Marsha. Same as before, I need you to find out if any of them have appeared anywhere recently. You know the idea, car hires, hotels, rentals…anything like that. I'd be surprised if one of them doesn't show up, but I don't know which one.' Take your pick.

'Yes, sir,' Marsha replied scanning the names on the paper. There were five of them and Marsha's logical brain noted that they were written in alphabetical order. Did that mean anything? Probably not.

'Again, no-one else needs to know. Just you and me okay?' Strong said, looking directly at Marsha, noticing that she looked different somehow, maybe her hair was a different style or did she have new glasses? Strong couldn't really pinpoint it.

'Of course,' Marsha replied, feeling herself beginning to blush as she could see Strong looking at her. She quickly looked down at the piece of paper again. 'I'll get onto it right away and let you know what I can find.'

'Thanks Marsha,' Strong replied and he turned back to face the computer screen sitting on his desk.

Marsha stood up and left the room quickly, closing the door quietly behind her and walking briskly back to her desk in the main office. It was in the far corner of the room, a nice quiet position, which she preferred so she could concentrate on her work without too many people walking past and disturbing her. She started on Strong's request straight away, keen to see what she could find for her boss. She knew there was other work, her day job, she should really be doing, but she liked doing these secret little missions for DI Strong. He'd given her, maybe five or six unofficial, off the radar, jobs over the last few years and she loved doing them. It felt like she was doing something useful for him and it made her feel a bit like a real detective, working undercover, but all from the relative safety of her own desk. She wasn't brave enough to undertake real police work, out in the field, there were too many scary people out there. But Strong had always been very good to her and she felt she owed him for that, as well as making her job that bit more interesting. Sometimes she imagined the two of them as characters in a TV crime series, Strong and Hughes, where the detective got all the credit for solving the crime but the viewer could see it was really the quiet, unassuming woman in his team that found the key evidence. No, not Strong and Hughes, Strong and Marsha – that was better. It reflected their relative statuses and Marsha wouldn't have minded that, she didn't like being in the spotlight and was happy for someone else to play that part, her in the background, knowing that at least she'd been useful.

Back at her desk, in the real world, she began with the top name on the list and typed it into her computer, waiting a few seconds as the software worked its magic in the background, checking the name against a number of databases Marsha had access to. It came back with the result "Not Found". Computer says no.

She felt a little disappointed but carried on, repeating the process for the next name, and after a few seconds the computer returned another negative result. Computer says no, again. She carried on, entering the third name on the list but once again it came back with the same message, “Not Found”. Marsha was beginning to get a little worried, she didn’t want to disappoint DI Strong, although she knew it wasn’t her fault, she didn’t want to be the one who brought him bad news. She decided to take a break and get herself a coffee, maybe that would bring a change in luck for her. She picked up her mug, “World’s Best Mum” it proclaimed in faded blue letters against a white background. It was the sort of thing you got as a present from your kids for your birthday or on mother’s day, but only she knew that she had bought the mug for herself. Marsha did have one son, but their relationship hadn’t always been easy. After his father had died, she’d had to bring him up on her own and she’d found that quite challenging. Maybe she’d been too soft with him at times, but it was hard not to be. He was all she had. Her only living flesh and blood. She knew what other people would say, but if they had been in her shoes she’d have challenged them to do anything different. It was always easy to criticise from the outside.

She walked out the main office, along the corridor and into a small room that served as a kitchen for everyone on that floor. The kitchen had a fridge, a coffee machine, a kettle and a set of cream-coloured cupboards with a built in sink. The standard office kitchen. As she waited for the kettle to boil, she washed up a couple of mugs someone had left by the sink and put them on the draining board. She didn’t like mess. Her house was spotless, always had been, even when her son had been living with her - even though he obviously hadn't inherited her cleanliness gene.

As she stood there watching the silver kettle, she wondered if perhaps she'd typed one of the names in wrong, but she was pretty sure she hadn't. Marsha was always very careful with her work and even more so when it was something she was doing for DI Strong. One of their secret missions. Strong and Marsha, Series one, episode four. Would there be a second series, she wondered? She put a spoonful of decaffeinated coffee into her mug and filled it with boiling water from the kettle, topping it with a splash of semi-skimmed milk she'd retrieved from the fridge. It was all semi-skimmed now, no full-fat, although Marsha had noticed a few cartons of Oatmilk appearing in the last few months. That seemed to be the latest fad. What was it though, Oatmilk? You couldn't really get milk from oats could you? Taking a sip of the hot liquid, she returned to her desk and sat back down with a degree of renewed optimism, ready to continue with her task. The caffeine, although there wasn't any, was doing its trick. Maybe it was all psychological, like the Oatmilk.

She looked at the fourth name on the list. Tom Randall, with two "l's". She carefully typed it in and sat back in her chair, taking another swig of her coffee and feeling the warm liquid trickle pleasingly down inside. The software seemed to be taking longer this time, or was that just her imagination? She had another drink and then the same box as before suddenly popped up on the screen. "Not Found." Computer never says yes!

That just left one final name. Marsha looked at the list, staring at that last name, imprinting it on her brain. Stephen Wallace. She took another sip of her coffee, hesitant. She didn't want to start, knowing it was the last one and it was probably going to return the same result as the others. Not Found. Computer always says no. And then what? There was nowhere else to go. She could try them all again, and she probably would, but she knew the answer would most probably be the same. Then she'd have to tell DI Strong that she'd failed. She hadn't been able to find any of the names on his list, even though he'd seemed pretty confident that she would. What would he think of her then? She'd never let him down before and maybe that would be the end of their secret little jobs. Maybe he'd use someone else next time. Strong and Dorothy, Marsha killed off at the end of the series? Surely it hadn't run long enough for that to happen yet? The viewers would be outraged.

She put her coffee down and slowly typed in the last name. Being extra careful to spell it correctly. She made a mental note to go back and try the alternative "Steven" if "Stephen Wallace" didn't show up. Wasn't there a comedy sketch about that, she briefly thought, something she'd seen on television, but she wasn't in the mood to give it any more time. She hit the enter key firmly and waited. Once again it seemed to be taking longer, but she chided herself for trying to outguess the computer. Suddenly a box appeared on the screen again, but this time it was different. It didn't say "Not Found". This time it had showed the name Stephen Wallace and there was a list of detail underneath it. This time it was finally computer says yes! Marsha smiled, she'd found Stephen Wallace and she'd been saved. There would be another series of Strong and Marsha after all! But, not just that, as she read the detail, she saw that he'd hired a car from Southend Airport on the same day that the man known as James Gilmour had flown in from Barcelona. It must be the same man, Marsha thought, DI Strong would be pleased. She could imagine him now, his smile as she delivered the good news. Another riddle cracked, another crime solved. Strong gets the plaudits but in the background you could see Marsha, just to the left, Marsha with a satisfied smile on her face. They'd have to commission another series now. Marsha relaxed back in her chair and looked around the office, taking a long drink of her coffee before starting to read more of the detail on the screen.

It got better and better. At least potentially. Wallace had given a home address when he'd hired the car and it was only a few miles away from the police station, from where Marsha was now seated. She carefully copied the detail from her screen and typed it into a more readable note for DI Strong. Thirty minutes later she was on her way back to DI Strong's office feeling very pleased with herself. As she walked past her colleagues desks she half expected them to stand up and applaud her, but of course they had no idea what she had been doing and she couldn't tell them. Marsha, the unknown and unassuming hero. She liked it that way.

When she left Strong's office a few minutes later, she was even more pleased. Strong had been delighted with the news that she'd found Stephen Wallace and that she had an address for him. Marsha didn't ask who this Stephen Wallace was or why Strong was so interested in him, that wasn't in the script. She was just happy that she'd managed to do something to help him again. She was his silent partner. He told her to keep a close eye on Stephen Wallace and the car registration to see if either came up again anywhere else over the next few days, as well as continuing to check the other names on the list. Marsha promised she would. That would be her number one priority. This episode wasn't finished yet, maybe she'd find more details or more names, the key piece of evidence that would lead to Strong solving the crime. But the viewers would know it wasn't just Strong, it was Strong *and* Marsha.

Inside his office, Strong was re-reading Marsha's note. It was good news undoubtedly, and he'd made sure Marsha knew that he was pleased with the work she'd done, and in such a short timescale. She was good, but he knew that what she'd found might not yet be the final answer. He knew that Stephen Wallace was definitely Andy Austin and that he had hired a car at Southend Airport. They had the model and registration number for the car and they also had a home address for him. However Strong also knew that Austin was no fool and, to Strong's regret, he had given Austin a lot of tips on how to avoid getting caught when they had first discussed Austin's idea. It was possible that Austin still had the car and that he was living at the address he had booked it under, but Strong thought both were unlikely. Austin had been a good pupil and had learned a lot from his discussions with Strong. Assuming he'd listened to Strong then it was likely that he had already switched cars and the hire car would turn up parked in a multi-storey car park in a few days' time, seemingly abandoned. The rental company would go on to waste their time trying to track down Stephen Wallace, before eventually having to give up and write off any debt accrued.

It was also likely that the home address Austin had given the rental company was a false one. But Strong would have to check it out. That's what police work was all about. Ticking off all the possibilities until you were left with just one. The right one. The one that meant you caught the criminal. They'd tracked him to the farm before and Strong was confident, now he had the list of names, that he'd find him again. But this time it would just be Strong and he wouldn't make any mistakes.

A few hours later Strong left the office and set off to find the address Marsha had given him for Stephen Wallace. It wasn't far away from the police station and he turned into Connolly Street just ten minutes later, slowing down as he drove along the residential road, trying to get a view of the house numbers. There were no numbers visible on most of the houses, but then he picked out a bright silver number twenty shining from a green door. He slowed down some more and counted the houses as he passed them. He was looking for number thirty eight and a minute later, he reckoned he was there.

It was a red door, but he couldn't see any number on it. He drove on, past a couple more houses, until he saw one with the number forty four proudly displayed in large black paint on a white front door. He stopped the car and looked around, counting back the houses which seemed to confirm that the one he wanted was indeed the one with the red door. Picking up his overcoat, he slipped it on as he got out of the car, buttoning it up against the cold November wind and started walking casually back towards the house. There was no obvious sign of anyone being there, no car parked outside, and he hadn't seen any movement as he passed the window although it was obscured by a pair of white net curtains. He walked up to the door and pulled back the silver knocker, giving it a couple of loud knocks. There was some movement from inside the house, some noise, and a few seconds later the door opened slightly to reveal a young dark-haired woman peering out. She opened the door further but held the door tightly to stop it blowing in the wind, and to keep the cold from getting into the house. Strong guessed she would be in her mid-twenties and she was wearing black leggings and a white, baggy sweatshirt with the words "Mummy knows Best" emblazoned in purple across the front. Over her shoulder, Strong could see a small child peering around a doorway, curious as to who their visitor was. When he saw Strong looking at him, he took fright and quickly disappeared back into the room.

'Sorry to bother you,' Strong started, 'I'm looking for a Stephen Wallace and was told he lives here.'

'Stephen Wallace?' the woman replied. 'No sorry he doesn't live here. I think you must have the wrong address. I've never heard of him.'

'Ah, okay, sorry, my mistake. Yes I guess I must have got the wrong address,' Strong replied smiling and he turned around and took a step away before suddenly stopping and turning back,

'What about Andy Austin?' he asked.

The woman stopped in the midst of closing the door and shook her head.

'Sorry no, haven't heard of him either. Not your day is it?' she smiled. A child's voice shouted out from somewhere behind her. 'Sorry got to go,' she said and she finished closing the door.

Not a surprise, Strong thought to himself as he got back in his car and unbuttoned his overcoat. He hadn't really expected this to be where Austin was holed up and it was obvious the woman had no idea who he was. In fact, a part of him would have been disappointed if he *had* been here. That would have been a sign that Strong hadn't taught him well enough. At least he had been a good teacher. Strong sat in his car for a few minutes getting his thoughts in order. He knew the game had just started again and these were just the early plays. Austin wouldn't know that Strong now had a list of all his possible false identities and he wouldn't know that Marsha was on the case. Next time a name popped up on Marsha's screen they'd be right on it. Every time they'd get closer and closer until one day Strong would inevitably find him. Austin would make a mistake, it was only a matter of time, and then Strong would be back in control.

Chapter 6

Andy Austin woke up with a groan. It had been another bad night. He couldn't remember the last time he'd had a good night's sleep. Yet again he had been dreaming about Lucy. This time they had been living together in a nice house in a nice street in a nice town. Probably called Niceville or Pretty town or something like that. Andy and Lucy had two kids and a big garden for them to play in. Being perfect parents, they'd put up a swing set and a slide and the two of them were sitting together on the patio with a cold drink, a cloudy lemonade, watching their children play. They were all laughing and the sun was shining. Everything was good. Then one day he came home from work, parked his four-by-four in the driveway. It was a German model, Mercedes or BMW, black, with all the optional extras thrown in. The sun was shining but they had sun shades on the rear windows for the kids. He got out and went into the house, but he was surprised to find it was empty. There was no-one there. In fact there was nothing there at all. There were just bare rooms with bare plaster walls and concrete floors. He went from room to room, calling their names, getting more and more anxious, but there was no response, just the echo of his voice bouncing around the empty house. He went out into the garden. The sun had gone and it was now cloudy and strangely dark. The garden was empty too, just a fence and a barren piece of ground. No grass, no plants, no swing-set. Just a wasteland. Then he heard a noise and he turned around. Standing at the patio door were two people, an older woman and a young man. He recognised them immediately. It was Hilary Potts and Peter Wilson, the two people he'd killed a year ago. They didn't say anything they just stood there staring at him from blank, white faces. That was when he had suddenly woken up.

He could hear the wind gusting outside and his head was aching again. He knew his condition was getting worse and the painkillers the doctor had given him seemed to be having less effect, even though he was taking more of them than he was supposed to. He reached over and grabbed two more from the packet, tossing them into his mouth and swallowing them with a gulp of water. He picked up the packet and, seeing it was empty, he threw it into the bin. He eased himself out of the bed and had a quick shower before getting dressed in a blue t-shirt and a pair of black jeans. He went to retrieve some more painkillers from the kitchen cupboard but when he opened the cupboard door, there were none there and he realised that he'd just finished the last packet.

'Shit,' he said, closing the cupboard door.

His plan for this morning was to drive around the areas where his two intended targets lived, just to check that nothing had changed from the last time. He liked to be sure that there was nothing new that could disrupt his mission. The mission that he knew he had to complete. Luckily the two families only lived a couple of miles apart from each other, and with him holed up just twenty minutes away from both of them, it wouldn't take too long to do his reconnaissance. Then he could get back to the house and rest up. If all looked well then he'd decided to complete the job the following week. He was ready. He didn't see any sense in hanging around any longer now, best just to get it finished and then....well, he didn't know. He couldn't think about that yet. Back to this morning and he realised he'd have to make time to get some more painkillers while he was out, and he picked up his prescription from the dining table, thinking he could probably get them from the local pharmacy on his return journey.

Austin left the house and quickly ducked into his hire car, the wind blowing annoyingly cold around his face. The car was a dark coloured VW Golf. Nothing flashy, nothing that people would particularly notice or remember. That was another thing that Strong had taught him. Make everything as plain and normal as possible, people don't remember that. Hidden in plain sight was how Strong had put it. Dark colours, nothing flashy, nothing distinctive, nothing that people would remember. As Austin set off towards the area where the Sears family lived, more specifically where

Arthur Sears lived, his head started pounding again and he wished he'd gone to the pharmacy first. Arthur Sears was the father of Dan Sears, one of the young men who had been in the car driven by Jack Wilson on that fateful night two years before. The night when Andy Austin's family had been killed.

As Austin made his way along the road, he pulled up at a set of traffic lights just as they turned to red. While he was waiting for them to change, he noticed a pharmacy sign in the parade of shops just beyond the junction, a green cross against a white background, in between a bookmakers and a charity shop. With his head now aching, he made the decision to get his painkillers there, so he could pop a couple straight away. Get them into his system and get them working. He parked the car outside the charity shop and went into the pharmacy. It was pretty quiet with just one man sitting to the side on a green plastic chair, apparently waiting for his prescription to be made up. He was old with thin grey hair, wearing a jacket, shirt and tie and dark trousers that looked baggy on him, falling over the sides of his thighs as he sat. He looked like he was about to fall asleep, his eyelids heavy. There seemed to be a lot of old people around nowadays. Andy walked up to the counter and handed his prescription to the young woman behind the counter. She was sporting a pair of thin black glasses and wearing a knee-length white coat covering a pair of black trousers. Her long dark hair was pulled back tightly and tied in a ponytail.

'Hi, can I have these please?' Andy said. 'It's a repeat prescription.'

The woman looked at the prescription and replied, 'Let me just check,' and she turned and walked behind a screen where Andy could hear her talking with someone else. It sounded like a man's voice.

The conversation seemed to be taking some time and then Andy heard a phone ringing and what seemed to be the same woman's voice answering it. His head was getting worse and he looked at his watch, wishing he'd kept a better eye on his painkillers in the first place, but also wishing this woman would hurry up with his medicine. He needed something now. It never took this long in his normal pharmacy. He looked at the old man sitting to the side. His eyes were now closed and Andy wondered if he'd been sitting there all morning, or even longer. Maybe he would just die there and no-one would notice until it was closing time? Andy could hear the woman continuing to talk on the phone and he felt himself getting more and more tense. His head was pounding. He stepped forward and rang the bell on the counter but the woman's voice carried on behind the screen.

'Excuse me,' he called loudly, startling the old man sat waiting in the chair. He gave a little grunt and shifted his position slightly, making the chair squeak, before closing his eyes again.

There was still no response at the counter. Andy pushed the bell again. Harder.

'Excuse me,' he shouted more loudly this time. The old man didn't stir.

Behind the counter, a man's head looked around the edge of the screen and then he appeared fully, also dressed in a white coat, dark trousers, and wearing glasses. Andy briefly wondered if glasses were part of the pharmacy uniform, or if working in a chemist's just wasn't good for your eyesight. But at this point he didn't really care, he just wanted his painkillers. The man approached the counter, he was older than the woman, and older than Andy. His hair was turning grey at the sides and he had thicker looking glasses. He looked across the counter at Andy, with an obvious frown on his face.

'Can I ask you to keep your voice down sir?' he said. 'This is a pharmacy, not a public bar. We will be with you in a minute.'

But Andy was too far gone to calm down and apologise. His head was too sore. He'd had enough of this waiting. Enough of everything. It was too much. He could hear the assistant still talking on the phone. She had some sort of accent but Andy couldn't quite place it, and that made him even more frustrated.

'Just give me my medicine will you?' he said angrily in reply. 'I can't wait here all day in your stupid little store. I need the tablets now.' He heard a cough from the old man sat to the side, but he didn't look at him.

Just then another woman came around from behind the screen, again older than the first woman he'd seen and again wearing a white coat and glasses. Red ones. She was a rebel or she'd not got the email about the required colour of glasses. She handed her colleague a small white package. She glanced at Andy, a look of concern on her face, then turned and disappeared back behind the screen. The pharmacist looked at the package and then lifted his head and spoke to Andy.

‘Can you just confirm your address please?’ he asked.

Andy told him the address and, taking the medicine sharply from the man, he marched out of the shop, head down, cursing under his breath. As he pulled the door open he almost collided with another man coming in and, glancing up, he noticed the man was wearing a dark blue policeman’s uniform. Andy carried on, out of the shop, the door catching the wind and slamming loudly behind him. He walked quickly back to his car, past the bookmakers, keen to get going.

‘Everything alright?’ the policeman asked the man behind the counter.

‘He got a bit angry at having to wait. I’m afraid we get that from time to time, seems to be on the increase,’ the man replied. ‘People don’t seem to have so much patience nowadays.’

‘Mmm.. that’s not right though, you shouldn’t have to put up with that. Especially in a pharmacy. Give me his details and I’ll check him out back at the station,’ the policeman replied. ‘Maybe I’ll pop round to his house and give him a bit of a warning if I have time. People don’t need to be rude.’

‘Okay, but as I said, it’s not that unusual now for that to happen. I wouldn’t be too hard on him. I think he was suffering a bit. He’s on pretty strong painkillers. I haven’t seen him in here before and I don’t suppose he’ll be back that soon!’ the pharmacist replied, smiling.

He wrote the man's name and address on a blank piece of notepaper and handed it across to the policeman. The policeman glanced at it.

'Stephen Wallace, that name doesn't ring any bells, it's not anyone I know, not a local I don't think. Must be an incomer. I'll have a look on the system when I'm back at the station see if we have anything on him,' he said as he handed over his own prescription to the pharmacist.

'All right Jack?' he said nodding to the old man sitting in the chair, who nodded back and grunted something incomprehensible in reply.

A few hours later a notification popped up on Marsha's screen at her desk in the police station. She'd set up several alerts on her databases to tell her if, and when, any of the names Strong had given her appeared on them in any way. For a couple of the older systems she had to manually search herself every day but this one had appeared from their own internal police database, which was fairly up to date and she had good access to it. Marsha had been in the middle of reading a long email about some new health and safety audit which was going to take place over the next couple of months and she'd been finding it difficult to concentrate on the details. She'd read the same paragraph two or three times now, without fully understanding it. It was like her brain was rejecting it as being too boring. Straight into its waste bin. They seemed to do these audits pretty regularly now. If it wasn't health and safety, it was data protection or something else. Everyone seemed to be checking up on everyone else. What would happen if the health and safety people found out that the data protection people were doing something wrong? Maybe they kept their fire doors wedged open with some boxes of data? Or the data protection people found that the health and safety people were sharing their passwords around? Who would win? Who took priority? Maybe they'd have to have a fight or do a quiz to decide. That would be a fun night out.

Marsha was both relieved and excited when the notification alert appeared on the corner of her screen. This could be the start of another episode. The viewers were waiting, it was all over social media. What would happen next, would there be a twist to the story? Whatever happened, Strong always got his man, with Marsha's help of course. Strong and Marsha – the number one programme on the box. Imagine.

She quickly shut down her health and safety email, relieved to have an excuse to do that, and clicked on the notification box. It opened up a new screen on her computer and she smiled with some satisfaction as she saw it was a short note on Stephen Wallace, just as she'd hoped it would be. Strong and Marsha, series 3, episode 1. It showed his name and a short description of what appeared to have been some sort of minor incident he'd been involved in, nothing serious, but most importantly it also gave a home address for him, which was different to the one she'd previously found. This time it said 27 Parkside Avenue and she tried to think of where that was, but she couldn't remember exactly. It was somewhere on the North side of town, she thought. She quickly took a screen shot and printed the information out, getting up from her desk to retrieve it from the printer behind her. Hopefully DI Strong would be pleased with her again. The viewers would be on tenterhooks. Marsha had come up with the goods again.

Chapter 7

Strong walked briskly up the pathway to the house and, using the silver door-knocker, knocked loudly on the door. Three times. A good solid knock. One that said, I'm here and it's official. He stepped back and waited. It was a bright sunny day, and the sun was reflecting off the silver number twenty seven on the door, but it was still bitterly cold and Strong pulled his overcoat collar up to cover his exposed neck. A few seconds after his knock, the door opened and a man he recognised, stood there looking at him, wearing a blue t-shirt and black jeans. He looked different, his hair was short and blond and he had a matching short beard. Beards seemed to be back in fashion now, most of the younger guys in Strong's team had one. Strong had considered it, but decided he was too old and it would just make him look older. The man at the door had a thinner face than Strong remembered, with a bit of a tan, but it was still the man he knew as Andy Austin. Austin looked back at him and then glanced beyond Strong, noticing that he appeared to be on his own.

'So you found me then,' Austin said simply. 'I guessed you would one day, you'd better come in,' and he turned back into the house letting DI Strong follow him through the doorway. Into the lion's den.

Strong closed the door behind him and followed Austin along a short hallway, past a staircase to the right and then turning right at the end before an immediate left turn, through a door into the kitchen. Strong was wary, staying alert, in case Austin tried something. He didn't think he would, but he'd misjudged him before and so he needed to remain cautious. Austin was a killer after all.

The kitchen was a small, but bright, room which made it appear larger than it actually was. There was a large window to the rear which looked out onto a garden and Strong could see a wooden fence and some bare trees blowing in the wind beyond that.

'Fancy a coffee?' Austin asked Strong, as he stood by a cream-coloured worktop.

'Sounds good, nice place you've got here,' Strong replied looking around the modern kitchen.

'Yeh, well it's not mine, just a short term rent, but I expect you know that,' Austin replied. 'It'll do for now.'

Austin made two coffees while the men chatted about nothing in particular. He put a plain white mug down in front of Strong, who was now sitting on a black padded, aluminium bar stool, his overcoat lying across his lap. Austin sat down on the other side of the counter on a matching stool. Strong took a sip of his coffee, it tasted good. He put the mug down and looked across the worktop at Austin.

'So you're back in the country,' Strong started, 'what's your plans?'

Austin laughed. A few lines appeared across his face and Strong observed that he was looking older. Comes to us all, Strong thought as he remembered seeing his own face in the mirror that morning. Where had all the years gone?

'You always were straight to the point,' Austin replied. 'I think you probably know what my plans are though. I've got a job to finish.'

'Mmm.. I was afraid that's what you were going to say. I can't let you do that though,' Strong replied, shaking his head. 'You've already gone too far with this one,' Strong added. 'I think you know that. It's time to stop. Too many people have suffered, it's not doing any good.'

'So why aren't you arresting me then? Why are you here on your own?' Austin asked the policeman and then took a drink from his coffee while watching Strong over the top of his mug.

Strong took another drink of his own coffee before replying. He'd given some thought as to what he was about to say and it was important that he got it right if his plan was going to work.

'The thing is Andy, when we discussed all of this in the pub a year or so ago, this … idea. It was born out of our mutual frustration at a lack of justice generally and, I suppose then more specifically for your situation. You felt, quite rightly, that the system had let you and your family down. That's something that I'm well aware of, this failing of the system, both for me personally and also through my long career in the police force. As police, we do our best, but then other people get involved, too many old judges, smart lawyers, people with money. Too many variables. And sometimes it doesn't work out as it should.'

'But in my mind,' Strong continued, 'what we agreed last year was that you'd maybe give the driver, Jack Wilson, a bit of a kicking and that would be that. Teach him a lesson. But you went too far. You killed two innocent people and it seems you are still intent on killing two more. I can't let that happen. It's too much. Those people didn't deserve that.'

Strong stopped speaking, picked up his mug and took another sip of coffee. Austin took that as a sign for him to respond.

'Maybe I remember it differently. We agreed that I would ensure justice was carried out for the killing of my family, and you told me how to avoid getting caught. You explicitly told me you didn't want to know what I was going to do. The less detail the better, you said. Give the driver a kicking? These scum killed my family and I needed them to suffer in the same way that I suffered. That was only fair. That was justice. That's why I did it.'

'I get that,' Strong replied, 'I understand. But it's too much Andy. We think the accident, maybe the bump you got on your head at the time, triggered some kind of PTSD condition which is driving you to these extremes. You must see that what you're doing is not normal. You used to work in an office. A guy that works in an office doesn't suddenly become a killer. You can't just go around killing people.'

Austin knew Strong was right. He knew the bang he had taken to his head when the car clipped him had probably started off the tumour and he knew that was probably causing him to act in the way he had over the last year. But he didn't know how to stop, and a big part of him still didn't want to anyway. He had a job to complete and it had taken over his life. He liked Strong and didn't want to cause him any trouble if he didn't need to, but he could see they were at diametrically opposite points on this.

'I know what you're saying and you're probably right about the PTSD. I've got a tumour. It's been growing and I probably don't have that much longer to live, probably just a few months. After that you can forget all about me. I'll be gone. Quite literally,' Austin laughed.

'Oh, I didn't know about the tumour, I'm sorry to hear that. Can't they operate on it?' Strong asked him.

'Maybe, but there's no point,' Austin replied. 'I just want to finish this off and then that's me done. I've got nothing else to live for now.'

'I can't let you finish it the way you want to,' Strong repeated, shaking his head slowly. 'I can't let any more innocent people die. I didn't sign up to that.'

Austin was feeling weary, the effect of his painkillers was beginning to wear off and he just wanted to sleep. Sleep for a long time and get away from this nightmare he was living in. Maybe this was it, maybe it was all over now, with Strong having found him, but if it was then he'd have failed. He was fed up playing games though and just wanted Strong to tell him what was going to happen next.

'So, what are you going to do, arrest me?' Austin asked him, shrugging his shoulders.

Strong finished his coffee and took a deep breath.

'I could do, or….' he said.

'Or what?' Austin replied intrigued by Strong's response, but just wanting an answer.

'Or we could do something else. Something that might satisfy both of us in some way. Something that will give us what we both discussed last year. Justice. We agreed that there were many cases where justice was seen not to have been done, including your one and mine too, and we both wanted to do something more about that - so maybe we can. If we widen this out a bit, don't just think about your situation, you've done enough there, think about the hundreds of other people that have suffered like you have. But they've suffered because of genuinely bad people, people who we haven't been able to put away because of their smart lawyers or stupid judges. They're not young men driving a car and having an accident, they're serious villains, evil men who will keep hurting people and they deserve to be punished. People we haven't been able to stop because the system isn't good enough. Maybe that's who you should be focusing on, not the old dad of a young man who happened to be sitting in the back seat of that car.'

Strong stopped talking, aware that he had said a lot and looked at Austin to see if the man across from him had taken it all in.

'So what are you saying?' was Austin's reply, intrigued but really still just wanting an answer.

'Okay, what I'm saying,' Strong began, 'is that I can arrest you now and you'll spend the rest of your life, however long that is, in a prison cell. Or we can do a deal. And the deal is that you stay out of prison and use your talents, with my help, to get justice for those other people, people like yourself who are suffering. Can you see Andy? It's the other side of the coin, instead of killing to make people suffer, you'd be killing to give other people justice. Give them what they deserve. You'd be doing something good.'

'You're crazier than me!' Austin said smiling.

'Okay, I'll arrest you then,' Strong replied, smiling back at him. 'I'm sure you'll enjoy prison.'

'Whoa, whoa…hold on,' Austin replied. 'I didn't say no, I just need to understand what you're saying a bit more. You've just hit me with this and, …well, to be honest it's a bit of a surprise.'

Austin made some more coffee and they talked for another hour, with DI Strong gradually convincing Austin that the four young men had suffered enough through his killing of two of the relatives. Strong explained that the families were all very close and so they had all been hurt because of the murders and his abduction of the two others. But, moving on from that, Austin now had a chance to do some good, to rid the world of some evil people who would always be evil unless they were stopped. Strong explained it was his only chance of escaping prison. If he didn't take it, Strong would make one call and it would all be over. Austin slowly began to see that he didn't have any alternative, he was never going to be able to finish the job now, but if what Strong had said was right, then maybe he didn't need to. He was feeling weary about it all anyhow and so it would actually be a relief to stop. And he liked Strong's idea of clearing out some criminals while he could. Doing something good for the world in his last few months of life. It harked back to their initial chats in the pub behind the courtroom when they'd discussed the weaknesses of the justice system and how they both wished they could do something about it. Although Austin had been thinking of it as specifically applying to his situation, maybe he'd done enough and, as Strong was suggesting, he should now move onto more deserving cases than him. Maybe it could even mean that he could see Lucy again, that would definitely make it worthwhile. He doubted it though, but he decided to voice his thought to Strong.

'Would I be able to see Lucy again, if I take your deal?' he asked.

Strong thought for a minute. He knew this might come up and he wanted to keep it as a future bargaining chip, should he need it with Austin. He was aware that, if caught, Austin could implicate him, although he was confident that he'd covered his tracks enough to prevent there being any serious fallout from that. He'd taken great care not to do anything that would lead back to him.

There was also the matter of Lucy's baby. Strong was sure that Austin was the father but it was obvious that Austin had no knowledge of the baby's existence. That could also be something he could use, if needed, at a future point.

'Let's hang fire on that for a bit, shall we. It would be dangerous for her if you made contact again. If she didn't report it immediately to the police, then she could be arrested for perverting the course of justice. Let's give it a bit of time and see how things go first,' Strong replied. 'Maybe later we'll be able to arrange something.'

Austin understood how his contacting Lucy again could cause all sorts of problems, for the both of them, but he desperately wanted to see her, just to talk with her, even if only for a few minutes. He had hoped Strong might have had some suggestion as to how they could do that safely, but he could see that Strong was right. It would be dangerous for Lucy and the last thing he wanted to do was to cause her even more upset.

They talked a bit further about how the new "deal" would work and agreed that Austin would leave the Reynolds and Sears families alone to get on with their lives without any fear of him attacking them. Strong would then provide Austin with enough details on a deserving target to enable him to carry out his retribution. They would do it one target at a time, taking stock after each one to see if they needed to do anything differently. There was also an unspoken understanding that Austin's current condition meant that the term of the deal might only be for a few months and so they might only be talking about a couple of victims, but even taking just a couple of these villains off the street would be a good thing in Strong's eyes.

'So…am I supposed to kill these people or just hurt them?' Austin asked Strong.

'I don't think it matters to be honest,' Strong replied. 'I think you need to hurt them badly, put them out of action. If that means they don't survive, then I wouldn't worry. They get what they deserve, whatever that is. They're not good people. You'll see what they're like when I give you the info on them. I don't think you'll have any qualms about delivering some justice for their victims. And believe me, there are a lot of victims from the activities of these people, whether it's through drugs, prostitution or just pure violence. More victims than we know about.'

Austin nodded his head. He was fascinated by the way Strong was speaking. He spoke with such passion. Austin knew that Strong had lost his parents many years ago to a hit and run driver who had never been found, but he could see that his lengthy police career had also increased his frustration at not being able to bring these types of people to justice.

'Okay, I'll do it,' he replied. 'It's a deal,' and he reached across the counter top and shook Strong's hand. As they shook hands, Strong noticed the trees blowing in the distance as a strong gust of wind caught the top, bare branches.

Chapter 8

Austin was sitting at his round kitchen table with a cup of hot coffee and a pile of documents spread out in front of him. He'd read them all a couple of times and he was making sure things were clear in his mind. Some of the papers had come from Strong, anonymously via a courier, and others he'd printed off the internet himself. They were mostly reports from newspapers and also a few copies of police documents that Strong had provided. At first he hadn't been sure about Strong's proposal, he had a few doubts, but then he'd come to the conclusion that he didn't really have much alternative. Maybe this was a good option. As Strong had put it, he'd be doing society some good instead of just taking out his frustration on more innocent relatives of the four men. Maybe they had suffered enough as Strong had said. And now that Strong had found him, the only likely alternative for him would really be a life in prison which wasn't something to aspire to.

In truth, part of Austin was pleased at this surprising development. He'd been getting fed up with the whole thing, just wanting it to be over, but not being able to stop himself as he'd been fully committed to doing it to get some sort of justice for his family. That was how he saw it, not revenge, but justice. Now Strong had made the decision for him, taken it out of his hands, he felt like a weight had been lifted off his shoulders. But of course his head still ached, a constant reminder that he wasn't well. That wasn't something that DI Strong could fix for him.

The man Strong had identified as Austin's initial target went by the name of Jed Sullivan. From what Strong had told him and the detail he had subsequently read about Sullivan, he was certainly an unpleasant, and probably dangerous, man. Although he'd never been convicted of any major crime it seemed pretty clear that Sullivan was heavily involved with drugs, extortion and a fair smattering of violence. However he always seemed to be one step away from getting caught and Strong had said that Sullivan had a strong legal team that knew how to play the system, always making sure he was never charged. He always had an alibi or there was some technicality, or potential witnesses suddenly went quiet or changed their stories.

'No, I didn't see anything, I must have been confused when I spoke to you before.'

Strong knew they were being intimidated but he couldn't prove it. In short, it appeared Strong's plan would be the only way Sullivan would pay for his crimes and the only way his victims would get any sense of justice.

Strong had also provided Austin with a set of photographs, showing Sullivan and his closest companions. Sullivan was thirty three years old and, to Austin's eye, a good looking man with short black hair and an even set of gleaming white teeth. He looked like he kept himself fit and indeed it seemed he was a regular attendee at a high class gym in town. Strong's notes explained that most of Sullivan's accomplices were low-life, petty criminals on his payroll and so Austin shouldn't be too worried if any of them got in the way, however Sullivan was the real target. There were also photos of two separate, very attractive, women. Their photos appeared to have been taken professionally for a modelling agency. Although Sullivan lived on his own, it seemed he had set these two women up in luxury flats and he visited both of them regularly, often arriving late at night, on his own, and leaving a few hours later or early the next day. Austin could guess what the purpose of these visits was. He wondered if the two women were aware of each other and the situation they were both in, or if they were just happy to have nice flats and a bit of spending money. Strong had also provided a detailed timetable showing Sullivan's regular movements. He seemed to be a very structured person, with a regular weekly routine and Austin spent a long time studying this. He knew the area where Sullivan was based really well, he'd actually lived there for a few years himself at one point, and he could visualise Sullivan's various journeys in his head. He realised he was feeling excited at the prospect of teaching Jed Sullivan a lesson and he was keen to get started. It was like a new phase for him and he was feeling more energised than he had been for a while.

He'd still also been thinking a lot about Lucy, trying to figure out some way he could see her but frustratingly he hadn't been able to come up with a solution to that problem. As far as he could see, Strong was right. Any contact with her would just cause her more distress and problems. He'd given her enough of that already. Besides she might not want to see him again anyway. She'd probably moved on with her life, maybe even found another man. She deserved to be happy. Who was he to come back and mess things up for her again? Hadn't he hurt her enough already? Although, before she found out what he was doing, they'd been very happy together. In fact Austin had never felt so happy or comfortable with anyone like he had with Lucy. And he really believed Lucy had felt the same. But how could she now? He was a murderer. It was a simple fact. Someone with a soul as beautiful as Lucy's would never be able to forgive him for what he'd done and, in truth, he'd be a bit disappointed in her if she did.

He'd thought about phoning her, just to hear her voice again, but he didn't know what he would say. There wasn't anything he could say really to make amends. He'd said sorry in the letter he'd left her, but of course that wasn't nearly enough.

He finished his coffee, gathered up the papers and put them back in the file. He had a plan for Sullivan fixed in his head now, he knew what he was going to do and when he was going to do it

Chapter 9

Strong tapped lightly on the solid, wooden office door and eased it open. He stepped inside, it was an office he had been in often. It was much bigger, much grander, than his own office. It had a nicer carpet, more luxurious, better quality furniture and a big, double window with a view out across some woodland. Everything paid for from a different budget to Strong's. A bigger budget. The Chief Constable was sitting on the other side of his desk reading, and occasionally signing, some paperwork, moving it from one pile to another. Right to left. As usual he was smartly-dressed, wearing a pin-stripe suit and white shirt with, what looked like an official police federation tie. Blue and white stripes. His official uniform was hanging up on a coat stand in the corner behind him, ready to wear if needed. He looked up as Strong entered.

'Ah, Mo, good to see you. Have a seat, I'll be with you in a minute. Just got to clear these first or Maria will just nag me again. It's never ending,' he said smiling before turning his attention back to the paperwork.

Strong wasn't sure if the Chief meant the paperwork or the nagging was endless, but he took the Chief Constable's advice and sat down at the end of the long table, which ran down one side of the office, waiting for his boss to join him. He felt fairly relaxed. You never knew with the Chief when he asked to see you, but Strong had learnt from past experience that when he addressed him using his first name, Mo, and not as Strong or DI Strong, then it was usually nothing too bad. Fingers crossed. Maria had just called him earlier that day and said the Chief Constable wanted to see him, no further detail, and so Strong had, of course, complied. And here he was.

The Chief got up from his desk, carrying a pile of papers and, without looking at Strong, he walked out of the office. Strong sat and waited, occasionally looking out through the large office window at the woodland beyond. It was another grey winter day, one of those days where it never seemed to get really light before it was dark again. The Chief Constable returned a few minutes later. He picked up a file from his desk and sat down at the long table, facing Strong at an angle and crossing his legs.

'So, our friends up North have a bit of a problem,' the Chief started. As always, straight to the point, Strong knew the Chief rarely engaged in small talk. 'The usual stuff, drugs and the like. But things seem to have got out of hand. Their stats aren't good. Too high for top brass's liking. I need you to go to Leeds and have a look at what they're doing and make some recommendations to get them back on track. Should be easy enough for you, with your experience. Just needs a bit of a shake up I think. Have a look in here, it's all there,' he said sliding the buff file across the table towards Strong.

'I need you to start straight away and it needs to be done quickly. Too many people are asking questions. People who don't understand how we work. I'd say six to eight weeks maximum. Anything you need, I'll clear it. I don't want any admin stuff delaying you.'

Strong flicked open the file while the Chief was speaking glancing at the detail inside.

'What about my ongoing work here?' Strong asked as he skimmed over the first few pages of the documents in front of him.

'Hand it over to DS Campbell. We'll make him an acting DI. It's about time we tried him out. I assume you're okay with that. You've told me before how good he is. Let's see what he can do,' the Chief replied.

Strong nodded. It was a sensible decision and he knew he could rely on Campbell to keep him in the loop on anything he needed to know. Better that than flying in a DI from another region and messing things up for Strong. Finding out things he shouldn't. He trusted Campbell and knew it was a mutual thing. It was the best solution for DI Strong. He'd still be pretty much in control.

'Okay, I'll fill Campbell in, I'm sure he'll do a good job,' Strong said to the Chief Constable.

'Grand, I'll leave you to get on with it, keep me updated on your progress, I'm sure you'll soon sort this out,' the Chief Constable said, leaving Strong in no doubt that was what was expected of him, before standing up and returning to his desk, immediately tapping something into his computer. Strong took that as a sign that the meeting was over and he gathered up the file, left the office and made his way back downstairs.

Although he hadn't seen this coming, he knew there was always the possibility of him being moved to do another job if needed. That was often how the police worked and he had built himself a good reputation, making him the right man to do this in the Chief Constable's eyes. Strong was happy that it was only a temporary move and that Campbell would be filling in for him. It meant he could still keep an eye on the Andy Austin situation without there being too much risk of anything happening without him knowing. He'd still have the control he needed.

Strong knew Leeds fairly well, his daughter Sophie was in her final year at university there and so he had made the trip up North a few times, dropping her off and picking her up, as well as a couple of stopover, weekend visits. He'd never been there on police business before though, so it would be interesting to compare their operations to how he ran his and, of course, find out where they were going wrong. Although it was a bit of a pain having to relocate for a short period, Strong had always liked new challenges and so he still felt a bit excited at the prospect of this new adventure.

Later that day, Strong called Campbell into his office and explained what was happening. As he had expected Campbell was quietly pleased, but at the same time a little nervous about taking over from Strong.

‘I’d like to have Dave Brown working with me,’ Campbell said, ‘he’s a good cop, can we make him an acting DS while I’m in this role?’

‘Yes, I’m sure that would be okay. Good choice. Don’t worry,’ Strong reassured him, ‘I’ll always be on the other end of the phone and I’ll expect you to keep me in touch with anything new, especially anything to do with our friend Andy Austin. Aside from that though, if there’s anything you’re not sure about or just need to discuss with someone, just give me a call. In fact let’s schedule in a regular weekly call just so we can catch up on anything major.’

Strong also knew he would have to tell Austin about his change of location, but now that they had made contact and agreed the way forward, he didn’t really see that as being a problem. There was no real reason for them to meet again in the foreseeable future and they could still contact each other by phone.

‘Thanks Guv, I appreciate it,’ Campbell replied thinking that it would be strange not having Strong around to chew things over with. They would often sit here, in Strong’s office, discussing cases, throwing around possible theories and coming up with an idea that would lead to them resolving the case. Campbell would miss that, maybe they could still do that by phone, but it wouldn’t seem the same and Strong would have his own work in Leeds to keep him occupied.

‘When are you going?’ he asked Strong.

‘Pretty much right away,’ Strong replied. ‘The Chief is going to get Maria to send an email around this afternoon so everyone will know. If they don't already. So congratulations acting detective inspector Campbell. I'm sure you'll do a great job. Just remember everything I taught you,' Strong said laughing as he got up and walked around his desk to shake Campbell's hand. Strong was confident that Campbell would be able to do the job while he was away, and also that he would keep Strong up to speed with any developments, meaning that Strong could continue to steer the ship pretty much as if he was still there.

Chapter 10

It was just after midnight and Andy Austin was sitting alone in his hire car, the VW Golf, in a visitors parking bay outside Melville Court, which, when built two years ago, was described as an exclusive development of luxury two and three bedroom apartments for professional people. To Austin it didn't look any different to any other block of flats that had been built in the last ten years - and there were a lot of them. Everywhere you went there seemed to be new buildings appearing, cranes abundant, and Austin couldn't understand who was buying them all. Definitely not people that needed them.

As always seemed to be the case, Austin was on his own again. He hadn't really spent any significant time with another human being since he'd walked out on Lucy. That did worry him a bit, his lack of social interaction, but he knew it was necessary. It was best to keep to himself to avoid having to answer too many questions. He was dressed all in black, from head to foot, only his face was visible and even then only partly, as he had a woollen hat pulled down tightly over his head and ears.

Outside the car, it was a clear night with a half moon and a few stars visible in the sky. Austin was looking up at them now but he didn't know what they were called. Maybe the Plough or something he thought, but he couldn't really see any resemblance to any farming machinery. Perhaps he should have paid more attention at school. Science hadn't really been his thing, he'd been obsessed with sport, playing for the school football and cricket teams.

He'd been parked there for around an hour and if things went to plan, he should only have another twenty or thirty minutes to wait. He knew Sullivan was a man of routine and so he should be appearing soon. It was cold sitting in the car but Austin didn't want to start the engine in case it drew any attention to him. He'd brought a blanket and he had it wrapped tightly around him, tucked in under his legs, partly covering his black jeans. The car was parked underneath a tree, away from any street lights and he had the car radio on at a low volume, just to give him some company. No-one had come or gone from Melville Court since he had arrived and he guessed most of the residents were in bed, or at least not intending to go anywhere at this time of night. Melville Court consisted of thirty apartments with ten flats on each of the three floors and most of those that he could see had their curtains closed, with no visible light from within.

Austin's eyes were moving back and forward between a particular third floor window and the entrance door to the block of flats. Just over an hour earlier he'd watched Jed Sullivan drive into the car park, park up in bay twenty three and go into the building. Austin knew he would now be in the apartment with that same number, with the young lady who lived there, Elena Adamcik. She was one of the women Sullivan regularly visited late at night and this, being a Wednesday, was one of her lucky nights. If lucky was the right term. Sullivan was nothing if not regular, Austin had discovered while he had been watching him, he was definitely a man of habit. Elena Adamcik described herself as a model/dancer and, from looking at her large portfolio of photos on social media, Austin could see it wasn't the type of dancing you could expect to watch on Saturday night TV.

There had been nothing to see at the window of number twenty three. The curtains had been closed when Austin had arrived and there had been no noticeable movement since then, not even when Sullivan had arrived ten minutes later. Austin glanced at the clock on the display of the car. If Sullivan kept to the normal schedule that Strong had provided for him, then he should be coming out of the building in about ten minutes. He sat back in the seat and waited, his gloved, left hand reaching across to feel the iron bar lying on a towel on the passenger seat. He wrapped his fingers around it feeling the smoothness of the iron. It would do the job nicely. Just then, the car park lit up as the headlights of a car belonging to a dark four by four turned in and made its way to the far end, stopping in the rear corner. Its lights were turned off. No-one got out and Austin assumed, and hoped, it was just a couple having an illicit meeting. It was a perfect place for it. He kept one eye on the car, but still no-one got out. Hopefully they were otherwise engaged and wouldn't notice his car. He looked at the clock again and decided it was time. He threw off the blanket and picked up the iron bar. He got out of the car, walking across to Sullivan's car, where he crouched down by the passenger door. It was cold and his breath was steaming up the car door. He wiped the passenger side window with his gloved hand and, looking through it, he could see the door to the building as well as the other car, which was about fifty metres further away at the far end of the car park. There was still no movement from the other car and Austin hoped the occupants were already too pre-occupied to care about anything else happening outside.

The entrance door to the flats opened and the security light came on, throwing a white blanket onto the courtyard outside. Sullivan stepped into it and turned to walk towards his car. He was wearing a long dark coat with a red, checked scarf around his neck. His breath floated out in front of him as he walked. He was talking to someone on his mobile phone which he was holding to his ear with his right hand. Austin watched through the window as Sullivan approached the car and he began to move to the rear end, still crouched down and breathing downwards so as not to give his presence away. He looked fit and Austin knew he might only have one chance to do this. The car's hazard lights flashed brightly as Sullivan aimed his key towards the car. He was twenty metres away. Austin was crouched at the back of the car, now by the driver's side. He had the iron bar firmly held in his right hand. Sullivan stopped ten metres away, still talking on the phone. Austin could hear what he was saying,

'Yes, sure, just do it. He's had his chance, he needs a lesson' a pause, then, 'good, call me later.'

Sullivan slipped the phone into his coat pocket and resumed walking towards his car. He was only a few steps away now. Austin was gripping the iron bar tightly. He felt tense, but excited at the same time. He could feel his heart beating in his chest. Sullivan was at the car. He opened the door and turned to get in. Austin sprang forward from behind him and swung the bar at his head. It connected with a loud crack on the top of his head. Sullivan crumpled, his legs gave way and he fell to the ground, toppling backwards, his head hitting the ground in front of Austin's feet. Austin looked down at him. His legs were bent, partly obscured by the open car door and his arms were splayed out on the concrete on either side of his body. His coat was still buttoned up, but his scarf had become loose and it was lying across his torso ending up by his right hand which was still holding the car key. His eyes were open and his mouth was open but he wasn't moving. There was a faint dark patch seeping out across the concrete from underneath his head.

Austin walked quickly back to his car. He got in and wrapped the iron bar into the towel, folding it up and placing it down in the passenger footwell beside the blanket. He looked across to the other car parked at the far end of the car park and was pleased to see that it still sat there with no movement from inside. His heart was racing and he had a big grin on his face as he drove out of the car park. Everything had gone to plan. It couldn't have been more perfect. He was elated.

Two miles down the road he turned into a retail estate and drove around to the rear of a McDonalds restaurant where he knew he would find two large skips, partly full with waste. He checked to see there was no-one else around and then he deposited the towel-wrapped iron bar into one of the skips, pushing it down as far as he could and covering it over with some of the other rubbish that was already in the skip. He'd done his research and knew the skips would be picked up in just a few hours time, to be replaced with new, empty ones. He turned back onto the main road, still feeling very happy, although his head was beginning to ache again. There was no other traffic on the road and pulling up at a set of traffic lights he glanced at the clock, it said twelve fifty. From start to finish the whole process had taken less than two hours. He'd be home in just a few minutes and he was looking forward to getting some sleep. The lights changed to green and he started off again. Looking ahead, down the road, he was aware everything seemed to be really bright and sharp. Maybe the adrenalin rush had made his senses go a bit hyper? Suddenly there was a bright flash, somewhere deep behind his eyes, and he slumped to his left side, falling towards the passenger seat, only restrained by his seat belt. The car kept going forwards until the next bend in the road where it mounted the pavement and crashed into a high brick wall with a loud bang.

Chapter 11

DI Strong had tried calling Austin again, must have been the third or fourth time, but he still wasn't answering. That was strange. He'd been expecting a call from Austin and he must know that Strong had been trying to make contact with him from seeing his missed calls. The two men hadn't spoken since Strong had made his move to Leeds, but Strong had heard from various sources about what had happened to Jed Sullivan and that pleased him greatly. His plan was working. And Austin seemed to have done a good job. In Strong's eyes, Sullivan was one less piece of scum to worry about, or to waste police time on. They'd been trying to nail him for years without success. And at least all of Sullivan's victims might now feel some sense of justice had been achieved when they heard what had happened to him.

Although Sullivan wasn't dead, he was now lying in a hospital bed, on life support, in a coma. The diagnosis was that he was unlikely to survive, and even if he did, he would have severe brain damage for the remainder of his life. Strong had spoken briefly to Campbell about it and Campbell had told him Sullivan had suffered a single blow to the head with a heavy object which had caused him a massive brain injury. He'd been found lying by his open car in a car park to a block of flats, early in the morning, and the forensics team thought it was likely he'd been lying there all night. He'd lost a lot of blood but somehow he was still alive. But barely. There hadn't been any witnesses to what had happened. None of the residents had heard or seen anything and no-one seemed to know why he was there. The young lady living in number twenty three had seemed a bit upset, but claimed not to know Sullivan, even though the police knew she was a "friend" of his. She'd been trained not to talk to the police and so that was what she was doing. She wasn't a suspect and so the police didn't press her and no-one else had come forward to report that they had seen anything. At this point the police had nothing to go on but the intelligent guess was that it was some sort of revenge attack for something that Sullivan had done previously. He wasn't short of enemies and a lot of people, including some of the police, privately felt he had got what he deserved.

'You can't blame people for thinking that,' Strong said.

'No, I guess not,' Campbell replied, 'but we can't have people going around acting as vigilantes and handing out their own justice though. That would be a lawless society.'

Or maybe a lawful one, Strong thought, if it delivered justice that the current system couldn't bring. Strong was still mystified by Austin's radio silence. He hoped he hadn't decided to go off radar again. But why would he? He'd agreed to Strong's deal and successfully carried out his first assignment by attacking Sullivan. Strong's guess was that Austin had attacked Sullivan when he'd been at one of his girlfriends. He knew one of them lived in a flat owned by Sullivan in the block where it had happened. It wouldn't make sense for him to change his mind now, not after what he'd done to Sullivan. Unless it had spooked him somehow. Maybe it hadn't gone as well for Austin as it had appeared to. It was also possible that Austin had been hurt by Sullivan at the time of the attack, had the two men got engaged in a fight? But from what Campbell had said there was no evidence to indicate that. There was only Sullivan's blood at the scene and no sign of any struggle. It seemed that one blow from behind to the back of Sullivan's head had been all that had happened. Strong could imagine it, Austin creeping up from behind, hitting Sullivan, watching him fall, then leaving quickly. He had killed twice before so he knew how to do it. But then why hadn't he called Strong? It didn't make sense.

Perhaps Austin had managed to hit Sullivan but then he'd been overpowered by some of Sullivan's men. Again, Strong didn't think that was likely though, because he knew that Sullivan usually travelled on his own and he was sure Austin would have picked a time when that was the case. If that had happened though, it would explain why Strong hadn't heard anything from Austin and in Strong's mind that wouldn't be the worst thing. At least they'd have got Sullivan off the streets first and Strong knew there was some personal risk in allowing Austin to do what he was doing. In fact, more than allowing, he was controlling him really, telling him what to do, and he knew it would have to end sometime. If Sullivan's people had somehow disposed of Austin then that would be one less risk that Strong would have to live with. But Strong hoped that wasn't the case. He wanted to use Austin to get shot of a few more scum first and deliver some justice for their victims, before it had to end. He already knew who the next one was going to be and was just waiting for the opportunity to tell Austin. Strong began to think he might have to make an excuse to return home for a day, so he could go to Austin's house and find out what had happened.

Andy Austin opened his eyes. He quickly realised he was lying in a hospital bed, it was the clean smell more than anything else. The disinfectant, or was it antiseptic? He felt stiff and sore and he could sense that there was some sort of bandage around his head. A doctor in a white coat with black glasses and curly black hair was standing by his bedside taking his pulse. Seeing the doctor immediately brought back memories of the accident that had killed his family. He hated hospitals.

'Hello, Mr Wallace, I'm Doctor Khan. How are you feeling?' the doctor asked him, smiling.

Andy had to think for a few seconds, he wasn't quite sure, and he couldn't remember what had happened for him to be here. He could only just remember the name he was using. Stephen Wallace.

'A bit groggy, a bit, ….I don't know,' he replied. 'What happened? Why am I here?'

'Ah, yes don't worry. You had an accident in your car. Hit a wall. By the fire station. Luckily a couple of the firemen came running when they heard the bang and got you out. They probably saved your life. You'll feel a bit sore for some time yet, but it will get better,' the doctor replied, writing something down on the clipboard he was holding.

'I can't remember much,' Andy replied hoarsely.

'No, that's understandable. Here have a little sip of water, that'll help your throat,' the doctor said, handing Andy a small beaker from his bedside cabinet.

Andy slowly brought it to his lips and took a little sip, then another, feeling his mouth moisten and his throat ease as the water trickled down inside. An image of a cold glass of lager sprang to his mind and for a second he wished he was back in Spain. Sitting outside a bar, sipping a cold drink and watching the world go by, without any worries. If only. He tried to move himself up the hospital bed slightly to get a better view of the area around him, but he didn't seem to have the strength and so he gave up and stayed where he was.

'We think you may have blacked out and lost control of the car,' the doctor continued. 'You hit the wall at quite a speed and you got bumped around a bit, but luckily nothing was broken. The seat belt probably saved you. However, while we were doing your scans, we did find a rather large growth under the right side of your skull, just above your ear, and we managed to remove most of it. We did quite a good job, even though I say so myself,' he said laughing. 'I take it you were aware it was there?'

'Yes…yes I was,' Andy answered warily.

'Ah well, you've saved yourself another trip to the hospital then, two for the price of one, so to speak. Has it been bothering you? Headaches, eyesight problems?' the doctor asked.

'Yes, …a bit,' Andy replied.

'Oh well, that should be a lot better now, now that it's out. It could well have been the reason why you crashed, it probably caused you to black out. I don't expect you'll remember. You'll need to have it checked regularly still, but there's no reason to suppose it won't be okay,' the doctor said.

'When was this,…emm, accident?' Andy asked.

'Three days ago,' the doctor replied. 'You've been awake on and off over the last couple of days, but again you probably won't remember. That's perfectly normal. Just the after effects of your crash. The rest will have done you good. It's amazing what the body can recover from with a bit of rest. You'll need to stay in hospital for a few days more just so we can check everything continues to improve after the accident, and of course, your brain operation. Try and get some more sleep now. Make the most of it, while you can, I know I would,' he laughed. 'One of the nurses will be along in a bit to check on you.'

The doctor replaced the clipboard on the bottom of Andy's bed and made his way along the corridor and out of sight. Andy tried to ease himself up on the pillow again but found he still didn't have the strength to push. He gave up and closed his eyes, taking the doctor's advice to rest while trying to remember what had happened.

He could recall attacking Jed Sullivan, and he was certain that had happened, but there was nothing after that. He couldn't remember getting in his car and driving away from the apartment block, but he must have if he crashed near the fire station. Andy estimated that must be about five miles away from where he'd assaulted Jed Sullivan. That was good because it meant he must have disposed of the iron bar, as he had planned, in the skip behind McDonalds. The doctor was probably right about him blacking out. His headaches had been getting a lot worse lately and maybe the adrenalin of the attack had tipped him over. It was lucky he'd crashed near the fire station and the firemen had been there to get him out. He remembered reading a newspaper report a long time ago about a man who had a heart attack in a street called "Hospital Road" and he thought at the time, "how lucky was that?" If you're going to collapse, Hospital Road must be as good a place as any to do it. Maybe he was just as lucky with the firemen being on hand. He must have drifted off to sleep then, because the next thing he became aware of was someone gently shaking his arm and talking to him.

'Mr Wallace, are you awake? Sorry but I just need to do a few checks. I've got you some water here too. Would you like a drink, I expect you're thirsty.'

Andy slowly opened his eyes and saw a nurse leaning over him wearing a blue and white uniform. She had short dark hair and a round, friendly looking face. She was smiling at him and she smelled of disinfectant.

'Ah there you are,' she said. 'Try a sip of this,' and she held a white plastic beaker up to his lips.

Andy opened his mouth slightly, his lips still felt like they were stuck together but he managed to sip a little bit of the water, feeling it trickle into his mouth, freeing his tongue.

'Thanks,' he managed to say.

'That's good. We'll see if you're ready to eat something a bit later, just something light,' the nurse said as she put the beaker back on Andy's green bedside cabinet.

'I just need to take your blood pressure. Is there anyone you'd like us to call now you're awake? We didn't have any details for you, other than your name, and there was nothing on our system. Perhaps your partner, or family, or maybe a friend?' the nurse asked as she set up the blood pressure monitor.

'Has anyone been in to see me?' Andy asked, wondering if DI Strong might have put in an appearance and knowing there wouldn't have been anyone else. If only he'd still been with Lucy. She would have been sitting by his bedside waiting for him to wake up.

'No, I don't believe so,' the nurse replied. 'As I said, we didn't have any details on you other than your name on a bank card in your wallet, so we didn't know who to call, if anyone. I think you had a mobile phone but it was locked. If you want I can bring it to you and you can make the call yourself if you feel up to it?'

Andy nodded, 'thanks, that would be good.'

The nurse returned a few minutes later with Andy's mobile and she handed it to him.

'There you go,' she said, smiling. 'I'll leave you to make the call, give you a bit of privacy,' she added and she pulled the curtain closed and walked away.

Andy switched the phone on and after a few seconds it buzzed into life. It still had a little bit of battery life left and Andy could see that there had been three missed calls, all from the same number. DI Strong. He was the only one who knew the number of this phone and so it could only be him. I'd better call him, Andy thought, he may not even know I'm in here, although he did seem to know most other things. Andy hit the number and waited a moment for it to connect. It started to ring and then it clicked as it was answered,

'Hello,' a man answered.

Andy immediately recognised it as Strong's voice and he explained what he knew about what had happened and where he was, taking care not to mention Sullivan's name. Instead he simply said that he'd carried out the task and it had all gone well. Strong confirmed that back to him and told him from what he had heard, it had been a successful job.

'Sorry to hear that, the accident I mean. Have they told you when you'll get out?' Strong asked.

'No, not yet, but I think it'll be another two or three days. I'll try and get out sooner but, to be honest, I probably need the rest,' Andy replied. 'Are you still in Leeds?

'Yes, still here, another few weeks then I'll be done. I take it you're in there as Stephen Wallace?' he asked.

'Yes, that's correct,' Andy replied.

'I take it there hasn't been any police involvement?' Strong asked. 'No-one's come to see you?'

'Not as far as I'm aware,' Andy replied. 'I've been pretty much out of it the last couple of days but I think they see it as a straightforward accident, nothing suspicious, no-one else involved and no connection to the other thing.'

'Okay, that's good. I think you're right, I'll make some enquiries just to be sure. Is there anything you need?' Strong asked.

'Just a charger,' Andy replied, 'but I expect they'll find one for me here.'

'Okay,' Strong laughed, 'give me a call when you're out and we'll talk more then,' he added before ending the call.

Chapter 12

'Who was that on the phone?' Emily asked her housemate Sophie as she wandered back into the room. 'You've missed a really good bit. You won't believe what he just asked her!'

Emily and Sophie shared a house with two other students, Josh and Olivia. Josh was very quiet and when he wasn't at university, he spent most of the time in his bedroom, reading, or "doing things" on his laptop. Some would think he was a bit of a geek, but of course they'd never say that out loud as it wasn't politically correct. The few friends he had all seemed to be similar to him and they'd never seen him out with a girl. Olivia was a mature student, doing a post graduate course and Emily and Sophie had come to look on her as being like a nice friendly auntie, although again, not out loud in case it offended her. Olivia had a boyfriend and often spent the weekend at his place on the other side of town. Emily and Sophie were both twenty one and in their final year at university. They'd met when they found themselves sitting together one day in a psychology seminar during their second year. They hit it off immediately, finding that they had a lot of common interests and, most importantly, shared the same wicked sense of humour. Things they could say to each other, but not to anyone else. The lecturer that day had been Professor Davey. He was probably only in his mid-thirties but he looked, dressed and acted like he was twice that age. He wore a red bow tie, checked shirt and sports jacket with brown corduroy trousers and brogues. Maybe he had been born like that, some people were. Emily and Sophie had nicknamed him Wavey Davey, for no particular reason other than it sounded funny and seemed to sum him up.

As well as having similar personalities, the two girls also looked alike and were often mistaken for sisters with their similarly styled, long blond highlighted hair, although Sophie was a few inches taller than Emily. Height was something Sophie had inherited from her dad who was over six feet tall. All height and no fat. The two of them had quickly become best mates and it had been a no-brainer for them to find a place together for their final year at university. Luckily they'd found this house in the main student area of town, ideal for walking into university, which was only ten minutes away. All four house-mates had their own rooms and shared the bathroom, kitchen and lounge. However, Josh and Olivia rarely used the lounge which meant that Emily and Sophie had come to think of it as being their own area and they were often to be found sitting there together, eating a takeaway, while watching something on You-Tube on the large flat screen TV.

'Ooh, can we rewind it please?' Sophie replied, 'just quickly. It was my dad on the phone.

Remember I told you he's going to be working up here for a few months, I think. Some sort of temporary transfer, I think he said.' She hadn't really been listening to him that closely, keen to get back to the programme she'd been watching. She picked up the remote and pressed the fast rewind button.

'Oh right, that's good. He's a policeman isn't he? Could be handy if we get in trouble I suppose,' Emily laughed. 'Those nights in town can get a bit rowdy sometimes, especially when happy hour's on.'

'Yeh, he's a detective in the CID. As far as I know, he tends to work on murders and stuff so hopefully we won't need him! Apparently they want him to sort something out up here. Don't suppose I'll see him much more though, he's always busy. Ah here we are,' Sophie said as she found the right place in the programme.

'Is your mum coming too?' Emily asked.

'No, she's staying at home. Makes sense, it's only a temporary thing and she has her own stuff going on at home,' Sophie replied, settling down to catch up with the story on the screen.

'Oh my god! Did he just say that that? Really?' she gasped. 'What a twat, no wonder he doesn't have a girlfriend!' she said and both girls laughed.

'Did Olivia call the landlord about the oven, do you know?' Sophie asked. 'I'm getting a bit fed up of sandwiches and salads to be honest and I can't afford another takeaway pizza this month.'

'Yeh, me too. I think she did. Yes, I remember now. In fact, I think she said something about a guy coming round tonight or something to look at it,' Emily replied, trying to remember the brief conversation she'd had with Olivia in the hallway that morning. To be honest, she hadn't been fully awake and so hadn't caught it all. Olivia was a morning person, often out on a run before eight a.m, showered, dressed and in the library not long afterwards. Emily definitely wasn't a morning person, she only started to fully function around three o clock in the afternoon.

Just as she finished talking there was a knock at the door.

'Ooh, maybe that's him now,' Emily said and she got up from the sofa and walked down the hallway to the front door.

Sophie pressed pause on the remote and she could hear Emily talking to someone at the door. A few seconds later Emily reappeared, followed by a man in a green boiler suit, carrying a large, blue toolbox.

'This is emm..,' Emily hesitated,

'Dave,' the man filled in.

'Dave, right, he's come to fix the oven, …hopefully,' Emily said, smiling at the man over her shoulder as she led him through into the kitchen. 'It's in here. There,' she said pointing at the oven, in case it wasn't obvious. Although if the oven repair man couldn't recognise an oven then there might not be much chance of him being able to fix it.

Emily re-joined Sophie on the lounge sofa and they resumed watching their programme. They could hear the man working in the kitchen and Sophie used the remote to turn the volume up slightly so they didn't miss anything. Both girls were intermittently looking at their phones as they watched, and as the programme came to an end they heard the man calling from the kitchen,

'Excuse me.'

The two girls got up and walked together into the kitchen. The man was standing by the oven, his mobile phone and a paper form lying beside him on the worktop, with the big toolbox sitting by his feet. He could do with a shave and a haircut, Sophie thought as she looked at him properly for the first time. Bit scruffy. Sometimes scruffy could be a good thing, but not that scruffy.

'All done,' he said smiling, a few stained teeth showing. 'Nothing major, it had just got a bit clogged up. Needed a good service that's all. Can one of you just sign this form, just to say I've been and carried out the work to your satisfaction? I've switched it on and it's working fine now.'

He took a silver pen out of the top pocket of his boiler suit and placed it on top of the form, taking a step to the side to give the girls space to move into.

Sophie moved forward and, without reading the form, signed her name in the space at the bottom.

'Thanks,' the man said. 'Oh, one thing. I found this phone behind the side panel. I don't know if someone put it there or it fell in somehow, but I don't know how it could have. Is it one of yours?'

he said picking the phone up from the counter top and handing it to the girls.

'It's not mine,' Sophie said.

'Mine neither,' Emily replied. 'Looks a bit old, maybe it's one of our housemates. We can ask them later,' she added.

The repair man picked up the form, pen and his toolbox and followed Emily back down the hallway to the front door where she thanked him and closed the door as he left. She walked back to the lounge where Sophie was sitting with the old mobile phone.

'Eww, he could do with using a bit of deodorant,' Emily said, 'he doesn't half pong.'

'Yes I thought that too, scruffy and smelly, not a good combination,' Sophie laughed. 'This mobile looks a bit old and basic, I doubt if it belongs to Josh or Olivia. It doesn't seem to have any charge,' she continued. 'I won't have a charger for it either, I've never had this make,' and she put it down beside the TV. 'Maybe Josh'll have one, he's a bit of a techy, bless 'im, I'll ask him in the morning.'

'Let me see it,' Emily said and Sophie handed her the phone. 'Yeh, maybe Josh'll be able to do something with it. If we get it working we might be able to see who it belongs to. Shall we watch one more episode of *Millionaire Celebrity Island of Love*?' she said putting the phone down and picking up the TV remote.

Chapter 13

Detective Sergeant Campbell pulled into the hospital car park, his wife sitting beside him in the passenger seat of his car. It was becoming a familiar journey for them, from their house to the hospital, one they could now almost do on autopilot. Turn the ignition on and then say “car take me to the hospital” and off it went. The technology probably existed to do that, Campbell had seen a bit about driverless cars on the news. They hadn’t spoken much on the way, both nervous and lost in their own thoughts about the procedure they were about to go through. This would be the fifth time they’d tried it and they’d both agreed it would be the last, no matter the outcome. Although they had said the same thing a few months earlier when they had been going through IVF for the fourth time. It was amazing how time could change things.

They walked across the car park arm in arm, huddled down, shielding themselves as much as possible from the bitterly cold wind, and entered the bright hospital reception. Once again, as if they were on autopilot, the two of them made their way across reception then, via the elevator, up to the Assisted Conception Unit. It was on level three of the hospital, in what was known as the Bedford wing, named after Sir Norman Bedford who had been a well-known twentieth century professor of gynaecology at the hospital. Campbell had read a bit about him online. They checked in at the ACU reception and took their place amongst the other patients in the plastic seated waiting area, facing the open door out to the corridor they'd just come in from. There were three other couples sitting there, no-one talking. All, Campbell assumed, hoping to become parents. Maybe for the first time, hoping to start a family. That was what life was all about wasn't it? You fall in love, get married, start a family. But for some it wasn't that easy. It hadn't been for Campbell and his wife. Of course you don't know that until you try, then you enter the medical process. Campbell noticed that two of the couples were holding hands and he reached for his own wife's, easily covering it with his large right fist. He felt her wedding ring in the palm of his hand and he smiled at his wife, she returning his smile nervously before looking away, waiting for their turn to be called.

As they sat in silence, Campbell began to get distracted by people walking along the corridor outside the waiting area, wondering what they were all doing here at the hospital. What was their story? Everyone had one. Some would be here as patients, some perhaps accompanying a partner or friend, or just visiting someone they knew. Campbell tried to categorise them as they walked past. It helped pass the time and fitted his logical police brain.

A man glanced sideways into the room as he passed the door. Something clicked in Campbell's head, something else, but he wasn't sure what. There was something familiar about the man, but he couldn't quite place him. What was it? His thoughts were interrupted as a nurse appeared from behind the reception desk and called their names. They arose from their chairs as one and disconnected their hands. DS Campbell walked a pace behind his wife as they followed the nurse along a corridor to the left of the desk and through a door into a room at the far end. They'd been in this room several times before and they sat, quietly listening, as the nurse explained what would happen. They'd heard it all before and didn't have any questions. Nothing had changed since the last time. They'd already asked all the questions they had, there was nothing else to say.

The rest of the day passed in a bit of a blur for Campbell. Having done this four times previously it all just felt like a process they had to go through. In some ways, it didn't seem real, but of course it was. It was harder for his wife though and he felt guilty (again) that she had to go through, what was an undignified process, with doctors and nurses poring over her – people she didn't really know examining her most intimate parts.

It was after it was all over and they were leaving the hospital that it suddenly came to Campbell. He hadn't even been thinking about it but it just popped into his brain. The man. He knew who he was, or at least thought he did. It was Andy Austin. He was almost certain of it. Something about the eyes. They were the same as those he had seen on the photos Austin's girlfriend Lucy had given them. His hair was different, short and blond and he had a beard.....but. The eyes. He stopped suddenly, his wife carrying on walking until she realised he was no longer there. She turned around to see him standing on his own in the middle of the hospital corridor as if in a trance.

'Come on, what are you doing?' she called back to him.

Campbell was frozen to the spot. He didn't know what to do. He needed to think. He walked forward again, catching up with his wife and grabbing her arm.

'Wait,' he said, 'I need to do something quickly. Do you mind, can you get a coffee or something? I'll just be five minutes.'

'What?' Campbell's wife replied sharply. 'What do you need to do? Can't we just go home, I'm tired. I need to just sit down and relax.'

'I know, I'm sorry. It's important. Just sit down in that café over there,' he said nodding his head towards an outlet promising fresh coffee and bagels. 'I promise I'll only be five minutes. I promise.' He kissed her forehead and turned back along the corridor in the direction they'd just come from before she could raise any further objections.

He retraced his steps until he was back outside the Assisted Conception Unit but instead of turning into the waiting area he kept on going along the corridor. The sign above him indicated he was heading towards the Neurology Department. He kept walking until he came to a door which he opened and stepped into a room which looked very similar to the waiting room he'd been sitting in, in ACU, a few hours earlier. Campbell walked up to the reception desk and produced his police warrant card from his jacket pocket.

'Hello, I'm detective sergeant Campbell,' he said to the young nurse sitting behind the desk. 'Can I see your list of appointments for today please? I just need to check the names.'

'Oh, em, …I'm not sure. I, em, don't know if I'm allowed to,' the young nurse replied, looking around to see if there were any other, perhaps more experienced staff members nearby. She'd never been asked anything by a policeman before. The patient records were confidential, but maybe the police were allowed to see them? She wasn't sure. She could feel her face beginning to turn red.

Campbell could see her hesitation and knew his wife would be getting more and more irritated by the minute as she sat waiting for him. He needed to exert his authority and do this quickly. He walked around the desk to stand beside the nurse and tried to reassure her,

'It's okay, I'm not asking to see anything confidential, just the names,' he said. 'Is that them there?' he asked nodding towards a sheet of paper lying on the desk in front of the nurse. The nurse looked down.

'Well, yes, it is…. I suppose that's okay,' she replied and she slid the list across the counter to DS Campbell.

Campbell glanced down the list until he came to the appointment times around when he had been sitting in the Assisted Conception Unit. The man had been walking away from the Neurology Department when Campbell had seen him, so if he was a patient, his appointment must have been before Campbell's. Campbell looked at the names of the three patients listed around that time. Two of them were women and there was only one that was a man. That must be him, Campbell thought. He looked across to the nurse.

'Do you have an address for this one?' he said pointing at a name on the sheet.

'Stephen Wallace?' the nurse replied and turned to look at her screen. She typed the name in and a new screen appeared showing Wallace's name and address.

Campbell reached across and grabbed a pen, scribbling the name and address down on a pink post-it note which he folded in half and put into his jacket pocket.

'Thanks,' he said to the nurse. 'You've been a great help,' and he walked off, keen to rejoin his wife as quickly as possible. He glanced at his watch, he'd been away for about fifteen minutes and he knew she wouldn't be happy, but he'd had to do it. If it was Andy Austin then it would be worth it. The nurse looked around and was pleased to see that no-one had seen their brief interaction, deciding not to mention it to anyone in case she'd made a mistake.

The next morning DS Campbell woke up early. His brain was already active. He got showered and dressed quickly, trying to be as quiet as possible so as not to disturb his wife. She hadn't been happy with him last night and he knew he still had some making up to do. But he couldn't just ignore his work. He couldn't ignore the fact that he might have seen the murderer the police were looking for. And that he now knew where he lived.

He made himself a quick piece of toast and washed it down with half a cup of strong, black coffee. He wrote a quick note for his wife telling her he loved her and that he would call her later, then he grabbed his jacket from the stairway bannister, quietly left the house and got into his car. He took the post-it note from his jacket pocket and typed the address into his satnav, saying it out loud as he typed,

'Thirty eight Connolly Street.'

The satnav software churned in the background before finding the location and displaying the directions on the screen. Campbell set off and fifteen minutes later he pulled up outside number forty two Connolly Street with the brightly painted, red door to number thirty eight visible in his rear view mirror. He sat there watching for a few minutes but there was no movement at number thirty eight. It was still early morning and the whole street was quiet, with no-one visible in either direction. The low sun was shining brightly as he got out of the car and walked slowly back towards the house, shielding his eyes but keeping them firmly fixed on the building. He decided to go straight in and hopefully catch him by surprise. He reached the door and gave it two firm knocks. There were somc sounds coming from inside and a few seconds later the door opened.

'Hello,' a young, dark-haired woman said, standing inside the doorway, a quizzical look on her face. She was wearing a sweat shirt and jogging bottoms, her hair was un-brushed and Campbell guessed she had just got up, or at least hadn't got herself sorted yet. He could hear more noise coming from inside the house. It sounded like a television, maybe a kids cartoon, he thought. He showed the woman his warrant card,

'Hello, I'm Detective Sergeant Campbell,' he said. He still hadn't got used to calling himself Detective Inspector and he wasn't sure if he should, given he was just "acting up". He didn't know what the rules were, if there were any, and he was too embarrassed to ask anyone at the station. He still thought of himself as one of the team and although DI Strong was currently elsewhere, he was still really the proper boss.

'I'm looking for Stephen Wallace, does he live here?' Campbell asked the woman.

The woman laughed and brushed her hair back off her forehead with her hand.

'No, he *still* doesn't live here, or at least not that I know of anyhow.' There was a child's scream from somewhere behind her and she said,

'Excuse me a minute,' and she walked back down the hallway, shouting something as she went. She reappeared a few seconds later.

'Sorry 'bout that, it's a bit early, bloody kids!' she said, smiling at Campbell.

'That's okay. Do you know a Stephen Wallace or an Andy Austin perhaps?' Campbell asked her.

The woman laughed again.

'No, I've *still* never heard of either of them,' she replied. 'they don't live here, just me and my two kids.'

'Okay,' Campbell replied. 'Can I just ask, why did you say "still" like you'd been asked before?'

'Well yes, because I have. I had another bloke round last week or the week before. He asked me about the same two people. Told him I'd never heard of them too,' the woman said.

'Did he say who he was, this other man?' Campbell asked her intrigued as to who else had been here.

The woman thought for a minute, replaying the incident in her head.

'No, I don't think he did come to think of it. He just asked about those two men's names and then, when I told him I didn't know them, he left. I kinda thought he might be a policeman, he sort of looked like one, but I don't think he actually said.'

'What did he look like, can you describe him?' Campbell asked the woman.

She paused for a moment, thinking again.

'Well, as I say he looked a bit like a policeman, quite tall, slim, a bit older than you, grey hair I think. He was wearing a grey suit, brown shoes.....that's about all I can remember,' the woman replied.

'Okay, that's good. Did you see his car?' Campbell asked her.

'No, I didn't see any car,' she replied, 'but I didn't really look. The kids were playing-up, as usual, he was probably only here for less than a minute.'

'Okay, thanks, you've been very helpful. If you remember anything else or if anyone else asks about these men, please give me a call,' Campbell said and he handed her his card before turning around and walking back to his car.

He climbed in and sat in the driver's seat gathering his thoughts. Trying to make sense of the conversation he'd just had with the young woman at number thirty eight. There were only a few people who knew Austin was back in the country and, although the woman hadn't given a full description of the man who had been here before, it sounded a lot like his boss, DI Strong. But how could that be? If Strong had found out the address Austin had given at the hospital, why hadn't he mentioned it? It just didn't make any sense to Campbell.

Chapter 14

Andy Austin woke up slowly. He turned to his right hand side and glanced at the radio alarm. The bright red digital display read ten fifteen. Ten fifteen! Austin couldn't remember the last time he'd slept in that long. Not since the accident, not since his life had changed. But not just that, he realised that he'd also slept all through the night. That just never happened. And, to cap it all, his head felt clear. There was no pain. None at all. He pushed himself up the bed, plumping up his pillow and smiled. Since he'd got out of hospital, he'd definitely been feeling much better. He still felt weak but he had been having less pain than he used to have, and today it was gone, at least for now. He had really cut back on his painkillers over the last few days and he was also much brighter, feeling much more positive than he'd been in a long time. Maybe things were finally changing. He knew they needed to.

He stretched his body out under the covers before swinging his legs around and getting out of bed. He had a shave and a long, hot shower, letting the heat soak soothingly into his skin. He carefully felt the scar on the back of his head where they'd operated to remove his tumour. It was still raised slightly but it felt like it was definitely going down and it would soon be completely covered by his hair. He returned to the bedroom and sat down on the edge of the bed thinking there was nothing that he needed to do today. He no longer felt the same overpowering need for revenge, for retribution. He was finally starting to put all that behind him and beginning to think about moving on with his life. But what did that mean? He didn't know. That was the one problem he had. The fact was, he was a double murderer and, only a few weeks ago, he'd carried out another serious assault. What he wanted to do with his life and what he could do with his life seemed to be poles apart. Even if he tried to settle down and lead a normal life, the police would always be looking for him and in effect he'd always be on the run. If he gave himself up he'd spend at least the next twenty years in prison and who knows what effect that would have on him.

The only other alternative he had was to keep doing what he was doing. In effect, working for Strong. Delivering some sort of justice to the villains that Strong and his colleagues couldn't bring about through their normal policing and the courts. While there was some merit to that, in Austin's mind the balance seemed to be tipping and he was thinking more and more that it wasn't right. He shouldn't be doing it. It wasn't him, he wasn't a violent man. What he'd done in the past was because he'd been ill. Some sort of PTSD Strong had said, and the more he thought about it, the more it made sense. The real Andy Austin was the kind, caring, loving man who had lived with Lucy Morris.

The man who had loved Lucy Morris. That was the life he wanted to get back to, but he couldn't see how. DI Strong seemed to hold all the aces and was able to control everything he could and couldn't do.

Just then, his mobile started buzzing on the bedside cabinet and he reached across to answer it. He knew it could only be that man, DI Strong, and he was tempted not to answer it, but he knew he would have to talk to him sometime.

'Hello,' he said, making his voice sound a little more hoarse than he actually felt.

'Hey,' DI Strong replied, sounding cheery, 'how are you doing, you okay?'

'Yeh, not too bad, getting there,' Austin replied, moving position so he could rest his back and head against the cushioned bed headboard.

'Good. I've got another job for you, are you ready for it' Strong asked.

'Emm, well, I guess so,' Austin replied hesitantly, 'I may need another week or two recovery time. The doctor said to take it easy after my op and I'm still feeling a bit weak.'

'Sure, no rush. The guy I have in mind will still be around in a few weeks unfortunately, I'm sure. He's escaped us enough times so far. This one likes young boys, we know it, but we haven't been able to prove it yet.'

The last time, they thought they had him. Banged to rights, as they say. They'd found a laptop in his house which contained explicit photos and videos, hidden away in a complex protected file, deep in the laptop. But not complex or deep enough to foil the expert police technology team. They'd found them and some of the images were awful. There was nothing else on the device, it was completely empty. The man claimed it wasn't his laptop and that it belonged to the cleaner, a young eastern European girl who couldn't speak much English. She claimed she'd been given it by a man friend, but she couldn't remember who. She had no idea that the file was on there, of course she didn't. They all knew it wasn't her laptop, but there was no way to prove it. The man had a smug smile on his face all through the interview, knowing they wouldn't be able to hold him if the cleaner stuck to her story, which he knew she would. She was being well paid and she knew the consequences if she didn't.

'Have you got any boys detective?' he'd asked Strong. 'Young, strapping boys I bet, better keep your eye on them, make sure they stay on the straight and narrow,' he said, as he smiled directly across the table at the detective.

Back on the phone call, Strong was keen to close off this new job for Austin, before he could back out.

'I'll drop you some details in the post. Plain brown envelope, as before,' he said.

'Okay, sorry, there's someone at the door. The postman I think,' Austin said and he ended the call.

He lay back against the headboard and closed his eyes. There was no postman, but Austin hadn't really been in the mood to talk with Strong. He needed time to think, and time to get stronger again, before he felt ready for a proper conversation with the policeman.

Chapter 15

She checked it again. Hardly able to believe what she was seeing. Every other time, before, when she'd done it, there had been one blue line and then just a blank space. Now there were two blue lines. Was it real or was she just dreaming? She shook her head to confirm she was awake. She was! Sitting on the edge of the bed, she checked the instruction leaflet again. It was definitely a positive reading. Her hand was shaking as she put the plastic tube down on the bedside table, subconsciously rubbing her stomach with her other hand. She picked up her mobile phone and dialled. She waited as it rang a few times but then it went to voicemail.

'Hi, you've reached the voicemail of Joe Campbell. Please leave a message and I'll call you back as soon as I can.'

Femi Campbell, the wife of DS Joe Campbell, was used to hearing that message. Whenever she called, probably nine times out of ten it went to his voicemail. Frustrating. He was always busy. Always working. The life of a policeman, and the life of being married to a policeman. It was annoying, but she was getting used to it by now. They'd been married for five years and she had come to learn how important her husband's job was to him. It's just that sometimes what she had to say was important too. Especially this time.

Femi and Joe had first met at a wedding. It was a big wedding, Caribbean style. Lots and lots of family. Femi was a cousin of the bride and Joe was one of the groom's many cousins. Yet another of Joe's cousins had introduced them and they'd hit it off straight away. They seemed to share the same sense of dry humour and Femi remembered him making her laugh until she was in tears. At that time he had just been promoted into the CID as a detective constable and Femi thought that sounded quite impressive. Her mum had thought so too and she was very keen for Femi to get to know this man better. It had always been her dream that her only daughter would marry a doctor or a policeman and so Joe Campbell fitted the bill perfectly. But Femi hadn't needed any pushing from her mum as she got to know Joe, she knew he was the one for her and luckily Joe thought the same way about her. Soon they were planning their wedding, well to be more accurate Femi and her mum were planning the wedding, with Joe trying to hang on to their coat tails. It was another big Jamaican style wedding and everything had gone perfectly, even her mum's insistence on making a speech and telling everyone how Femi had once flashed her pants at the minister when she was three years old.

It had always just been Femi and her mum growing up, her dad had decided family life and the weather in the UK wasn't for him, and he returned to Jamaica not long after Femi was born. Femi had only seen him once since, when she was seven, he'd come to visit one day but she hadn't felt anything for him. He was just a stranger to her and they'd not had any contact since. She didn't need him, just her mum. Joe had asked her if she wanted to invite him to the wedding but she said no, it had always just been her and her mum and that was good enough for her. It had been hard for them at times, trying to fit in. A single black woman and a black daughter. Lots of racism, both obvious with name calling and direct comments, and less obvious with just how they were often treated as some sort of second class citizens. Still they had made friends too and built up their own social circle and made it through. Femi's childhood memories were mainly happy ones and that was largely down to her mum. They hadn't needed her dad then and they didn't need him now.

'Hi, it's me. Give me a call back. I've got some news,' she said and hung up.

She hoped he would call back soon, but knowing him that wasn't a definite. Maybe she should have given him more of a hint. But surely he would guess? He was supposed to be a detective after all! They'd been trying for a baby for the last three years and, fingers crossed, it looked like it might be happening at last. She knew it was early days and she didn't want to get too excited and tempt fate, but it was difficult not to. Especially after all they'd been through. Fifth time lucky, please let it be, she thought. They'd never had a positive test result before. Please let it be right. She wanted to tell her friends too but she knew she had to tell Joe first and then together they could decide what, and when, they did after that. After all it was his baby too. Their baby. After all this time, all the pain they'd gone through, she still couldn't believe it and she couldn't stop smiling.

DS Campbell walked along the hospital corridor and turned through the doors into the Neurology department waiting room. He'd seen the missed call from his wife but he hadn't listened to the voicemail yet, deciding he'd call her back later. After he'd finished what he was doing here. This was important. This could make his police career. It had been a hard slog for Campbell to get the level he was now at in the police and he knew he'd have to do something extra to warrant his next promotion. There were three men sat on the brown, plastic chairs in the waiting area. All on their own. All quietly waiting their turn to be called. None of them were Andy Austin.

Campbell marched up to the reception desk and the young nurse looked up from her computer. He was pleased to see it was the same nurse he'd spoken to before and he gave her his best smile.

'Hi, DS Campbell, we met last week. I just need a little bit more information on one of your patients. Can I come round?' he asked and did so without waiting for her answer.

'Oh, right,' the nurse replied, beginning to blush. She hadn't been sure if she should give him the information last time, but it seemed to be okay. At least no-one had said anything. Although she hadn't actually told anyone. But now he was back again asking for more. He seemed to know what he was doing. She wasn't sure what to do, but he was a policeman and so maybe that was okay? She looked around for help but she knew she was the only member of staff there at the moment. Everyone else was either with patients or on a break.

‘I just need to know if one of your patients has an appointment coming up, and if so, when it is. His name is Stephen Wallace. Can you check please?’ Campbell asked with, what he hoped was an authoritative tone. He could sense the nurse was wavering and he didn’t want to give her the chance to say no.

Thoughts ran through the nurse’s head, “that’s not too sensitive, not anything personal, should be okay, if I do it quickly” and she typed the name into her computer. After a few seconds the screen changed and she looked up at the policeman standing in front of her.

‘Emm, he’s actually due in later today, but I don’t want any trouble. He is a patient and I’m not sure what the rules are on confidentiality and that,’ the nurse said.

‘Don’t worry, there won’t be any trouble,’ Campbell answered confidently. ‘Nothing will happen in the hospital. I just need to see him, that’s all. I’ll talk to him outside when he leaves. What time is his appointment?’ Campbell asked.

‘Oh, okay, well it’s two thirty this afternoon,’ the nurse replied.

‘Thanks, you’ve been a great help,’ Campbell said.

As he turned and walked out of the room, he glanced at the clock on the wall which read one thirty. He walked back to the café by the hospital reception and decided to sit and wait with a sandwich and a coffee. The barista informed him that if he opted for a “meal deal”, he could also get a chocolate bar or a bag of crisps, and it would be cheaper, so he quickly picked up a mars bar. After paying, he positioned himself at a table towards the rear of the café and sat on a chair facing the hospital entrance. He hadn’t met Austin before and so he didn’t think Austin would know who he was, but he didn’t want to take any chances so it was safest staying out of sight at the back. He had about an hour to wait and he took his time eating lunch, chewing it slowly and taking small sips of his coffee. He watched the people coming and going through the hospital entrance. Some with obvious ailments, sporting bandages or limping or being pushed along in wheelchairs. Others with no obvious, outward signs, of there being anything wrong with them, but maybe they were concealing something on the inside. Physical or mental. Or, they could just be visiting someone. Campbell could only imagine, but it passed the time. He noticed that the great majority of people coming and going were elderly. There were a few young men and women, some with children, but not many. It should be easy to pick out Austin amongst them.

He finished his chocolate bar and glanced at his watch, it was almost time. If Austin was going to keep his appointment then he should be coming in pretty soon. Campbell had a sudden panic that he might come in through another door, but he quickly convinced himself that was highly unlikely. This was the main hospital entrance and he doubted

Austin would have any reason to think about sneaking in any other way. He knew he could have called it in and got some back up, but time was tight and he didn't want to miss the chance. His chance. If Austin saw police cars arriving in the car park just as he arrived himself, it might scare him off and they'd have missed their opportunity to get him again. Campbell didn't want that to happen and he was confident that he'd be able to apprehend him on his own. Campbell was fit and strong, an ex-boxer, and of course he had the element of surprise. He would just pick the right moment, when Austin least expected it, and quickly arrest him. Then he could call in the cavalry.

There was a steady flow of people coming in through the entrance door, many of them in hospital clothing, mainly greens and blues, probably a change of shift Campbell thought. His eyes were now completely focused on the reception area and sure enough, a few minutes later, he saw Austin come through the revolving door. It was definitely him. Campbell had no doubt. He walked slowly across the reception area and headed down the corridor. Campbell stayed seated. He knew where Austin was headed and there was no need to follow him. Having thought about it while he waited, he'd decided that his best course of action would be to follow Austin out of the hospital and trail him back to wherever he was currently holed out. Campbell knew that might be slightly more risky but he wanted to catch him in his lair so that they could get the maximum amount of evidence to be able to secure a solid conviction. Campbell was sure there would be incriminating details in his house. There would be stuff on his phone or his laptop, as well as the possibility of them finding some sort of weapons there. If he arrested him at the hospital they might never find out where he was staying and so miss out on potentially decisive evidence they might need to convict him.

Campbell still had a little coffee left in his cup, but it had gone cold and he'd been sitting at the table for over an hour since he'd first arrived and bought his lunch. No-one had asked him to leave, but the café had got busier and he felt conscious he was still taking up a four chair table. Maybe someone else needed it and it wasn't fair that he was just sitting there. He glanced at his watch again and guessed he still had another ten or fifteen minutes to wait, but he didn't want to leave the table as this was the perfect spot to see Austin reappear. He decided he had enough time to get a coffee top-up and he rose from the table, leaving his coat on the seat, and went up to the counter, ordering a flat white and glancing back to the corridor every few seconds to make sure he didn't miss Austin. As he waited for his coffee to be made he saw Austin coming back down the corridor. Walking briskly. Shit, he thought, that was quick and he grabbed his coat and started walking slowly out of the café towards the reception area. A family of four had already sat down at his table and as he left the café area he could hear a woman's voice shouting behind him.

'Joe,… Joe, …flat white for Joe.'

He kept walking, keeping Austin in his line of sight, over to his right. As Austin reached the reception area, Campbell fell in step about ten metres behind him, partly obscured by an old man with a patch over his right eye. He followed the two men through the hospital door, overtaking the old man as they left the building, and then followed Austin up a few steps to the main hospital car park. He watched as Austin took a car key from his jacket pocket and aimed it out in front of him. The lights flashed on a black hatchback and Campbell quickly took a mental note of the car make and registration number. He walked quickly to his own car, which was in the next row, and drove to the exit, pulling into the side of the road as he left. A minute later he watched as Austin's car drove past him and turned out of the car park onto the main road. Campbell put his car in gear and went after him.

He stayed a few cars behind but always keeping Austin's car in sight. He had trailed a number of cars during his career in the police and he knew what he was doing. Eventually he saw Austin take a right into a residential street called Parkside Avenue and when Campbell arrived at the junction he noticed that Austin had stopped about fifty metres down the road. There was nothing behind Campbell so he sat there waiting until he saw Austin get out of the car and walk through a gate to the house adjacent to where he'd parked. Campbell turned into the street and pulled into the kerb on the other side of the road, giving himself a view of the front door, number twenty seven, and he watched as

Austin opened it and disappeared into the semi-detached house.

Campbell sat there for a few seconds thinking. Really he should call this in and get proper back up, organised with a suitable plan to enter the house and capture Austin safely. But that would all take time and Campbell was excited. He didn't have Strong to tell him what to do any more and that felt kind of liberating. He could make his own decision without having to ask for any approval. If it all went well and he arrested Austin, no-one would care whether he followed the correct process anyway. He would just bluff his way through it saying he'd just happened to spot him and he seized the opportunity while he had it. The fact that Austin had been arrested would cancel out any other questions that might have arisen. He would be the hero. He liked this feeling of power, of being the one in charge. Austin was only one man and Campbell was physically stronger than him. With the element of surprise he should be able to overcome him quickly and get a set of handcuffs on him before Austin realised what was happening. Then he could call for support and it would be all over. The arrest of the Anniversary Killer. At last. What a start it would be to his term as an acting DI. They couldn't not make him a DI after that, surely?

Campbell had convinced himself it would work and, feeling confident, he got out the car and walked towards the house, staying on the other side of the road. He walked past it, glancing to his left as he did so to get an idea of the layout. There was a gate and a short path leading to the front door which displayed a silver number twenty seven on it. To the right of the front door there was a double window and above that there were two further windows. The house attached to the left of Austin's was a mirror image. Campbell guessed the front room would be some sort of lounge with a kitchen and dining room at the rear. The detective didn't see any movement in the house as he walked past it. He stopped a few metres further on and took out his phone, pretending to make a call, but keeping one eye on the house. After a minute he put his phone back in his pocket and crossed the street, heading back towards Austin's house. He didn't have any great plan, but didn't think he particularly needed one. He'd simply knock on the door, Austin would answer it, he'd overpower him before he realised what was happening and that would be that. It would be all over in a few seconds.

He opened the gate quietly and walked quickly up the path to the front door, watching the downstairs window as he went. There was no movement at the window. He knocked firmly on the door and stood close to it, waiting, his eyes fixed on the door jamb, waiting for a gap to appear. Poised and ready to move. The door began to open and Campbell immediately stepped forward. Using his shoulder, he pushed hard on the door, forcing his way in and he hit Austin square in the chest. Austin staggered backwards along the hallway and Campbell's momentum carried him forward with his target. Austin fell over, his arms flailing outwards as he hit the floor. With nothing to stop him, Campbell stumbled and fell too. As he went down, he hit his head against the staircase bannister with a loud crack, knocking him out cold. He rolled onto the hallway floor, landing at Austin's feet, lying face up. Blood started to ooze out of a gash on his forehead and trickle down his left cheek. Austin scrambled to his feet, bent over trying to catch his breath. He looked down at the man lying bleeding on the floor in front of him, wondering what had just happened. He didn't recognise the man. This man who had just barged into his house, knocking him over. Once he had regained his senses he bent over the man lying there to have a closer look at him. He was out cold but still breathing. He reached inside the man's jacket pocket and took out his wallet, opening it up. He immediately saw the police warrant card with the man's photo, looking a bit younger with the words Detective Sergeant J Campbell written underneath.

'Oh shit,' Austin said out loud, 'a bloody policeman.'

So they had found him, but where were the rest of them? There didn't seem to be anyone else just this one policeman on his own. That was strange, maybe the rest were on their way or waiting outside for him. "We have you surrounded, come out with your hands up." But no, he looked outside and there was no one else there. The street was deadly quiet. He went into the kitchen and came back with a towel, placing it on the policeman's wound to stem the flow of blood. He wasn't a doctor but it didn't look too bad, he'd seen worse.

He decided to phone Strong and tell him what had happened. He knew he had to get out before this policeman woke up, or his colleagues finally arrived. DI Strong would probably know the best way to do it. He couldn't just leave this Campbell guy lying here, but he knew if he called for an ambulance, more police would definitely come too and they'd want to ask all sorts of questions which would probably lead them to realising he was a wanted man. The Anniversary Killer.

Strong answered on the second ring then told Austin to wait while he found a quieter place to talk. Austin explained what had happened, and that DS Campbell was now lying on his hallway floor. Strong sounded shocked. He appeared to know Campbell but claimed to have no idea how he had found out where Austin was living. Austin reassured Strong that his colleague didn't look bad, it had been an accident, probably just a superficial cut, but he had knocked himself out and he was still unconscious. The phone went quiet as Strong thought for a few seconds, then he told Austin he should pack his stuff and get out of the house as soon as possible.

'I don't know how much Campbell knows at this point so let's assume he knows a lot. Take your car and then leave it in a side street, or a car park somewhere. Somewhere it won't be seen as being obviously abandoned, or easily found. Then use public transport, or a taxi if you have to after that, and check into a hotel somewhere, using another ID. You've got other IDs I take it?' Strong asked him.

‘Yes, yes, I have a few I haven’t used yet,’ Austin replied. ‘What about this Campbell. What should I do about him?’

‘How does he look?’ Strong asked.

‘I think he’s fine, just unconscious, he’s breathing okay, he’ll probably wake up soon with a sore head,’ Austin replied..

‘Okay, I’ll call an ambulance,’ Strong sighed. ‘You’ve got ten minutes to get out. Call me tonight when you’ve found somewhere to stay and we’ll talk more then.’

Austin put his phone into his pocket and started packing everything he needed into two large sports bags. Ten minutes later he was in the car, making his escape. After a short ride, he parked it in a small car park at the back of a block of flats and then started walking towards the train station, on his way to his next place of refuge. He was getting used to this now but it didn’t make him feel any better about it. He desperately wanted to somehow have a normal life. But how would that be possible, maybe Strong could tell him.

Chapter 16

'Shhh...' Sophie giggled as Emily noisily tried to get the key in the door. 'You'll wake up Josh and Olivia.'

'Bloody key won't fit, has someone changed the locks?' Emily said as she put her hand over one eye and tried to focus on getting the key in the lock. She knew one-eyed people had better eyesight and now she could see there was only one lock to try and open.

'Give's it here,' Sophie replied, 'it's bloody freezing out here and you're too drunk. You shouldn't have had those last shots.'

Sophie took the key from her housemate and quickly opened the door, with Emily stumbling in behind her. They walked along the hallway into the lounge and collapsed together laughing on the brown sofa. It was Monday night, which was "student night" at one of the bars in town. A good marketing ploy to sell more alcohol on what would otherwise have been a quiet night in the bar. Students didn't care what night it was as long as the drink was cheap. Four shots for a fiver was the special offer this week, and it had gone down well with the student crowd. In a previous life the bar had once been a police station and the owners had imaginatively called their bar The Old Police Station. Or maybe they'd employed a marketing agency to come up with the name, but that was doubtful, as they'd more likely have called it The Banana Bush or something equally obscure.

In the Old Police Station, on a Monday night, if you had a student card, or got someone to lend you a student card, or had a fake student card made for you, then you usually got half-price drinks as well as whatever the special offer happened to be that week. Emily and Sophie went there most Monday nights and knew a lot of the other people that did likewise. All students. Tonight had been a good night. As usual they'd had a bit to drink, not too much, or at least Sophie hadn't, Emily had made the most of the shots offer, but more importantly they'd had a good laugh.

'Who was that guy you were talking to at the bar, earlier on?' Sophie asked her friend as they sat relaxed together on the sofa.

'Oh, I don't know, some twat and his mates,' Emily replied. 'He tried some chat up line, claimed he was a student and that they were going to a party after, and I should come too. Bring my mates, he said. But I don't think they were students. They didn't look it and I doubt there was any party. Who has a party on a Monday night for god's sake?'

'No, that's true. Rookie mistake that. And I've never seen them around Uni before,' Sophie replied. 'Probably got hold of some dodgy student cards. I think I saw the bouncer talking to them later on and then I never saw them after that. I'm guessing he threw them out.'

'I think I'll get myself a glass of water,' Sophie said to her friend. 'Do you want one?' she called back as she walked through to the kitchen.

Emily flopped further down on the lounge sofa and called back,

'Yes please mum.' She let out a loud burp and started laughing hysterically.

Sophie returned with two glasses of water and sat down beside her friend.

'Here you go, better drink that, we've got a nine o' clock English Lit seminar tomorrow,' she said.

'Eeargh, don't remind me,' Emily replied, 'and it's Mister bloody pinky Potter that's doing it, the old perv. I swear if he leans over me again tomorrow and looks at my tits, I'm gonna elbow him in the balls. That'll stop him ogling me.'

'Haha, aww, he's alright Potter, he knows his stuff, he's probably just a lonely old man,' Sophie responded. 'He's actually quite a good lecturer.'

'Yeh, right, lonely old perv you mean. What's that, over there by the TV? Lying on the table?' Emily asked her housemate, suddenly distracted.

Sophie pulled herself up on the sofa and looked across the room.

'It looks like that phone, you know the old one the cooker man found the other day. Wait though, it's plugged in. I asked Josh if he had a charger and he said he'd look in his cables drawer. He must have found one that fitted.'

'Cables drawer!' Emily laughed. 'Who has a cables drawer? I've got a bra and pants drawer, but that's about it!' she shrieked. 'I wonder if he has a separate drawer for everything? We need to check his room one day. I bet he has a plugs drawer too.'

'Yeh, but not just one. He'll have one for two pin plugs and another for three pin plugs I bet!' Sophie replied, laughing. 'Ah bless him, he's alright really. At least he found a charger.'

Sophie got up from the settee, walked across to the TV table and picked up the phone, disconnecting it from the charger and returning to sit beside her friend on the sofa.

'Look, I think it's pretty much charged,' she said as she pressed the power button.

After a few seconds the screen on the phone lit up.

'Oh good, it's working,' Sophie exclaimed.

'Ooh, let's see,' Emily replied leaning into her friend. 'Let's see if we can find out who's phone it is.'

Sophie pressed a few buttons with Emily looking on and after a few seconds she turned to look at her friend.

'It doesn't seem to have been used much, well there's not much on it, just one contact number with the letter "K" as the name but no call history. Let's see if there's any texts,' she said.

'Ooh, yes there are some texts to and from that number, look,' she said handing the phone to Emily, 'Hold on, I need the loo.' Sophie pushed herself up from the soft sofa and walked out the room. When she returned a few minutes later Emily was still looking at the phone.

'Found anything?' Sophie asked.

'Well, yes, it looks like these two have been getting up to no good. Some sort of secret liaison by the look of things,' Emily replied.

'Ooh, really? That's so cool. Let me see,' Sophie said, edging closer to her friend to get a better look.

'From what I can see it looks like this one, whoever owns this phone, was married, or at least had a partner. Look, it says things like "is he out tonight" and "how long will we have" and when is he back" stuff like that. Maybe that's why the phone was hidden by the oven. She was hiding it from her husband or boyfriend.'

'Really, that's cool. We've stumbled on a secret affair. How cool is that?' Sophie said, sitting back up and taking a long drink of her cold water.

'Yeh looks like it. Did you meet the people who were in here last year?' Emily asked while she continued to scroll through the phone.

'No, it was empty when I came to look at it. I think the agent said that it hadn't been let out before, they'd been doing it up or something,' Sophie replied.

'Mmm…looks like it's all finished though,' Emily replied, still reading through the texts. 'Look the last one was over six months ago and she hasn't replied. He's texted three times asking why she's not replying and then I suppose he's just given up. I wonder why she didn't reply?'

'Maybe he was getting too heavy, or her boyfriend found out or something?' Sophie suggested.

'Yeh, maybe, could be all sorts of reasons I suppose. Shall we text him now?' Emily said, smiling mischievously at her flatmate.

'What? No, you can't do that. And say what? You might stir up all sorts of trouble,' Sophie exclaimed, her mouth open, staring at her friend.

But Emily's fingers were already moving, her tongue poking out of the side of her mouth as she focused her eyes on the little screen. She hit send.

'Oh my god, what have you said?' Sophie asked.

'I said, sorry haven't been in touch, needed a break. Time to think.' Emily replied.

'Oh my god,' Sophie repeated. 'I wonder if he'll reply.'

The two girls sat there for another five minutes chatting, whilst keeping an eye on the phone, but there was no response. The phone stayed silent. Sophie looked at the clock on the wall and decided it was time for bed and, bidding her friend goodnight, she headed upstairs. Emily waited another ten minutes but there was still nothing from the phone so she too gave up and, picking up the charger, made her way upstairs to her room. Ten minutes later there was the sound of low, gentle snoring coming from both rooms.

Chapter 17

DS Campbell woke up in a hospital bed. He was still feeling a bit groggy, but the doctor had told him that there was no serious damage to his head. He'd given it a good crack against the wooden stair-post but they'd scanned him and there was no internal damage. Thankfully. The doctor had told him that they wanted to keep him under observation for another twenty four hours just to be sure. Campbell told the doctor that he wanted to leave as soon as possible, that he had work to do. After a bit of discussion, they agreed on a compromise that the doctor would come and see him again later that day and they could review it again then. Campbell knew that whatever the doctor said, he was determined he was going to leave.

He was annoyed with himself. He had Austin in the palm of his hands and he'd let him go. He felt like an idiot, falling and knocking himself out like that. What a rookie. If word got around the station of what had happened, he'd be a laughing stock. Thankfully though, because he'd been on his own, it would be unlikely that anyone else would find out the truth. With what had happened, he felt he didn't deserve to be a DI, Strong would never have done anything like that. He'd have organised it properly with the team, made sure they had the proper back-up and Austin would be behind bars now. Maybe he should have done it properly. Of course he should have. He'd just got carried away with the excitement of it all. Bringing Austin in. For once in his life he'd have been the main man. Now he just felt totally incompetent.

Campbell hadn't told anyone that Austin had been there at the house where he'd knocked himself out. No-one had brought it up and he'd managed to bluff his way through any of the questions as to why he was there, by saying he was just meeting one of his informants and he'd tripped over. One of the advantages of being an acting DI, he was finding out, was that nobody really questioned you too deeply. He was learning that the higher you went, the more you could get away with. The police force ran on a hierarchical basis and you very rarely questioned a superior officer.

He'd been awake, but still annoyed with himself, when his wife had come in and told him that she was pregnant. It was great news, of course, but Campbell had found it hard to show much enthusiasm given that he was lying in a hospital bed with a sore head, and he'd just let Austin, The Anniversary Killer, escape. He wished he'd got the news when he'd been in a better frame of mind, but he knew you couldn't plan these things. He was genuinely happy for his wife, who he knew was desperate to start a family. And he was happy for himself too. It was what he wanted – to have a beautiful wife and family. He just couldn't get Austin out his head at this point in time.

'You don't seem very happy,' his wife had said.

'What? Of course I am,' he'd replied trying to lose the negative thoughts in his head and forcing a smile. 'I'm still a bit, you know…' he said, screwing up his face.

'You need to be more careful, now you're going to be a dad,' she told him. 'Maybe you should look for a safer role, get a transfer away from serious crime? I don't like the thought of you being in danger.'

That had irritated him more. It was bad enough lying here, feeling like a failure with no-one to talk to about it, and nothing he could do while he was stuck in his hospital bed. Now his wife was telling him he should transfer out. Did she think he was a failure too, not good enough for the job? Maybe he wasn't, maybe she was right. He had messed up on Austin after all. He should have waited and organised it properly. He'd got carried away, imagining it would be easy and he ended up knocking himself out! What a fool! If he was the Chief Constable he certainly wouldn't make himself a DI now. He couldn't help comparing himself with DI Strong and he knew Strong would never have made such a mess of things. That's why he was a DI and Campbell wasn't. Maybe his wife was right, maybe he just wasn't cut out for the role?

Overall, it had been an awkward visit from his wife and she left early saying she had things to do, but he could see she was upset with him. She'd been annoyed at his lack of reaction to their baby news. They'd been trying for years and in her mind it was the most important thing in their lives, but that didn't seem to be the case for her husband. Campbell knew he'd let her down and so he resolved to make it up to her with a proper celebration as soon as he got out of hospital.

However, as soon as she'd left, his mind drifted back to Austin and the earlier events of the day. He'd run it over and over in his head. Time and time again. He could remember going to Austin's house and confronting him in the hallway, and he could remember stumbling, falling as he grappled with Austin, but nothing after that until he woke up in the hospital bed. How had he got here? He didn't think there was anyone else in the house, which would suggest that Austin had called an ambulance for him before he escaped. Why would he do that? He decided to call his colleague DS Brown.

'Can you do me a favour? Can you find out who called the ambulance for me. I guess it must have been the guy I was going to see, but I just want to check. Ask them for a copy of the recording and then bring it to me,' Campbell said.

'Yes guv, I'll get right onto it,' DS Brown replied.

Two hours later, DS Brown came marching down the corridor towards Campbell's bed. Campbell could hear him approaching, he was a big man, over six foot and probably weighed about seventeen stone. He could be really useful in some situations, those where a strong man was needed, but he'd never be very good at sneaking up on people, as his big size twelve feet echoed down the corridor.

'Quick, let's get out the back door,' the thieves would say, 'I can hear detective sergeant Brown running down the street.'

DS Brown stopped at Campbell's bedside and Campbell could see that his cheeks were flushed.

'You're gonna want to listen to this,' DS Brown said excitedly and he pushed the play button on his phone, turning the volume up. The sound boomed out of the phone.

'Emergency, how can I help you?' a woman's voice said.

'I need an ambulance immediately,' a man's voice said. 'The address is twenty seven Parkside Avenue. There's a policeman unconscious there. He's had an accident. Fallen and hit his head.'

'Can I just take some details sir. What's your name?' the woman asked.

DS Brown stopped the recording.

'That's it. He just hung up at that point. An ambulance was sent to the address and that's where they found you,' DS Brown explained.

Campbell made no attempt to respond, he just sat motionless in his hospital bed, thinking.

'What do you think? Do you recognise the voice?' DS Brown asked him.

'Not sure, I don't think so, do you?' Campbell replied.

DS Brown looked around the room, checking that no-one else was in earshot of the two men before replying.

'Well, I guess it must have been this guy you were seeing, but I can't help thinking it sounded a bit like our old guv, DI Strong,' Brown said, fairly certain that it was him, but not wanting to say it out loud to his boss, Campbell, lying in the hospital bed, in case it broke some protocol. He knew Campbell and Strong were close.

Campbell didn't respond but he knew the voice wasn't Andy Austin's. In his mind, it was definitely the voice of DI Strong. Strong had made the emergency call. But that didn't make sense. How did Strong know where Campbell was? To know that, he'd need to know Austin's address. And to know Campbell needed an ambulance, he'd also need to know that Campbell was injured. How could he know that? There was only one person that could have told him all of that. Andy Austin.

Chapter 18

Emily was giggling to herself. She was sitting on her own on the bus heading back to the house after a long law lecture. The rain was battering against the bus window and it was steaming up on the inside. Law! God how she hated that subject. How could anyone do that as a job, day in, day out. There were too many books, too many cases, too many confusing rules. And Latin! What was the point of that? Why didn't they just use English like everyone else? She was certainly glad she only had to do it for one term as part of her overall course. She hadn't really been listening to the lecturer today, she'd been too busy on her phone. Well, technically not her phone. It was the phone they'd found in the kitchen. Things had moved on since she had sent that initial text, and it was getting interesting. She was having fun. That was what life was all about.

The man at the other end of the texts had replied a few days ago and Emily had carried on with the conversation, still pretending that she was the original phone owner. It hadn't been too difficult to trick him, just keep the messages short and don't be too specific. She could pick up on some of the things he said in his texts and it was enabling her to build up a fuller picture. The two people had obviously been having some sort of secret affair and the woman Emily was now pretending to be had definitely had a boyfriend at the time. On one text exchange, Emily had suggested that she might be thinking of dumping the boyfriend, thinking that would tease him further, but to her surprise it seemed to put him off a bit. Maybe he liked the whole secrecy thing, she thought. It certainly didn't look like he wanted their relationship out in the open or have any sort of commitment. She wondered if maybe he was married or had a girlfriend too, but there was never any indication of that in the messages. He was still a bit of a mystery.

As the bus journey continued, another text came in. This one suggesting that they should meet. He'd asked this before but Emily had put him off, saying the boyfriend was getting a bit suspicious and she couldn't get out on her own. He'd offered a number of suggestions, like she was meeting a girlfriend or she was going to the shops, but she'd managed to come up with reasons why she couldn't. He seemed to be able to meet at any time of the day or night and that made her wonder what he did for a living. Maybe he had his own company, a self-made millionaire, although at the other end of the scale he might just be unemployed with no money. From some of the things he'd said in his texts, she guessed that he was fairly young, in his twenties, she thought. He was getting more and more persistent about meeting though and she was running out of excuses to put him off. Of course he didn't know that she wasn't the woman he thought she was, and she knew if they did meet then it would all come out.

'You've changed.'

'Oh yes, you mean my hair, I had it done last week.'

'No, I mean your skin colour. You weren't white last time we met.'

Of course Emily didn't know that, but she couldn't really text him with questions like,

"What do I look like?"

She was really enjoying the game though and didn't want it to end just yet. She knew she could just finish it anytime if she wanted to. He had no idea who she really was and if she just stopped texting him or even threw the phone away that would be the end of it. But she didn't want to. Not yet anyway. It was too much fun, leading him along like this. She hadn't told anyone what she was doing, not even Sophie. She'd only have persuaded her to stop. In fact Sophie seemed to have forgotten all about the phone, not even noticing that it wasn't lying around the house somewhere. It was Emily's secret game.

Of course the other alternative would be to agree to meet him. A big part of her was intrigued to find out who this man was and what he looked like. She knew that could be risky, but it would seem like an unfinished story if she just stopped the messages and never discovered his real identity. She couldn't think of any way to ask him anything personal in the texts. It was obvious he'd met the woman a number of times previously and they'd been intimate, so Emily couldn't ask anything that he would presume she already knew. The more she thought about it though, maybe she could meet him. If she took care and did it on her terms. She could arrange to meet him in a public place like a bar maybe. Surely that would be safe enough? He'd come across as quite a nice guy in the texts, even though he'd obviously been having some sort of secret affair. She was pretty sure he wasn't a serial killer or anything and if he took offence at her playing him along, she could just up and leave. He still wouldn't know who she was and it was unlikely they'd ever see each other again. If he was good looking and saw the funny side of what she'd been doing, well, he might turn out to be a nice guy and….well, you never know. He could be young, fit, rich and available!

Chapter 19

Austin scrolled down his contact list for the sixth or seventh time. It was his old phone and there were people there he hadn't spoken to since before the accident. Most of them in fact. After he'd made the decision to get justice for his family, he'd had to disappear and re-invent himself and so now they were all people from his past, from another life. All except one. He was looking at that name now. Lucy Morris.

He couldn't stop thinking about Lucy and although Strong had warned him off from contacting her, knowing that to do so would put her in a difficult position, Austin had done a lot of thinking over the last few days as he recuperated. He realised that, in purely practical terms, there was nothing to actually stop him from contacting his ex-girlfriend. He wanted to speak to her and Strong couldn't stop him from doing that. In fact Strong didn't even need to know. But, on the other hand, he knew that Strong was right. Maybe *he* wanted to talk to Lucy again, to try and explain to her why he did what he had done, but maybe *she* wouldn't want to talk to him. Didn't *need* to talk to him, like he felt he *needed* to talk to her. Maybe he was being selfish. If he had any respect or feelings for Lucy, perhaps he should just let her get on with her life. She'd probably moved on now, put Austin in her past, maybe found another boyfriend and was living a happy life. He did hope she was happy, mostly, but a small part of him also hoped that she still thought about him and even missed him a bit. He thought about the time when they had lived together, when he'd moved in to her flat. It had been the only time he had been content in the last few years, since the accident. And he had been happy, truly happy. He hadn't seen it coming but then, of course, you never do. That day, when he realised she had found out what he had been doing, who he really was, had been one of the worst days of his life. Almost as bad as the day of the accident that had wiped out his family, although nothing would ever be as bad as that. Part of him had thought he'd be able to explain it to her and maybe she'd understand, but deep down, knowing how pure and honest Lucy was, he knew that could never be the case. He'd left her a letter trying to clarify his reasons, why he had to do it, but he knew that wasn't enough and she deserved better than that. At that time, he couldn't tell her everything without putting her in a potentially compromising position with the police. They might have thought she had known what he was doing and charged her as an accomplice and he'd been very careful to keep her out of it all.

Now, when he thought about what he had done at that time, killing two people, even he found it hard to understand. He still didn't believe justice had been done, somehow the four men in the car should have had to pay for what they'd done, but maybe he had gone too far. He definitely didn't feel so aggressive anymore. At the time it had taken over his life, but now he was just glad he'd stopped. He had felt completely different since he'd got out of hospital and the more he thought about it, the tumour and the PTSD Strong had told him about, could they have been what made him do it? The truth was he didn't know, and even if there was some sort of medical explanation for it, did it matter? He'd still killed two innocent people – there was no getting away from that. If he got caught no jury would let him off. He'd been a dangerous, violent man, no matter what the reason, and now he was in an impossible situation.

There were a lot of things Austin didn't know, and would probably never find out. A lot of them outside his control, but there was one thing he could still do. He could call Lucy. Just once. What was there to lose? The worst she could do would be to hang up on him, and he realised that was a real possibility, but unless he tried, he'd never know. Maybe she would talk to him, listen to him, that would be a start. A start to what, he wasn't sure but he'd never know unless he tried and, if he didn't, he'd always be left wondering. For the rest of his life. In that moment he knew his mind was made up, it's now or never, he thought, and he hit the call button.

Lucy had just put the baby down for an afternoon nap and was making herself a welcome cup of coffee in the kitchen, when her mobile rang. It was on charge in the living room and she really wanted that coffee. No, she *needed* that coffee, so she decided to just let it ring out. Whoever it was would call back, or once she'd sat down, she might ring them. Depending on who it was. It had been a long morning after a long night. Carl, or CJ as she mostly called him, hadn't settled and she'd not had much rest herself. It wore you down after a while and now that he'd finally gone down she was determined to just have a bit of a chill herself and recover. A bit of "me-time" as they called it on daytime TV. She made her coffee in a pink mug emblazoned with "Mum" in white letters, and walked back through to the living room, slumping down on the settee and taking a few sips of the hot drink. She breathed in the aroma and immediately felt herself begin to relax for the first time that day. The baby monitor was sitting on the coffee table in front of her, the light blinking away, but thankfully it was all quiet. She took another drink of the coffee, feeling it course through her body and she could feel her eyes getting heavy. She let them close and for the first time that day the world felt good again. She stayed sitting like that for what seemed a long time, slowly sipping her drink and listening to her own breathing. She felt very calm. One of her friends had told her about some meditation techniques, but she'd always found them hard to get into. If you had to focus on doing them, how could they be relaxing? After a few goes, Lucy had given up and reverted to caffeine and a soft sofa. That seemed to work best for her, when she could find the time to do it. It had certainly been a crazy couple of years.

She leaned forward and put her, now, empty mug on a coaster, beside the baby monitor and her mobile phone and sank back into her comfy settee. Just as she felt herself about to drop off to sleep, her phone rang again. She reached forward for it with her right hand and deftly disconnected the charging cable without opening her eyes. It was too much effort to see who it was calling so she just held the phone to her ear and answered the call.

It was her best friend Jane calling for a chat from work. Jane worked in a travel agency and she was one of the funniest people Lucy knew. She had so many stories to tell, and most of them were true, although sometimes with a slight bit of exaggeration. They chatted for a few minutes before Jane announced that she had to go and attend to a "bloody" customer. Jane had often said she loved her job and it was only the stupid customers with their stupid questions that almost drove her to drink. Although, she probably wouldn't have needed much driving. In Lucy's experience a night out with Jane usually involved copious amounts of alcohol.

Lucy smiled to herself after the call with her friend ended. Jane had always had a way of cheering her up when she was feeling a bit down. She'd been especially helpful after the situation with Andy Austin, practically dragging her out of the house and getting her drunk, but more importantly making her see she could start to enjoy life again. And then she'd taken her away on holiday to Spain and that was just what Lucy had needed. A nice relaxing week in the warm Mediterranean sunshine. She was a great mate.

While they'd been talking on the phone, Lucy had apologised for not answering Jane's earlier call, but Jane responded that she hadn't actually called her before. Now that their call was over, Lucy had a look at her missed calls and saw that the call before had been from a number she didn't recognise, certainly not one in her list of contacts, otherwise the name would have shown up. Probably someone trying to scam her, she thought. Apparently there were a lot of calls like that, although Lucy hadn't actually had any at all. Why don't people want to scam me, she thought, laughing to herself. There was probably a help line for that somewhere. She could imagine the advert.

"Has no-one tried to scam you lately? We can help. No scam no fee. Dial now, or send us your number and we'll call you and try and get you to give us your bank details."

Well, whoever it was that called, if it was important they'll call back. That's what her mum always said and it seemed pretty logical to Lucy. Right now, she'd rather just rest and make the most of her time while CJ slept.

Across town, Andy Austin was still sitting on his sofa, his phone lying beside him. He wasn't sure what to do now. Did it mean something that Lucy hadn't answered? Was there some higher meaning? Could it be fate dictating that they should never talk again? Of course he knew logically that there were all sorts of possible reasons for her not answering. It had gone to her voicemail, so that presumably meant it was still her phone, he still had the right number. He hadn't left a message though. He didn't think that would have been right. There was too much to say. It couldn't be summarised in a thirty second message. He needed to speak to her directly to have any chance of getting a conversation going. One where he could start to explain to her why he had done what he had done and how he had changed and then…..what? Austin didn't know the answer to that, but he knew he had to at least try and get it started. And that first call would be the most important call he'd ever made. I'll give it one more try, he thought and he picked up his phone and dialled the number again.

Lucy was just about drifting off to sleep once more when the phone started ringing. She felt for it with her hand and automatically answered it, again too tired to look at who was calling.

'Hello?' she said sleepily.

There was a moment's pause and then she heard a man's voice.

'Hi, is that Lucy?'

Her heart skipped a beat and she sat upright, her eyes now wide open and she felt herself grip the phone tightly, her other hand also grabbing at the sofa cushion, like she needed something to hold on to. She could feel her heart thumping.

'Yes, who….who is that?' she replied, knowing really, but not sure if she wanted to know.

'It's me, Paul, please don't hang up,' the voice said quickly. Austin felt strange calling himself Paul again. It had been a while, but that was the name Lucy knew him by.

Lucy moved forward on the sofa, not knowing what to do. Should she hang up? She stood up and walked to the window, looking at the street outside. It was raining. She clenched her left hand into a fist to try and stop herself trembling.

'What do you want?' she asked him.

'I… I, just wanted to talk. Just wanted to see if you were all right. Are you?' he replied, relieved that at least Lucy hadn't just hung up on him. He thought she might have.

'Yes, I guess so. It's a bit of a shock when you find out that your boyfriend is a murderer but after a while life has to go on,' Lucy replied, shakily.

'I know,' Austin replied. 'I know I did you wrong and it's hard to explain why I did what I did, but I was ill. And I'm not using that as an excuse, but it's the truth.'

He waited for Lucy to reply but she stayed silent and he realised he'd need to keep talking or she might just hang up.

'I had a brain tumour, but I had it removed and I'm okay now. But it's not that simple. I'm not saying it is. I'd really like to try and explain it all to you but it's not going to be easy over the phone. Could we perhaps meet, just for a coffee or something? I owe it to you to try and explain and then I promise, if you want, I'll never contact you again.'

'Oh right, you say you had a brain tumour and that's what turned you into a murderer. Is that what you're telling me Paul? Really? In fact Paul isn't even your real name is it? It's Andy Austin.

Why don't we start with that?' Lucy replied angrily, her voice rising as she spoke. She didn't want to have this conversation, she desperately just wanted to hang up but something was stopping her. There was still too much unfinished business. Stuff she'd been suppressing, trying to forget, but it was still there, biding its time and now that time had come.

'Yes, my name is Andy Austin, but it's not as straightforward as that. Just give me ten minutes of your time and I'll tell you everything. I never meant to hurt you, you have to believe that,' Austin replied.

But he had hurt her, he had hurt her badly and it had taken Lucy a long time to recover and get back to where she was now. It had been a strange situation, not just a normal break up. In fact they hadn't really broken up. The man she'd known as Paul Smith, her boyfriend, had just walked out and disappeared when he realised that his cover had been blown. When it had all come out, none of Lucy's friends had known what to say, or how to treat her. And she didn't want to discuss it with them, it was all too painful. Everyone felt sorry for her but she sensed that they were also a bit confused. *Could she really live with him, not knowing what he was doing? He was a murderer!* She didn't blame them, she'd probably have thought the same if the tables had been turned. She'd learned to put a "brave face" on it. No-one had died, although that wasn't true, but she hadn't lost anyone – unless you counted the man she thought she was going to spend the rest of her life with. But he was still alive somewhere and she couldn't explain her sense of loss. It was like he'd died, but of course he hadn't. That made her feel even more guilty when she thought about the families of the two people he had brutally killed. They had really lost someone they loved. Lucy had lost someone, it turned out, she didn't even know. He was a fraud, both versions of him.

So after a while she just had to get on with her life, there was nothing else she could do. The baby had helped, despite it being his baby. It had given her something else to focus on, and over time she found herself thinking less and less about its father. She didn't think she would ever see him again and so it would always be just the two of them, unless she met someone else in the future but at this point in her life that wasn't on the cards.

But then the police had come round and warned her that Andy Austin might try and make contact, and now here he was, on the other end of the phone. It was bringing back all the memories of her time with him. All the things she'd tried to forget, to move on from and build a new life. When they'd been together, her time with Paul had seemed perfect. He had seemed perfect, and she had found herself thinking about a long term future with him. Even he'd talked about it a bit, although in retrospect she could see that it was more her that had initiated those conversations, and he'd been pretty non-committal about it. Of course he must have known all along that there was no future for them as a couple. He'd just been using her as cover. Somewhere to hide and appear normal. Playing her all along. And then it had all ended. She'd found out that he wasn't the man she thought he was. Not at all. She hadn't even known his real name. It was really Andy Austin, the police had told her. And he was a murderer. A serial killer, which she'd looked up to confirm that he fitted that definition. It seemed to, if you carried out the murders in the UK, but you needed to kill at least three people if you were in the USA to qualify, presumably they had too many murders and had to raise the bar.

When she'd realised what he'd been doing, Austin had just walked out and disappeared. Leaving her devastated. Devastated that he'd left. Devastated that he wasn't who she thought he was. Devastated that she'd been taken for a fool.

'So Andy Austin, are you back to finish what you started, killing more people and hurting those poor, innocent families?' Lucy asked, her whole body now trembling.

'No, no, of course I'm not. That was all in the past. I promise you. I know now what I did was wrong but I didn't know that at the time. I was ill, not thinking straight. Can I come and see you? I promise, just ten minutes and then I'll go. I just need you to hear my side of the story,' Austin pleaded.

Despite knowing that she should just say no. Just hang up. She couldn't. She needed to finish this off. Somehow. He can't come here, Lucy thought, he would see little CJ, his son. Even if she left him with her mum, there was still all the baby stuff, the baby smell in the flat. It was obvious. He'd work it out and she wouldn't be able to lie to him. She'd never been a good liar. Maybe he had a right to know about him, his son, but not yet. That would have to be further down the line, if at all. Lucy needed time to think about that.

'CJ, this is your daddy, he's wanted for killing two innocent people. Look he's brought you a cuddly bear.' She just couldn't reconcile it in her head. It was all still too difficult.

But what if he'd already been to her flat? He knew where she lived, she hadn't moved since they lived here together. Maybe he'd been spying on her and seen her with the baby? Maybe he was sitting outside right now, and she glanced back out into the street looking for any strange cars, but not really knowing what a strange car looked like. She couldn't see anything unusual but she didn't really think he would be outside, otherwise he would have said something, wouldn't he? She guessed this phone call was his first step.

Part of her wished he hadn't called, that she just never heard from him again but when he had, Lucy began to realise that, somewhere deep in her brain, she had been waiting for this moment. She knew it would come, had to happen. That was why she couldn't hang up. There was still unfinished business. Things she needed to know and despite it all she couldn't deny that she still had some feelings for this man. Maybe it was just the memories, but she wasn't sure. He'd given her more love, and more heartache, than any other man she'd ever met.

She decided maybe she would give him his ten minutes, she felt she needed to hear it, and see what happened then. But she still felt strongly that he should pay for what he'd done. He'd killed two innocent people and even if he had been ill, surely that wasn't an excuse. Or, if it was, then the judge would consider that when they sentenced him. Either way, he should still pay for the hurt he'd brought on these poor people. She'd always been brought up to be honest and do the right thing, it was in her genes.

'Okay, we can't meet here, but I'll meet you in the local park,' she said. 'Ten minutes you say and that's it. How about tomorrow, three o' clock at one of the benches by the swings?'

'Yes, of course. Thank you. I know it's not easy for you to say that,' Austin replied with a great sense of relief.

'Tomorrow, three pm then,' Lucy said and finally hung up, her hand shaking as she dropped the phone onto the floor.

Lucy sat back down on the sofa. Her mind was racing, full of conflicting thoughts about what she should do. She'd give him his ten minutes, let him talk and see what he said. She wanted to hear it from him. After that she wasn't sure, but there were some things she needed to know. Some things she needed to get answers to. Things that had lain hidden, somewhere in her brain, waiting for this point, and now they were re-surfacing. Had he used her all along just as a safe hiding place while he carried out his killings? Had he really had any feelings for her or was it all just an act? If it was then he was certainly a very good actor, but maybe Lucy was blind to it. She had fallen in love with him, or at least she thought she had at the time. She'd gone over it time and time again in the early days, the days after he'd left and it had all exploded.

But she didn't know, she couldn't decide, and the only way she could find out would be to hear it from him and look him in the eye while he was telling her. Then she'd know. And after that.....what? She wasn't sure.

Chapter 20

Emily was heading into town. She was wearing her favourite ripped white jeans and a short blue denim jacket. Double denim was back in fashion. Had it ever not been? For once the weather was okay, dry, sunny and no wind so it wasn't too cold for the time of year, so far it had been a mild, wet winter. All down to global warming they said. Emily had chosen what to wear carefully, not wanting to look too smart or too scruffy, and she was happy her selection was ideal for the bar she'd decided to meet the mystery man in. Her mystery phone guy. Ooh, it was exciting. It was quite a trendy bar, busy enough, but not too busy so she should be able to find the man she was meeting fairly easily. The man at the other end of the mobile phone.

He'd been pressing her to meet, and after she'd thought about it a bit more, she just decided to do it. That was typical Emily. It was too exciting not too. After she'd met him, it would be a great story to tell all her friends. Sophie would be shocked. Emily felt a bit guilty at keeping it secret from her best friend, but she knew it would be worth it to see the look on her face when she did tell her. Sophie would never have had the courage to do anything like this, but Emily's moto was YOLO and, to her, it was the most exciting thing she'd done in ages.

So she'd texted him to say she could meet him for half an hour, she thought it best to keep it short just in case, in Rolly's bar. If she didn't like him, then thirty minutes would be survivable. She'd chosen Rolly's because it was one of her regular haunts and she knew a couple of the people that worked behind the bar. They were also students, trying to make a bit of money to see them through university and maybe at some stage in the future pay off their student loans. Emily hadn't needed to work, her parents were pretty well off and they'd been able to provide the funds Emily needed to get her through the three years in Leeds.

Although she'd decided to meet her mystery man, Emily didn't really have a plan for what she was going to do when they did actually meet, other than to just play it by ear and see how it went. If you could call that a plan. It was at best a loose plan. That tended to be the way Emily lived her life. Just do it and see what happens, whatever it is, just deal with it. Sometimes it worked and sometimes it didn't, but it made life more interesting.

However, although her plan might not have passed the FBI's requirements for a proper plan, she had put at least a little bit of thought into some aspects of what she was about to do. Apart from choosing a safe place, she'd also given some thought as to how she was actually going to meet him, given that she didn't know what he looked like, and he was expecting to see some other woman. The woman he'd originally been texting a few months ago. She could see there was potential for things to go wrong.

So, she'd told him to make sure he was there on time, as she didn't have long, and he'd said he would. Emily then arrived ten minutes late and as she entered the bar, she rang the man's number on the old phone. She stopped and scanned the inside of the bar looking for someone in the process of answering their mobile. The bar wasn't that busy, there were probably about twenty or thirty people in it, and only about six or seven of those were men seemingly on their own. But, frustratingly, she couldn't see anyone answering their phone and she couldn't hear any phone ringing either. Her call started to go to a standard voicemail and she ended it before it went any further. That's strange, she thought, and she tried again, this time focusing on the two most likely men she thought it might be, willing one of them to pick up their phone. They both looked in their twenties and both on their own. But neither of them made any move towards answering a phone, they both just sat their drinking their drinks, looking bored. Emily was beginning to panic a bit now. Her half-thought plan A hadn't worked and she didn't have a plan B to hand. She checked her watch to make sure she'd got the right time and saw that it was now twelve minutes past. Where was he? Why wasn't he here? Or if he was here why wasn't he answering his phone? Maybe she could text him and see where he was, perhaps he couldn't answer his phone. She quickly typed out a message.

"Where r u?"

She could sense a few people looking at her as she stood on her own in the middle of the bar, but none of them made any move towards her. They'd probably seen her making the calls, guessing that she was waiting to meet someone or, even worse, been stood up. Some of them would be feeling sorry for her, others wondering if it might be an opportunity to try and chat her up. A bit of sympathy sometimes worked. Emily decided to wait outside to see if he replied. If he didn't reply within five minutes then she would just go. A shame, but his loss. As she turned to leave the bar, she bumped into a young man coming in and the phone span out of her hand and landed with a thump on the floor.

'Oh, shit, I'm so sorry,' the man said as Emily bent down to retrieve her phone. 'I didn't see you there, is your phone okay?'

Emily picked it up and looked at it. It looked like there was a slight crack across the screen and it appeared to be switched off. She pressed the power button and held it for a few seconds but nothing happened.

'Is it broken?' the man asked. 'I'm so sorry, let me get you a drink, it's the least I can do.' He took hold of Emily's arm and guided her towards the bar. He ordered two glasses of white wine and turned to face Emily.

'Let me have a look at it,' he said, holding out his hand.

Emily passed him the phone and he took it, turning it around in his hands, examining it closely. She took a sip of her cold drink and, for the first time, took a proper look at the man stood beside her. His head was bowed down looking at the phone so she couldn't see his face properly but from what she could see he looked okay. Seen worse. He had dark hair, gelled down and a very light growth of beard, or maybe he just hadn't shaved that morning. Emily liked beards so that was a tick in the right box. He was wearing a dark suit, light blue shirt and a dark blue tie and a pair of black brogues. Very smart and city-like. Maybe he had a good job with a good salary? Her mystery mobile phone man was already fading in her thoughts.

'It's, emm, quite an old phone, isn't it? You had it a while?' he asked, still looking down at her mobile.

'Haha, yes,' Emily replied. 'It's emm, not, emm, it's not actually mine. It's a friend's. I'm just using it for a day as mine was needing charged.'

'Oh, I see,' the man replied, and Emily noticed that he had taken the back off her phone and he was fiddling around with it.

'Sometimes just taking the battery out and putting it back in again works,' he said. 'Ah there we go, it seems to be working again now. That's done the trick.'

He replaced the rear cover on the phone and handed it back to Emily, their fingers touched slightly and he looked up with a smile.

Emily thought she recognised him, but she couldn't think from where. Cute smile though.

'Do I, …do we, emm, know each other from somewhere?' she asked him. 'You look kinda familiar.'

'No, I don't think so,' the man replied, still smiling.

Well, you don't know me, but I know you, Kyle thought. She was the cow who had got him thrown out of the Old Police Station bar. He'd only tried to chat her up, and he was sure she'd said something to one of the bouncers, as it wasn't long afterwards that he and his mates had been asked to leave. Bloody students, think they're better than everyone else, sponging off the state. He paid taxes to let them have their three years dossing around at university. And now he also knew her as the girl who had been texting him from Sally's phone. Sally was a girl he had met a couple of years before, on a drunken night out, and they'd ending up having sex. After that, they met up every now and again, just for sex. They both knew it wasn't going to be a long term thing, Sally had a boyfriend, and after a while it just naturally petered out. Kyle had been thinking about ending it anyway, he was getting bored with her.

But this girl wasn't Sally, this was somebody else. He'd known from the wording of the texts, right from the start, that it hadn't been Sally texting him again. He'd never really expected her to. In a way he was glad and he was intrigued to find out who it really was, and why they'd been doing it. Maybe he could get something out of it.

But Kyle wasn't stupid, okay he hadn't gone to Uni, but he knew that today's meeting could have easily been a trap. Maybe Sally's boyfriend had found out about their affair and he and his mates were waiting to give him a beating. So he had taken some precautions. He'd waited outside the bar until his phone rang. When it rang the second time he was looking through the bar door and he could see this girl with her phone at her ear. Then he saw her texting and sure enough a few seconds later a message popped up on his phone. After that, the rest was easy. Just bump into her, apologise, get talking, buy her a drink. Find out who she was and why she was pretending to be Sally. He hadn't meant to knock the phone out of her hand, but that had turned out as an unexpected bonus as the phone definitely confirmed it was her, and it also made it easier for him to persuade her to have a drink. He had been her knight in shining armour. And, to be fair, although she'd got him thrown out of The Old Police Station, she wasn't that bad looking so that was a bonus, maybe something would come out of this. Shame she was a student though. He'd met her type before, loads of them, all a bit snooty. Thought they were better than everyone else, more clever, well we'll see. Let's see who's the clever one now. It could be a good challenge and, besides, he'd nothing much else planned for the rest of the day so might as well see how it goes.

They were both standing at the bar, sipping their drinks, and Emily was trying to size him up over the top of her glass. Not too bad looking, she thought, nice smile. Don't like the suit but I guess that's maybe what he has to wear for his job. Pretty fit looking, could definitely have bumped into someone worse and he's bought me a nice glass of wine. Perfect....probably still a bit too early for shots, Emily thought smiling to herself.

'Thanks for the drink, my name's Emily by the way,' she said, holding out her hand.

'Hi Emily, I'm Kyle,' the man replied smiling and shaking her hand. Nice strong grip.

The two of them stood with their drinks, chatting at the bar, and Emily found herself telling him her life story. He was a good listener, laughing in all the right places and making a sympathetic face at other points, as required. Kyle didn't talk a lot but told her that he worked in "the entertainment business." He name-dropped a couple of fairly well-known singers, and that had impressed her. Of course he knew it would. It had worked for him before, and he had no doubt it would again. He didn't have to go into too much detail though as she just seemed to like talking about herself, with an annoying habit of pulling on the ends of her hair as she rambled on. He'd met plenty girls like her before, all about themselves, how clever they were. All the fun things they'd done.

Back in the real world, Kyle worked in sales at an estate agency, and for him it was an ideal job. He was pretty much his own boss, able to get out of the office any time he wanted on the pretext of looking at a house. What he really liked about it though was that he got to meet lots of women, often in their own homes, usually bored with their husbands being away all day at work. He'd learned just to sit, listen and laugh with them. Make a few obligatory compliments and smile and more often than not, after a couple of visits, they ended up giving him a detailed look around their bedrooms. Most of them he never saw again, or if they became a bit clingy he would pass them on to one of his colleagues. They usually got the message. They couldn't really complain without confessing to what they'd done with him and so they generally didn't say anything. There had been a couple of awkward ones who'd made complaints, but he'd managed to talk his way out of it, and he knew his excellent sales record would always stand him in good stead. No estate agent would want to lose their top salesman, especially to a competitor, so he'd always got the benefit of the doubt. After all, it takes two to tango.

Kyle was starting to get bored with this one though, god she couldn't half talk and he was struggling to keep focus on what she was saying. What was her name again, he couldn't remember. He finished his drink and put the empty glass down on the bar, with an exaggerated look at his watch. It was time to move things on. See if she was game.

'Oh, do you have to be somewhere?' Emily asked laughing, having noticed him looking at his watch and for once not talking about herself.

'Oh, sorry yes, actually I do. I need to sort something out for a client. Can I give you a lift somewhere, my car's outside,' Kyle replied smiling at Emily.

'Only if it's a Porsche or a Ferrari,' Emily laughed and she got down from her bar stool, smoothing her jeans down as she stood up. Maybe I should have worn my new skirt she thought, showed off my legs a bit. Everyone said she had nice legs, but the weather was still a bit cold for that. She stumbled a little as she stood and giggled. I'm not used to drinking this early, she thought, it's rather nice! The couple walked out of the bar and Kyle led Emily round to the car park at the rear. There were only about three or four cars parked there at this time of the day and Emily tried to pick out which one might be Kyle's. There were no Porsches or Ferraris unfortunately but Kyle pointed and clicked a key fob and Emily saw the lights flash on a large dark four by four.

'Is an Audi Quattro good enough for you?' Kyle asked, smiling.

'Well I suppose it'll have to do,' Emily replied, grinning back at him.

Most of her friends in Leeds were students and so she hadn't been in many nice cars for a while. Not since she'd been back home at her parent's house. The few students that did have a car in Leeds tended to have fairly run-down hatchbacks. Usually Vauxhalls, or Fords, sometimes the occasional VW. Internally they were all a bit like overflowing dustbins, with empty water bottles rolling around alongside discarded crisp packets and chocolate wrappers. Kyle's Audi was a different story though. As she got in she immediately noticed how clean it was and how nice it smelled. The aroma of leather. She breathed it in and smiled as she settled into the big, comfortable passenger seat. She looked down into the footwell in front of her. Nothing there, perfectly clean. Just like new. As she clipped her seat belt on, she felt her seat warming up. Nice, she thought. She glanced over her shoulder and saw that the rear of the car was equally clean with just a pile of leaflets lying on the long back seat. The top one had a photograph of a house and some writing underneath it.

'Are you looking at houses?' she asked Kyle as he reversed out of his parking space, a dashboard screen giving him a full colour view of the area behind the car.

'Oh, yeah, sort of. I kind of keep an eye on houses for myself and a few of my clients,' Kyle replied as he accelerated smoothly out of the car park.

'Cool,' said Emily. 'I'd love to do that, you know, look round rich people's houses. I'd have a good snoop around them and definitely do a wee in their loo,' she laughed.

Kyle grinned, 'actually I could show you one now, if you like, I need to go there today anyway. Might as well pop in now. It's only a few minutes away.'

Emily smiled and let herself relax into the comfy, heated seat. It was so nice, I could just sit here all day, she thought. This was turning out to be a good day. When she'd set out to meet the mystery mobile man, she'd been a bit nervous, not sure how it was going to pan out. She knew it could have gone badly wrong but she felt she'd taken enough precautions. She was still a bit disappointed when he hadn't turned up, she would have liked to have seen him, just to satisfy her curiosity. Still, if he had appeared, then she probably wouldn't have met Kyle. Emily was a great believer in fate, sometimes whatever happened was meant to happen. Sitting here in this lovely, luxurious car she'd already decided that, as soon as she could, she was going to dump the old mobile phone. It had been fun for a while and it would have been good to find out who the man was, but it obviously just wasn't meant to be. He had his chance and in her mind, she'd already moved on.

A few minutes later Kyle made a couple of turnings down some roads that Emily had never seen before. She'd never been in this part of town in the three years she'd been in Leeds. It looked very nice. There were more trees and the houses were bigger, at least the ones that you could see. A lot of them were hidden behind high walls and even more trees. There were no cars parked on the road either, Emily noticed. That wasn't like where Emily and Sophie lived at all, in the student area of town. In their road, every space by the kerbside was taken up with nose to tail parking, and if a slot ever became available it would be filled up again very quickly by a triumphant driver delighted to get a parking space.

Kyle slowed down and turned the Audi into a short driveway, stopping the car as he reached a set of tall, wooden gates. He leant out the window pressed a few buttons on a metal post and the large, solid gates in front of the car slowly swung open.

'Wow,' said Emily, 'impressive. Whose house is this?'

'Oh, just a guy I know. He works in the music business. He's a producer. Does records and stuff.'

'Wow, has he worked with anyone famous?' Emily asked.

'Oh, yeah, plenty. Elton John and Rag and Bone Man, ...a few others,' Kyle replied.

'Wow, cool,' Emily replied smiling. Wait till she told Sophie about this, she'd be so jealous.

They drove on for about another fifty metres, up a narrow tree lined road, and stopped in front of a large Georgian style house with two imposing white pillars either side of a solid looking black door. Kyle jumped out the car and Emily followed him. They walked up to the front door and Kyle produced a key from his jacket pocket and turned the handle, pushing the door easily inwards. He stepped inside and Emily followed him into a tastefully tiled entrance hall. Kyle closed the door behind them.

'Jeez, this is gorgeous,' Emily exclaimed, looking around the entrance hall, astonished by the detail of the decoration. Everything looked just right. It was like a photograph from one of those interior design magazines you only find in Dentist's waiting rooms.

'This hallway is as big as our house. Who is it that lives here?' she asked Kyle.

'Well, technically no-one at the moment,' he replied. 'I've just got to check something out for a client, come on you better stay with me. I don't want you breaking anything,' and he started walking up the staircase.

Emily was still mesmerised by the decoration as she followed Kyle up the ornate staircase, feeling the silky smoothness of the bannister on her hand as she went upwards. At the top of the staircase Kyle turned to his left and walked along a cream-carpeted hallway, glancing behind him to make sure that Emily was still following. He slowed down as he approached a white door and let Emily catch him up. He opened the door and stood to the side to let her enter and he followed her into the room, closing the door quietly behind him.

Emily stopped a few steps inside the room and looked around. In front of her there was a huge four poster bed, probably the biggest bed she'd ever seen, with white drapes hanging from the structure and matching white bedding. Again it looked like a photo from a design magazine, everything just looked perfect. To her right, there was a modern, grey coloured dressing table with a matching stool in front and a long mirror across the rear. Past that, nearer the bed, there was another white door which was slightly open and Emily could just make out that it led into an en-suite bathroom. I bet that's huge too, she thought. She looked around to the left side and saw some more doors, which she imagined was the entrance to some sort of walk in wardrobe or dressing room. She'd never seen a walk-in wardrobe before, only on TV. Further on from the doors there was a huge window, with white drapes, overlooking the garden outside.

'Wow, this is unbelievable,' she said. 'I have never in my whole life seen anything like this. It's so beautiful. This whole room is as big as some of the student flats I've been in. I need to have a place like this!'

As she stood there looking around, she suddenly felt an arm circling her waist and a body press up against her from behind.

'What, …what are you doing?' she said as she tried to break free and turn around, but he was holding her too tightly and his other hand was now moving her hair and she could feel his lips touching her neck.

'Get off of me!' she shouted and pushed herself back into him, loosening his grip slightly.

Kyle stepped back, letting her go free and laughed.

'Come on, stop playing around. You know you want it,' he said. 'Why else would you come here with me?'

'What? You've got to be joking! We've only just met and we're just having a bit of fun. That's all. Doesn't mean you can come on to me like that. I'm not a slag.'

'Come on, I didn't say you were. Like I said, we're both adults, just having a bit of fun. Look at that bed, it'd be a shame to waste it,' Kyle replied, smiling and he took a step forwards towards Emily.

'Get back, I warn you. I'll call the police if you take one step closer,' Emily said forcefully, feeling in her pocket for her mobile, while taking a step backwards away from Kyle.

'Go on then, call the police,' Kyle laughed, 'I'm sure they'd be interested to hear your story about identity theft. It's a big thing for them at the moment. Even you poor students might have heard about it. Do you know you can get ten years in jail for that?' Kyle sneered.

'What are you talking about? I'm leaving now, don't try and follow me and don't ever come near me again or, or….you'll be in trouble,' Emily stammered trying to appear braver than she was feeling.

Kyle laughed again, this time louder.

'Sure, you can go if you want, no-one's stopping you. But I can't guarantee you won't see me again. Have a think, you've got my number. Give me a call when you're ready. I promise you it'll be enjoyable. I've never had any complaints,' he laughed again, clearly enjoying the moment. He carried on.

'Of course you don't have to call me, but if I don't hear back from you by this time next week then I'm afraid the police will be coming to talk to you. There goes your student life, your career. I'm sure your mum and dad won't be so proud of their little Emily then, will they?'

'The police? What are you talking about?' Emily said, feeling confused.

'All those texts you've been sending me, leading me on, pretending you were someone else. They'll want to know all about that I'm sure. And then arranging to meet me in the pub and coming here with me. It'll all come out,' Kyle replied, feeling completely in control and enjoying the moment.

'What, you're…..you're the guy I've been texting….on the mobile?' Emily uttered as she began to understand.

'Correct, now you've got it, not so clever now are you?' Kyle replied laughing as he spoke.

Emily didn't know what to do, but she had to get away from here, she knew that. She walked forwards determinedly, her face bright red and her head firmly pointed downwards, staring at her feet. Kyle stepped to one side to let her pass and she left the bedroom and then ran quickly down the stairs and out of the house. She was sure she could still hear Kyle laughing as she went through the gate, back out onto the quiet residential street.

Chapter 21

Lucy was doing her make-up in the bathroom mirror. It was taking her a bit longer than normal because she couldn't stop her hand from shaking. She was now on her third attempt at blusher. Today was the day she was going to meet Andy Austin and listen to his attempt to explain why he had deceived her. Why he had pretended he'd loved her, but really used her as cover while he carried out two horrific murders. She didn't want to have to go through with it, but at the same time she knew it was something she needed to do. She needed to hear it to stop all her wild imaginings. Just when she'd thought she had got over him and moved on with her life, he'd suddenly re-appeared and stirred up all the old memories she'd been hiding away at the back of her mind. She needed to clear out the clutter. After a few more tries, she finally finished her make-up. Not great, but good enough, she thought and she walked through to the living room and sat down resignedly on the sofa.

Since he'd called the day before, she'd thought of nothing else. What to do? How to play it?

Was she doing the right thing? Of course she couldn't discuss it with anyone else. No-one else could know that she was planning to meet him. Except, of course, the police.

After a lot of thought and a lot of to-ing and fro-ing, Lucy had come to the decision that she would let him have his ten minutes and then hand him over to the police. She was hopeful that she would get what she needed from spending that ten minutes with him. She wanted him to give her some answers, something that would lead to some sort of closure, if that was possible. But, whatever he said, whatever excuses he had, he still deserved to face justice for the hurt he'd put those two families through, killing a wife and a mother, a son and a brother. She felt she owed it to them to ensure that he faced a judge and jury. That was how she'd been brought up. If he had some sort of excuse, some sort of reason for killing them, then of course that would be taken into account. But he needed to face justice, of that she was certain. She'd convinced herself it was the right thing to do, yet a small part of her worried that she was just using all this need for justice, this honesty, as a simple excuse to get her revenge. Maybe she just wanted to hurt him. To hurt him, like he'd hurt her. There was probably some truth in that. She'd hand him over to the police and probably consign him to spending the rest of his life in jail. But she knew revenge wasn't the overriding factor and it wouldn't give her any satisfaction. The key thing was that he should face justice for his horrific crimes.

She hatched a plan in her mind to ensure that she would get the brief time she needed with Austin before the police moved in to arrest him. She ran it over in her head a few times and when she was happy that it could work, she walked through to the spare bedroom. She opened the top drawer of the dressing table and inside, lying on top of a few pens and note-pads, she retrieved the card the policeman had given her when they had visited a few weeks before.

'Detective Sergeant Campbell, Serious Crime Squad,' she read out loud.

There were two telephone numbers on the card. One was a mobile number and the other a landline, presumably a phone on Campbell's desk in the Serious Crime Squad office, or maybe just a general switchboard number, she wasn't sure. In her head she pictured a busy room with police officers sat at various desks answering each other's phones when they were out, or busy elsewhere. Lucy wanted to talk directly to DS Campbell and so she decided to try his mobile number first. She punched in the number and waited for it to connect. After a few seconds she heard it ring and then it went to voicemail. She didn't want to just leave him a message, it was too important that she got this right, and so she hung up. She was somewhat reluctant to try the landline number in case she ended up talking with someone else. Another policeman, someone she'd never met, who might not go with her plan. The fewer people that knew what she was going to do, the better, less chance for anything to go wrong. Anyone else might have different ideas which would prohibit her having the time she wanted with Austin. She decided to leave it and try Campbell's mobile again later. She looked at the card once more and decided to add DS Campbell into her phone as a contact so she could easily call him when she needed to, at short notice, which was what she'd have to do if her plan was going to be successful. As she started typing in the word "Detective", another name appeared and she stopped and read it. Detective Inspector Strong. Of course, he was the other policeman. Wasn't he Campbell's boss? She thought that was the case. She must have got his number when it had all happened last year, and she'd spent the day at the police station, telling them everything she knew about Austin, which turned out to be a lot less than she thought she did. She cast her mind back to that day and remembered Strong had given her his number and told her to call him directly if anything else came to mind, or if she heard from Austin.

She finished adding Campbell's number into her contacts and then tried calling him but it went straight to voicemail once again. She wanted to get this done while she had it straight in her mind and so she decided to try calling DI Strong. She dialled the number, another mobile, and it started ringing. Strong answered on the third ring and, after a few minutes of general familiarities – "How are you?", "I'm fine, you?" - she told him that Andy Austin had been in touch. Lucy said that it had only been a quick call but she felt that he would probably call her again soon. She said that when he did she would try and get him to agree to a meeting somewhere, a neutral space – maybe a café or a park or something and then she would let the police know so that they could arrest him. She told the detective that she felt strongly that he needed to be brought to justice for what he'd done. She didn't mention that she was in fact meeting him later that day. That was going to be part two of her plan to ensure that she had her time with him first. She'd expected the detective to come up with some alternatives to her plan but, surprisingly, he hadn't. She thought he might say something like "we'll allocate someone to watch you so they can follow you to the meeting" but he hadn't. In fact he'd said her plan sounded good, and that if there was any obvious police presence it might scare him off. Better to get him relaxed with you and then we can move in and arrest him. Just let us know when he calls again and when and where you are going to meet him, leave the rest to me, he had said. It's best you don't know any details so you can just act naturally with him. It all seemed pretty straightforward and Lucy was relieved when she ended the call, she hadn't expected it to be that easy.

After taking the call from Lucy, DI Strong had sat quietly on his own for a few minutes, his hands on the desk in front of him, his fingers interlocked and his thumbs rotating around each other. He was thinking. There were a number of options here, he thought. He could end it now for Austin, but he was still useful and Strong was enjoying the fact that he could use him to get more scum off the streets. It was a great way of getting those criminals that managed to continually avoid the normal justice process and he also liked having that extra advantage, that bit more power, that no-one else knew about. It was his way of overcoming the flawed system he had to work in.

Lucy picked up her coat and left her flat, she was feeling nervous, but at the same time excited. She wanted to hear what Austin had to say and then what happened after that would be interesting. She didn't feel she was in any personal danger. She couldn't imagine the man who had lived with her, who had said he loved her, could do her any physical harm. Even if he was a double murderer, she was sure she couldn't be that wrong about him.

Earlier that day Lucy had called her mum and asked if she could look after baby CJ that afternoon as she had a "kind of business" meeting she had to go to. It wasn't an interview but just an idea for something that might develop into something else. She kept it vague and of course, as she'd known, her mum, CJ's granny, was delighted to have the chance to spoil her grandson for the afternoon. Lucy wasn't planning to mention CJ to Austin when they met. She would tell him at some point, she knew it would come out in the lead up to the trial anyway, and it should really come from her. The fact that he had a son. But for now, she wanted it to be just her and him. She needed to hear what he was going to say to fill in the blanks, so she could move on.

Five minutes later she arrived at the park and a couple of minutes after that she'd got herself a coffee from the van that always parked up near the swings. She sat down on one of the benches, sipping her drink slowly through the little hole in the white, plastic lid, feeling nervous. She pulled her coat tighter around her. The van was doing a roaring trade, as always, it was obviously a great catchment area getting all the mums, and a few dads, as their children played in the swing park. It seemed you couldn't go out anywhere now, without buying a coffee. It had become a way of life. And there were so many varieties. Lucy's mum and dad were old school, anytime she went out with them they either had a tea with milk or a regular coffee. None of these new fangled drinks for them. PG Tips or Nescafe, what more did you need?

Lucy slowly looked around the park over the top of her coffee cup, trying not to make it obvious to anyone that she was looking for someone. She couldn't see him, or anyone that even looked like him. Maybe he had changed, but surely not that much that she wouldn't recognise him? She'd seen him that one time in Spain, across the road in a café and she knew it was him immediately by his smile. Little things like that were unmistakeable when you really knew someone. Their eyes, how they opened their mouths, how they laughed. Everyone was unique and you couldn't hide that with hair dye or a beard.

Lucy had wondered what Austin's plan would be. She was pretty sure he would come, he had asked to meet her after all, but she didn't know if he was already here, watching to make sure Lucy hadn't betrayed him and there were plain clothes police hanging around waiting to arrest him. Lucy had also thought about that after her call with DI Strong, but even if he was planning that she was pretty certain he wouldn't have had time to organise it yet and she hadn't told him the meeting was today. He had no reason to think that she wasn't telling him the whole truth and he was probably expecting the meeting to be in a few days, or the following week, which would give him plenty of time to organise all the paperwork and resources he would need to run the operation properly. Lucy had seen it on TV detective programmes, there would be processes, approvals, authorisations to go through before they could do it. They had to make sure the general public wasn't put in any danger and here they were in a park, by a kid's playground. That would score high in any risk assessment. Despite that she looked around, taking note of everyone there, but as far as she could see none of them looked like police. You could usually tell.

Lucy took another sip of her coffee and checked her watch, it wasn't quite three o'clock yet. In her nervous state she must have walked more quickly than usual and got to the park a few minutes early. She glanced around again and still couldn't see anyone that looked like Andy Austin, or a plain clothes police officer. Although she didn't really know what a plain clothes police officer would look like and of course the whole idea was that they shouldn't be noticeable. Everyone just looked like normal mum's and dad's. Normal families. Just here to play on the swings, not like Lucy, here to meet an ex who was also a double murderer. She was the only one doing that, she presumed. She was about to check her phone when she felt a hand lightly touch her shoulder and it made her jump.

'Hi, sorry,' a voice said from behind her. A voice she knew very well. She turned her head round and looked up into the face of Andy Austin. He wasn't smiling, he looked tense, but he still looked just as handsome as she remembered him. In that other lifetime, when she'd known him as Paul Smith.

He walked around the bench and sat down beside her. He was wearing a long dark overcoat which he pulled over his knees and he turned sideways on to face Lucy.

'It's good to see you,' he said, 'you're looking well. I like your new hairstyle. It suits you.'

Lucy returned his compliment with a small smile. He was also looking well, maybe even better than when they'd been a couple, but she wasn't going to tell him that. He seemed brighter and his skin had more colour to it. Maybe he had been ill, like he had said.

'You've got ten minutes,' Lucy said, a bit more sharply than she'd intended and she could see from his face that her abruptness had shocked him slightly.

'Yes, okay, ….well I've thought long and hard about this time. What I would say, if we met again. You know? All sorts of things. I even tried writing it down but I guess at the end of the day all you want is the truth. So I'll just try to do that, tell you the truth, and…' his voice trailed off as he thought "and what?"

He turned to face Lucy and reached for her hand, but she kept her hands clasped tightly on her lap. Seeing that, he withdrew his hand and started talking.

'Okay, well I guess some of this you already know from the police and stuff and some you won't know, but I'll just start at the beginning and try and tell you everything from my side of things. The truth, which is all I can do.'

He gazed at her when he spoke, but Lucy could tell he wasn't really seeing her, he was looking through her. His mind was focused on what he wanted to tell her and nothing else. What he needed to tell her. He started by talking about the accident that had killed his family and how the driver, Jack Wilson, had got away with just a careless driving charge and a one year ban. She knew some of this already and she couldn't help but feel sorry for him. She tried to imagine how she would feel if it had been her mum and dad that had got killed in the accident, and the thought made her shiver. It was horrendous. But surely it wouldn't have turned her into a killer? He then explained how he seemed to go through some sort of personality change which he now thought had been caused by the head injury he'd sustained in the accident. Some type of PTSD, he said. Lucy didn't know that he'd been injured, no-one had said, but she guessed it might explain his headaches. When they'd been together he'd suffered badly with headaches and he'd been taking some strong painkillers, but Lucy had never been able to get him to talk about it. Now she understood why. If the headaches had been caused by the accident then he couldn't tell her, otherwise the whole story would have come out.

Then Austin told her how he found out that maybe it hadn't in fact been an accident, that the driver, this Jack Wilson, might have driven into them deliberately because Austin had once had a brief fling with his younger sister and she'd been upset when it ended. This was also news to Lucy and she momentarily wondered if the police knew about that. Austin's sense of injustice had grown and he wanted revenge on the occupants of the car. But it was more than that, it had become an obsession. It became his life's purpose, even when he was with Lucy. Now, in retrospect, he believed that it was the tumour, causing the PTSD, that had driven him to this obsessive behaviour. He'd wanted to tell her thousands of times, he said, but he couldn't without dragging her into his mess and she didn't deserve that. He knew what he'd done was wrong, terribly wrong, and he said he'd do anything now to reverse that and live a normal life again, but he said too much had happened and he was now trapped.

Lucy glanced briefly at her watch, realising they'd already had their ten minutes, but knowing she had other questions she needed answers to.

'So I guess it was all an act with me then?' she said, again more aggressively than she'd meant to.

Austin gasped and sat up straight, staring wide-eyed at Lucy.

'No, no, of course not. It wasn't an act, not at all,' he replied, shaking his head. 'I didn't set out to meet you, or anyone else, but everything we did, everything I said to you, I meant. It was all true. I loved you more than anything and I didn't know what was going to happen. I was too scared to think about it. I,.. I guess I knew it couldn't end well. We couldn't live as a normal couple with the lie I was hiding from you. But I didn't know what else to do. I needed to get justice but… I loved you. I, …I still do….'

Lucy had been watching him as he spoke and he looked, and sounded, sincere. She almost believed him, but then how could she? Maybe he was just a very good actor. He had fooled her before, big time. How could she trust a man who had deceived her so easily? This man had killed two innocent people while he had been living with her, and surely you can't get away with that by just saying you had a bump on the head? She was torn, she didn't know what to think or say. She needed time to think.

'I, emm, I just need to go to the loo,' she said and she got up from the bench and started to walk across the park to the toilet block which was on the far side of the swing-park. She walked with her head down, just focusing on getting there and trying not to think about what had just happened. It was all too confusing.

Austin stayed sitting on the bench and watched her walk past the colourful swings, all red, blue and yellow, until she disappeared inside the small, red brick built building. Inside, Lucy stood by the washbasins and splashed some cold water onto her face. She'd known this meeting wasn't going to be an easy one for her but she was surprised at the level of feelings she still had for this man. As soon as she'd looked into his eyes, she knew there was still something there, something deep, and she couldn't deny it had thrown her a bit. When they had been together, she had been completely in love with him, more, much more, than with any other man she had ever met. A couple of times she'd dreamt about them getting married and starting a family. Buying a house, going on exotic holidays, everything normal couples did. They'd even tentatively spoken about it on occasion, but now she realised that it was all a sham. He must have known that they would never be able to have that life, but he had played along. Played her like a fool just so he could carry out his violent crimes. She felt the anger rise up in her and in that instant her mind was made up. Okay, maybe she was looking for a bit of revenge, but right now she didn't really care. He had really hurt her. And he'd killed two innocent people. She couldn't let herself be deceived by this man again, no matter how she felt about him. She took her phone out and dialled DI Strong's number, after a few rings it went to voicemail.

'Shit,' she exclaimed loudly and then looked around to make sure there was no-one else in the ladies with her. Thankfully it was empty. She never, ever swore in public, Until now.

She decided to try the other policeman instead, DS Campbell. She hit his number and waited a few seconds as the call connected. It rang three times, Lucy's heart was pounding, hoping he answered and no-one else came in to the toilet.

'Hello?' a man's voice came out, loud and clear.

'Is that DS Campbell?' Lucy asked, cupping her hand around the phone and bowing her head down towards the washbasin, noticing how scratched it was.

'Yes, who is this?' Campbell answered.

'It's Lucy Morris, Andy Austin's….emm, his ex-girlfriend,' Lucy replied hesitantly and as quietly as possible.

'Oh, right, I can't hear you very well, how are you?' Campbell answered politely.

'Listen,' Lucy said, 'I only have a minute. Andy Austin is in Greenfield Park, by the swings, five minutes from where I live. Do you know it?'

'Greenfield Park? Yes, …yes I do,' Campbell replied, visualising the small park in his mind. A children's playground, a grass area, a few trees and bushes. He'd never actually been in it but he'd driven past there many times on his way to the hospital.

'Okay, he's here now,' Lucy cut into his thoughts. 'I can try and keep him here for as long as possible but he may get suspicious. How soon can you get here?' Lucy asked nervously.

'I'm leaving now, should be there in about ten minutes, Campbell replied as he threw his coat on, his phone wedged between his chin and shoulder as he ran down the corridor towards the police station car park.

'Okay, I have to go back to him now. We're sitting on a bench. Be as quick as you can,' Lucy replied and she ended the call and put the phone back in her pocket. She was nervous and excited and she thrust her hands into her coat pockets to stop them from shaking. She felt a text message buzz on the phone in her pocket as she let go of it, but she knew she needed to get back to him before he began to speculate about why she had been so long. She'd been gone almost five minutes and she imagined he'd now be starting to wonder where she was. She was happy she'd done the right thing though. She'd tell him the toilets were busy, or there was only one cubicle in operation, or something. As she exited the toilet block and looked across to the bench where they'd been sitting, she was surprised to see that it was empty. She stopped, confused, and scanned around the park, but he was nowhere to be seen. Lucy walked across to the bench and looked all around it, even underneath, although she knew he couldn't possibly be there. She couldn't understand it, it was as if somehow he was there and she just couldn't see him. He had to be. But he wasn't. She looked slowly all around the park again, but he was nowhere to be seen. He'd gone. She took her phone out to call DS Campbell and saw the text notification. She clicked on it and read the message.

"Sorry. Had to go. Hope you understood what I tried to say. Love A xx"

She stared at the text for a long time, trying to understand it. Trying to analyse it. Why had he gone? Did he know her plan? But he couldn't have. She had hardly said anything, certainly nothing that would give him any hint that she was going to turn him into the police. She'd let him do all the talking. It didn't make sense. Maybe she'd been in the toilet too long and he'd got suspicious? Surely that couldn't have been everything that he wanted to say to her? He couldn't expect her to understand him, why he'd done what he'd done, why he'd hurt her, who he really was…in just ten minutes? She tried to remember everything he said and she kept coming back to the same thing, and it kept repeating over and over in her head, "*I loved you, I still do.*" Lucy felt confused, this wasn't how she'd expected it to be. She thought she would see through his act, but she hadn't really. He'd seemed genuine, like he was telling the truth. But was he, or was he just a very good actor? He certainly had been when they lived together but when was he acting and when was he real? Lucy just didn't know. And now he'd gone again, out of her life, just like before.

But the most disturbing thing for Lucy was the realisation that she had felt excited to see him again. She'd convinced herself she was over him, but she now knew that wasn't completely true. She still had feelings for him. She'd managed to bury them deep inside somewhere, but as soon as she saw him, sat with him and listened to him, they all started to creep back. She tried to suppress her emotions, but she couldn't, they were too strong. She looked at the text again and thought about replying, but then she thought "why don't I just call him, if he doesn't answer, at least I can leave a message and he'll maybe reply." She rang the number from the text and waited for it to connect. She could hear it ringing in her ear, but at the same time she could also hear a phone ringing somewhere else. It was close by, in the park. She stood up confused and looked around, expecting to see Austin with the phone, but there was no-one there. She focused on where the sound was coming from and started walking towards it until she reached a green bin a few yards away from the bench. She realised the ringing sound was coming from inside the bin. She looked around to check that no-one was watching her and then slowly reached in through the gap at the top of the bin, feeling around with her hand. Her hand touched something that felt like paper, maybe a coffee cup, and then her fingers brushed against a cold hard object. It was vibrating and, as she hooked her fingers around it and pulled it upwards, the ringing sound got louder and louder. It was a mobile phone. Lucy ended the call on her own phone and the second phone fell silent. She looked closely at what seemed to be just a normal, cheapish, mobile phone. The no frills version. What was it they called them on TV detective programmes – a burner phone? She'd never quite understood that term, but she knew that it just meant a cheap, untraceable phone.

Lucy walked back to the bench and sat down, holding the phone on her lap in front of her. It was unlocked and she quickly scrolled through it. No contacts. One call from the previous today to her number. One text today, again to her number. Apart from that, the phone was empty. *"Nothing to see here"* it seemed to be saying to her. Lucy sighed. After she'd gone to the toilet, Austin must have got up and walked off, sending her the text and then throwing his phone into the bin as he passed it. Maybe that had been his plan all along – but then he wouldn't have known she was going to go to the toilet. He obviously didn't want to be traced, maybe he suspected Lucy was going to get the police involved. Perhaps he just knew that's what she would do? He had known her very well. She'd never kept any secrets from him, pity that hadn't worked both ways, she thought with a wry smile.

A few minutes later she saw DS Campbell striding across the park and she gave him a small, somewhat hesitant, wave. He was a big-looking man, even from a distance. Not tall, but wide. He made his way over and sat down beside her on the bench, taking up most of the empty space.

'I take it he's gone?' he said.

'Yes, I'm afraid so,' Lucy replied. 'I called you from the ladies, over there.' Lucy motioned with her head and Campbell looked across at the square brick building. 'When I came back, he'd gone. He sent me a text and then dumped his phone in that bin over there.'

'What did the text say, can I see it?' Campbell asked her.

Lucy clicked on the message, opening it up, before handing over her phone. He looked at it for a few minutes and then handed it back to her.

'Is that the phone he used?' Campbell asked, nodding towards the other phone lying in Lucy's lap, 'can I have it?'

Lucy nodded and handed it to him. Campbell spent a few minutes looking through it before putting it in his pocket and turning to face Lucy.

'So I've seen the text he sent and it looks like he called you yesterday too?' Campbell asked her.

'Yes, that's right. I tried to call you, but I couldn't get through so I spoke to detective Strong instead.'

'You spoke to DI Strong?' Campbell interrupted her.

'Yes, I tried your number but there was no answer so I called him, why?' Lucy asked seeing that Campbell was looking surprised. 'Didn't he say?'

'No, he's working up in Leeds at the moment so we don't see each other so much,' Campbell replied thinking he still would have expected Strong to tell him. It was his case now after all.

'Ah, okay, I expect he was going to tell you. I told him I was going to try and get Austin to agree to meet me next week so I expect he thought it wasn't that urgent.'

'Yes, I expect so, but you met him today?' Campbell prodded.

'Yes, but I didn't know that was going to happen. He must have been following me. Obviously he knows where I live and I guess he just saw me coming for a walk in the park and the next thing I know he's sitting beside me on this bench, just like you are now. We used to come here together occasionally, in the…, you know, when we lived together. Anyway, that's when I excused myself and called you from the ladies but when I came out, he'd gone. He must have got scared I guess. Maybe I took too long.'

'What did he say to you?' Campbell asked.

'Not much, just that he wanted to explain stuff. He felt he owed it to me,' Lucy said laughing ironically. 'After a minute or two I said I needed to go to the toilet so I could call you, and then when I came out again, he was gone.'

'I see. Why did you call me, not DI Strong?' Campbell enquired.

'I did try calling detective Strong,' Lucy replied, 'but he didn't answer, so I called you.'

'Okay, and what do you think his text meant?' Campbell asked, 'the bit where he said I hope you understood what I tried to say. What did that mean?'

'I'm not sure,' Lucy replied cautiously, thinking. 'He was starting to say he had been ill but now he was better....maybe it was something to do with that. But he really didn't have time to say much, it was literally only a minute or two before I left him to call you.'

'Mmm, okay,' Campbell replied. 'Well, let me know if he contacts you again. It sounds like he may think he has some unfinished business with you. Do you want me to walk you back to your flat?'

'No, I'll be fine thank you,' Lucy replied, 'I think I'll just sit here for a few minutes longer. It's nice and peaceful.'

DS Campbell got up from the bench and walked slowly across the park, back towards his car. He had an uneasy feeling, something wasn't quite right. For some reason he didn't think Lucy had been telling him the whole truth. Yes, she had met Austin and yes, she had called Campbell, but the rest of it just didn't seem right. The bit in-between, but he couldn't put his finger on it. They'd had a policeman watching Lucy for a couple of days in case Austin turned up, but when nothing had happened they'd had to pull him off to work on another case. These things were always easy in retrospect, but if only they'd kept him on her for a few days longer they might have got Austin. And why had Strong not let him know about her call, that was strange. Sure he was working in a different region, but that shouldn't stop him making a call. Maybe Lucy was right in that he thought he had time to let Campbell know. Could've, would've, should've, Campbell thought, feeling a bit down, as he got in his car and drove away.

Chapter 22

Sophie walked into the busy bar. It wasn't one she'd been in previously, she had only been in this part of town a couple of times since she'd started at Uni. This was mainly the business area of Leeds and you didn't find many students here, except for the ones working behind the bar, trying to fund their education. The bar was full of people, all smartly-dressed in suits or fashionable clothes and she immediately felt out of place, like everyone was looking at her. There's a student they were all saying, what's she doing here, is she lost or something? Shouldn't she be studying, we don't pay taxes for her to be coming in here. Although in reality, she knew they probably hadn't even noticed her enter, and they were all continuing with their normal business talk, whatever that was, demonstrating how clever and important they were.

She saw her dad sitting at a table on his own in the far corner. It was so easy to pick him out, not just because he was her dad or that he was tall and slim, but more that he was a policeman. Somehow he just looked like a policeman. If she'd asked everyone in the pub to pick out the "policeman" in the bar, she reckoned most, if not all of them, would point straight at her dad. He'd definitely never be able to work undercover, or at least not without dramatically changing his appearance.

Sophie walked across to where her dad was sitting and they briefly, slightly awkwardly, hugged. Her dad had never been that good at physical contact stuff. Although she didn't really want anything, he insisted on buying her a soft drink and he went to the bar, returning a few minutes later with a coke. They chatted for a bit, catching up. Him, asking how university was going and her asking about his police work and what he was doing in Leeds. He never really told her much about that though and she didn't mind. She didn't really want to hear about some of the horror stories that he no doubt had to deal with on a daily basis. She'd seen enough of those on-line. Rather him than me she'd always thought as she grew up and began to get a better understanding of what he actually did. You had to have a strong stomach for it, especially in the area he worked in. Let's face it "Serious Crime Squad" didn't exactly sound like a bundle of laughs.

After a while the dad/daughter conversation began to dry up, with longer and longer pauses between each, increasingly shorter, piece of discussion. Sophie decided it was a good time to bring up the main reason she'd arranged to meet her dad. That being the unfortunate saga of Emily, the mobile phone, and the sleazy estate agent.

Sophie had known straight away that something was wrong when Emily had returned to the house that night. She'd gone straight to her room and, standing outside her door, Sophie could hear her crying. She'd never seen Emily like that before. Emily was the one who just got on with things. If something went wrong, she just moved on and did something else. But not tonight, something serious had happened and it obviously wasn't good. Sophie went to the kitchen and returned with two cups of hot chocolate. Whatever it was, hot chocolate would always help. She tapped lightly on Emily's door and pushed it open. Emily was lying on top of her bed in a foetal position. She'd stopped crying and her eyes were open.

'Brought you some hot choccy,' Sophie said as she sat down on her friend's bed, putting one of the mugs on the bedside cabinet.

'Thanks mate,' Emily replied, forcing a thin smile as she sat up on the bed, hugging her knees, before reaching over and picking up the mug. She took a sip of the hot drink.

'Ah, that's nice,' she said.

It had taken a while, and a lot of listening and coaxing on Sophie's part, but eventually the whole story had come out as they sat on Emily's bed, and the two girls had ended up hugging each other for a while until everything felt just a bit better.

'What am I going to do?' Emily asked. 'He's got me trapped. If I don't see him, and I know what he wants with that, then he's going to report me to the police for identity theft. I don't know what my mum and dad will say. They'll be devastated, I'll have to give up Uni and I'll never get a job' and her eyes began to tear up again.

'Don't worry, it won't come to that,' Sophie replied smiling. 'I have a plan,' she said confidently.

'What is it?' Emily replied hopefully.

'Emm,… well…I'll tell my dad. He's a policeman, he'll know what to do,' Sophie said, trying to sound convincing for her friend, although in truth she didn't know if that would do any good at all. She'd never asked her dad for help on anything like this before. 'Don't worry, he'll sort it out,' she said, smiling.

The next day, the two girls had done a bit of their own investigation on-line and found out that Kyle Smith worked for an Estate Agent's in town, which explained the leaflets in his car and how he had access to that big house, the one he'd taken Emily to. However, as hard as they tried, they couldn't find out anything more useful about him which might help. So they'd reverted to the original idea, which was in fact their only idea, Sophie contacted her dad and arranged to meet him. He seemed happy to hear from her, if, as usual, a little distracted, but he had said he could meet her for half an hour in the New Inn, near where he was stationed, which was where they were now sitting.

Sophie told her dad what had happened with Emily, from the start when they had found the phone right through to the incident with Emily and Kyle in the big house, and he listened carefully until she'd finished. Then he looked her straight in the eye and said,

'Tell me truthfully, did this really happen to your friend Emily and not you?' and he continued to stare at her.

'What? Yes, of course it was Emily,' she replied irritably, thinking he hadn't been listening.

But DI Strong had been listening and he'd wanted to make sure this man, this Kyle Smith, wasn't harassing *his* daughter. If that had been the case then he was going to be in really big trouble, but he could see his daughter was telling him the truth. He shook his head.

'You know, I hear about this sort of thing more and more regularly now. Not so much with a mobile phone, but more through social media. Especially with people your age and even younger. Someone contacts you, over a period of time they somehow become a friend, even though you've never actually met. And then you do meet and find out they're not who they said they were. I'll spare you the worst, but I hope you and Emily realise what danger she could have put herself in. I know it might have seemed like a good laugh to her at the time, but she should never have used that mobile phone. Sounds like in the end she had a lucky escape.'

'I know,' Sophie replied, 'she realises that now, but what can we do? He's threatening her and she's worried if she doesn't contact him, he'll accuse her of identity fraud or something. We looked it up on line and it says she could get ten years in jail for that. She's really worried and so am I.'

'Okay, leave it with me,' he said smiling reassuringly. 'Tell Emily she's got nothing to worry about. He's just bluffing with the whole identity fraud thing. She won't get done for that. She's just been a bit silly, that's all, but lucky too. I hope she knows that. It sounds like this Kyle Smith needs to learn a lesson, I'm guessing Emily might not be the only woman he's done this to. We don't know what happened to the previous person he was texting. I'll get one of my men to have a quiet word with him. She won't hear from him again, I promise. Tell her not to worry but tell her not to do anything like that again.'

Strong finished his drink and looked at his watch.

'I have to go now,' he said, 'got some more work to do I'm afraid, but it's been nice catching up. We should do this more often while I'm in Leeds, although if all goes well I might be finished here quite soon.'

He stood up, bent down and kissed his daughter lightly on the cheek.

'Don't tell mum about this,' Sophie said as her dad straightened up again, 'she'll only worry.'

Chapter 23

Lucy was busying around in her flat, trying to tidy it up a bit and make it more presentable. She'd done the bedroom and the kitchen, now all that she had left to do was the lounge. She'd put that off till last as it was the messiest. There hadn't been time to clear up her breakfast dishes from that morning, which she'd left on the coffee table, and on top of that there was a variety of baby paraphernalia lying around on the sofa and chairs, as well as the floor and most other surfaces generally. It had never been like this before CJ came along, but now she just didn't seem to have the time, or often the energy, anymore. It seemed to be never ending, like the proverbial painting of the Forth Railway Bridge. As soon as you were finished you had to start all over again. Lucy had always prided herself on keeping a tidy house, it was how she'd been brought up. One of her earliest memories of her mum was her hoovering in the lounge and telling Lucy to lift her feet as she sat on the settee, frustratingly trying to listen to the TV over the sound of the hoover. Why did she always hoover when Lucy's favourite programme was on? Now Lucy yearned to get her flat back into a neat and tidy state but knowing it might have to wait until CJ was a few years older and needed less looking after.

Not that any of her visitors seemed to care about how tidy her place was, all they seemed to want to do when they visited her was to see the baby and make funny noises at him until he started crying - and then most of them would quickly hand him back to Lucy. There were exceptions to that though - obviously her mum, aka granny, and a few of her closest friends who had children of their own. One other exception was Lucy's best friend, Jane, or Auntie Jane as she'd now come to be known. Jane was a frequent visitor and, although she didn't have any kids herself, she was brilliant with little CJ. She just seemed to know how to handle him.

Jane had called Lucy earlier that day and invited herself around for a cup of coffee in the afternoon, as she often did. 'I'll bring the cake,' she said and Lucy didn't mind, it was always good to see Jane, she was such a positive person and always seemed to be able to cheer Lucy up if she was feeling a bit fed-up or down.

Lucy looked around the living room, it looked okay. Okay'ish. Her arms were full of baby things – mainly clothes and toys along with a couple of packets of wipes, two dummies and a feeding bottle. She walked through to her bedroom and laid the baby pile down on her bed, pulling the door closed behind her as she left and returned to the lounge. If you couldn't see it then it must be tidy, she laughed to herself. That was a good rule for all young mothers. Lucy glanced up at the clock on the wall as she sat down on the sofa. The clock seemed to rule her life at the moment, telling her what to do and when. Feed, change, play, sleep. Sleep was a big one. When the baby was asleep, that was the time when Lucy had to try and do everything else. Washing, dressing, cleaning, eating. If she was lucky and the baby slept for a bit longer than normal then she might get a bit of rest too. That was a luxury though and it didn't happen too often.

Knowing that Jane would be here shortly, and the baby would soon be awake again, she decided to try and grab a few minute's rest now. As she sat there her mind began to drift to the other major thing that had happened to her lately. The return of Andy Austin.

She'd thought a lot about him since they'd met that day in the park. During the short period between setting the meeting up and it actually happening, Lucy had thought it would be pretty straightforward, a bit like a business meeting or a chat about something with a far-flung acquaintance. Someone she only slightly knew. Very matter of fact. You did this, I did that, sort of thing. Then she'd call in the police and that would be that. But it hadn't been like that at all. As soon as he'd sat down beside her on the park bench, something else had kicked in and her emotional side had taken over. She hadn't been expecting that. This wasn't a remote acquaintance or someone she worked with. This was the man she had lived with and loved - and also the man who had hurt her more than anyone else. Two sides to the same coin. She had tried to stay calm and let him talk, but at the same time she could feel her heart racing and her mind was all over the place.

Thinking about it since, the only explanation she could come up with was that she still had strong feelings for this man. She didn't want it to be that way, but that seemed to be how it was. Maybe she was still emotionally tired and weak from looking after little CJ? She certainly could do with getting more sleep but she wasn't convinced that was the reason for her unexpected reaction to seeing him again. This man. This Andy Austin. This murderer. She didn't want to admit it to herself but it was hard to deny. She thought about women who wrote to prisoners on death row in the United States, she'd seen it in documentaries on TV. Was it the same thing? Did she have some weird fascination for a killer? But, no it wasn't like that, and she wasn't like that. She had fallen in love with this man without knowing what he'd actually done. Who he really was. If she had known, then of course there was no way she would have got involved with him at all. He'd tricked her and probably used her, there was no doubt in her mind about that. Yet she still couldn't reconcile the man she'd lived with, who she'd known as Paul Smith, who she'd imagined her future with, to the man who in reality was a killer, known as Andy Austin. How could he be the same person and how could she still have feelings for him? It just didn't make sense.

Not being able to clear her mind, but not wanting to think any more about him, she got up and walked into the kitchen, looking for something to do. Some sort of diversion. She switched the kettle on and wiped the work surfaces, although they were already spotless, but at least it seemed to help. A few minutes later there was a knock at the door and she opened it to the welcome sight of her best friend Jane. They hugged each other warmly and then returned to the kitchen where Lucy boiled the kettle again and Jane unwrapped two pieces of lemon drizzle cake she'd brought with her. The two women sat chatting, eating the cake and drinking their coffees and Lucy immediately felt much more revived. Jane was in the middle of another funny story about one of her customers from the travel agency, when they heard little CJ begin to stir. He always started with a few sniffles and then there would be the noise of him moving around, stretching himself, before there was a little whimper, which was usually when Lucy went in and picked him up. Once she'd been in the room when he started stirring and she was astonished how quickly he awoke. His eyes had just suddenly popped wide open. She'd stared at him then for a minute or two, thinking how beautiful he looked and also how much he reminded her of his father. He had the same eyes and same shaped mouth.

'Ooh, can I get him?' Jane asked as she eased herself off the bar stool, and without waiting for Lucy's reply she was on her way to the bedroom.

'Ignore the mess in there,' Lucy called, 'I am going to sort it out later.'

'Hello, little man, your Auntie Jane is here to see you again,' Jane was saying as she came back into the kitchen, the baby in her arms. 'Oh, Lucy, I know I say it all the time, but he really is the most handsome baby I think I've ever seen. You should send his picture to a modelling agency, I bet they'd take him on.'

Lucy laughed and getting off her stool, she picked up the two mugs and walked through to the lounge, telling her friend to follow. Jane walked after her, cradling the baby, and they sat down together on the settee, both gazing fondly at the little boy snuggled up in Jane's arms.

'You need to have a baby of your own,' Lucy said laughing, 'you'd be a great mum. You're a natural.'

'Maybe sometime, but not yet,' Jane laughed back, 'I'd need to find a good man first....oh, sorry I didn't mean....' Jane stopped talking and could feel herself starting to blush.

Lucy had never discussed CJ's father with anyone, not even Jane, but maybe with all that had happened recently, maybe it was the right time. Suddenly, from Jane's comment, in that moment, she realised she'd been keeping it all to herself for too long, she needed to share the load and who better with than her best friend Jane.

'Can I tell you something, but it's just between us, no-one else, you have to promise,' she began, not sure where she was going to go next.

'Of course you can, you know that,' Jane replied, reaching across and holding Lucy's forearm, her look suddenly serious.

'Paul's back. Well I should say Andy Austin I guess, as that's his real name,' Lucy said and she also felt herself begin to blush.

After that opening line, Lucy carried on talking, she couldn't stop herself and it all just tumbled out. She told Jane almost everything. About the police coming round to warn her he was back in the country. About him calling her. Then their meeting. Her calling the police. Him disappearing.

'Wow, c'mere, you should have told me this before, you poor sweetheart' Jane said and she reached across and gave her friend a sympathetic hug with the baby wedged between their two laps.

They sat like that for what seemed a long time before Lucy gradually eased herself free and picked up the baby from her friend's lap.

'He's due a feed now, I better do it or else he'll just get grumpy,' she said.

'Typical man, always thinking about food,' Jane laughed.

'So what happens now with Austin, what's next?' Jane asked as Lucy began feeding her baby.

'Well I don't know. I've no way of contacting him so I guess the ball is in his court. He knows where I am, but of course he may not want to see me again. Maybe he said all he wanted to say in the park. Maybe he thinks it'll be too dangerous and he'll get caught if he tries again. I just don't know what he's thinking.' Lucy said, staring across the room. She gave a big sigh.

'Do you want to see him again?' Jane asked her.

Lucy was quiet for a few seconds, still staring straight ahead, then she turned to look at her friend.

'Honestly, I don't know. I just don't know' she said, shaking her head. 'What would you do?'

'Do you still have feelings for him? Knowing who he really is?' Jane asked.

'I know, I shouldn't have, He's a murderer, I know that. But seeing him again that day, I didn't think I would but.... And of course there's CJ too,' Lucy replied, looking down at her baby.

'Ah, okay, I take it he's the father,' Jane said and Lucy nodded, 'I assumed he must be, unless you'd been visited by an angel during the night and I think you'd have told me that,' she said smiling at her friend. 'But I'm assuming he doesn't know, you haven't said anything to him yet?'

'No, I haven't told anyone at all, not him, not even my mum. You're the first and only person I've admitted it to, although I'm sure a lot of my friends would have guessed it, and just didn't want to say. But Austin, do you think I should tell him he has a son?' Lucy replied, hoping her friend had the answer.

Jane exhaled deeply, 'well that's a tricky one. As you say, you've got no way of contacting him so I guess if he gets in touch with you again you'd just have to....'

Suddenly they were interrupted by the ringtone from Lucy's mobile phone. The two women looked at each other in surprise and Lucy picked it up. It wasn't a number she recognised. Her hand was shaking as she hit the green button.

'Hello,' she said quietly.

'Yes.'

'Yes, this is Lucy.'

‘Is that right?’

‘When?’

‘Why?’

‘Look….just piss off will you,’ she said suddenly and ended the call.

Lucy put the phone down beside her and looked at her friend who had been staring at her throughout with her mouth hanging open.

‘Who….was it…him?’ Jane asked her friend, unintelligibly but still getting her meaning across.

Lucy looked back at Jane and started to laugh.

‘No, it was a man claiming to be from Microsoft telling me I had a problem with my computer that needed fixing urgently,’ she replied, now laughing uncontrollably.

‘Oh, you cow,’ Jane replied, joining in the laughter and hitting Lucy with one of the sofa cushions which made her laugh even more.

Chapter 24

Strong dialled the number on his mobile phone. Austin had just come back from a morning jog and was in the kitchen making a cup of coffee for himself when it rang. He was feeling positive after his morning run, the endorphins he guessed, and he was tempted to not answer it, knowing it could only be DI Strong as he was the only one who knew his number. It wouldn't be good news, but he knew he had to. They exchanged brief pleasantries before Strong explained that he had another "job" he wanted Austin to take care of. Austin tried to think of some excuses why he couldn't, but Strong was determined. He said it was for his daughter, some sleazebag estate agent had been bothering her and her flatmate and he just needed to be warned off, nothing too serious.

'What, so I'd have to come all the way to Leeds to tell this bloke off? Can't you get someone up there to do it?' Austin asked, still looking for reasons not to get involved.

'I'd rather not. I don't want to involve anyone else up here, especially when I am reviewing their whole operation. Could put me in an awkward position if I start asking them for favours.

Besides it's best if only me and you know about this, remember our deal. You'll just need to do an overnight stay, should be pretty simple. It shouldn't take you long. In fact you can stay at my place, I've got a spare room. Should be okay for one night, no-one will know you were here. This guy just needs a little reminder to behave better when he's around women,' Strong said. 'Nothing too violent.'

'Listen, I'm, I'm....Look, is it always going to be like this? You calling me up? To be honest I'm feeling a lot better now, a lot less angry. What I did last year…I'm not sure I've still got the appetite to do this,' Austin said.

'Look, just do this one, as a personal favour to me. Then we can talk. Maybe we'll have a break, see how it goes. I'll send you the details. It needs doing in the next few days. Best come today, call me when you get here,' Strong said and the line went dead.

Austin sat for a few minutes thinking. The scar on his head was itching a bit but he resisted the temptation to give it a scratch. The doctor had warned him about avoiding infection and he'd taken care to keep it clean. His hair had now re-grown over it and it was only faintly visible without moving his hair aside. It did itch though and more so when he was feeling stressed, as he was now. He knew Strong had the upper hand on him and could have him arrested practically anytime he wanted. Sure, he could go on the run again but then it would be like that for the rest of his life until he slipped up and got caught. He'd never see Lucy again and that was the one thing he most wanted to do. Although

Strong had all the aces on him now, he was also the one who could help him get out of this mess and live some sort of normal life again, maybe even with some sort of contact with Lucy, if she would agree to that. Austin began to think about that a bit more, maybe if he kept Strong sweet for a bit longer, he could get him to stop. Maybe Strong had the authority to close the Anniversary Killer file, or at least put it on the back burner so that no-one was actively looking for him. Strong might be his only hope of some way out of this mess and he needed to think carefully about how he could get Strong to help him achieve that.

Since he'd met Lucy in the park, he'd not stopped thinking about her. She'd looked even more beautiful than he remembered. More radiant, more mature. And, although she'd obviously been angry with him, he thought he'd noticed a little bit in her manner, how she was, that indicated she was also pleased to see him too. Maybe he'd just imagined that, but she'd really looked at him intensely when he'd been talking and she looked sympathetic, maybe even loving. Still? Could that be possible after he'd hurt her so badly? Maybe he just wanted that so much that it seemed real. He had known all along that it was only going to be a very brief meeting with Lucy. Strong had warned him about what she was planning to do, and when she made her excuse to go to the toilet, he knew it was time for him to go. He couldn't really blame her and he had expected that she would do something like that. That was how she was. That was the Lucy he'd fallen in love with. He knew she would feel that he deserved to be brought to justice and he couldn't argue against that. However, she had at least let him talk a bit, and hopefully explain some of it to her, why it had happened, how he had been ill, before she'd gone to make the call to the police. He saw that as a positive. She could easily have just set a trap for him to be arrested as soon as he arrived in the park, but she hadn't. She'd let him have some time to explain. Just the two of them, together again. That must mean something.

He hadn't tried to call her back since then, although he had been tempted, and a couple of times he'd started dialling her number on his new pay-as-you-go phone. But he'd stopped, deciding it was better to leave her to think about things for a bit longer before he tried again. This might be his last chance. But he knew at some point he would call her. And soon. Even though he knew it was risky, what was the alternative? He had to give it another try. He needed to get a feeling for there being any chance of some kind of future with her, even if it was a very slim one.

Maybe a trip to Leeds would be an ideal diversion to take his mind off Lucy for a day or two - and then he could call her when he got back. It would also give him a chance to talk directly with Strong and see if he could persuade him to stop, or at least have a break from this situation, as Strong had hinted to him. He would certainly press him on that and hopefully that would give him the chance to move on to some kind of more normal life. Whatever that was. His life before the accident had been pretty normal. He had a good job, a nice house, lots of friends and a good social life. But he knew that was all in the past, there was no way he could ever go back to that. To all of those people in his past, he was now The Anniversary Killer. It would be impossible to come back from that. The only good thing that had happened since the accident had been meeting Lucy. If only he'd known her before. His friends would have loved her. But would he have met her if the accident hadn't happened. Austin had read about the principle of "the butterfly effect" where everything is in some way connected and a small change in one situation can be the trigger for bigger changes somewhere down the line. If the accident hadn't happened would he have been in the café on the day when he first saw Lucy? Probably not. It was a Wednesday and he would have been in his office at work, as normal. Or what had been normal. He wouldn't even have been in that part of town and so he might never have met Lucy. Despite that he couldn't accept that anything good could possibly have come out of the accident that had wiped out his family, his mum and dad, brother and cousin. Maybe he would have just met Lucy some other time. In a bar or something. Another flap of the butterfly wings. His mum and dad would have loved her.

A few hours later Austin was sitting on a train, heading North, towards Leeds and DI Strong. He was reading the documentation that had arrived by courier in a plain brown envelope earlier that day. Luckily, the train wasn't busy so he was able to lay it out on the table in front of him without anyone seeing it and perhaps connecting the dots afterwards. The target was a young man, Kyle Smith, who worked at an Estate Agent's office in the centre of the town. He was in the sales team and part of his job was to value houses for his clients who were looking to sell, and then finding potential buyers for the houses and persuading them to make an offer. It was really a balancing act, finding the right price that satisfied both the seller and the buyer and then pushing the deal through as quickly as he could so he could get paid on it. However it appeared Kyle Smith wasn't satisfied with just the commission he got from completing the deal, he had also developed an unhealthy habit of expecting more from his clients. Extra benefits from his female clients. And it seemed to Austin that a lot of Smith's clients were women. Probably not a coincidence. Maybe some of them did find him attractive – he was young, fit healthy, confident, not bad looking, probably charming – but it appeared that he didn't like to take no for an answer. Somehow Strong had managed to get details of Smith's personnel record and it showed there had been a number of complaints against him, all from women clients, and probably more that hadn't come out. There were accusations of inappropriate behaviour, sexual comments and even a couple of times where it had been claimed he had physically touched them. Smith had denied it all and said they'd all misread his "sales patter." And nothing had been proven, it was the women's word against his and it seemed they didn't want it to become public. That was understandable. On top of that, Smith's excellent sales record meant that the company didn't want to lose him, so no further action had been taken. The file was closed for now. It would appear that Sophie's flatmate Emily hadn't been Kyle Smith's only victim. He was a serial sexual predator and Strong had made a note, perhaps to justify their planned action, that these types of men very rarely changed and often progressed on to carry out more serious acts of sexual violence. Austin didn't really care. Smith was obviously not a nice man and if Strong wanted him warned off, he could do that, and then he would be in a better position to negotiate a way out of the deal he'd agreed with the detective. That was the plan Austin was formulating now.

Austin read through the documentation a second time and finished just before the train trolley service reached his seat. Kyle Smith hadn't killed anyone, but he was a nasty guy with little or no respect for women and certainly needed teaching a lesson. At least Strong wasn't asking him to be particularly violent this time, maybe just a little slap if Smith needed it. If Lucy had been one of his victims, Austin would certainly have wanted to teach him a lesson and so he imagined that some of the women were just like her.

'Anyone for snacks or hot drinks?' a voice called out and Austin gathered his papers together into one single pile and looked up at the woman pushing the trolley. She was wearing a dark blue skirt and waistcoat with a white blouse and red, white and blue cravat. She had, what Austin could only describe as, a disinterested look on her face.

'Yes please, what sandwiches have you got?' he asked her and she stopped the trolley suddenly, seemingly surprised that someone had spoken.

'Sorry, sir, no sandwiches left,' she replied, without smiling and appearing ready to move on.

'Oh, do you have any crisps then?' Austin asked her politely.

The woman bent down to the reach into the lower half of her trolley then stood up again.

'Yes,' she said.

'Oh, right, well can I have a packet of cheese and onion crisps and a decaf coffee please?' Austin asked her smiling.

'Sorry, no cheese and onion crisps left,' the trolley woman replied.

'Okay, what do you have?' Austin asked, feeling a mixture of amusement and frustration.

The woman bent down again and pulled out a lower tray. 'Plain crisps,' she said, 'or cheddars.'

'Okay, I'll have plain crisps and a decaf coffee please,' Austin replied.

'We only do regular coffee,' came the reply.

'Regular it is then,' Austin said, trying hard to suppress a laugh.

The woman poured out a cup of coffee and put it down in front of him along with three small cartons of milk, a variety of sugars and a plastic stirrer. Austin didn't have the heart to tell her that he drank it black.

After the trolley lady had moved on, Austin settled back down in his seat to his crisps and coffee, a dark looking liquid, which was just about drinkable. He put his pile of papers back in the brown envelope and in turn put that into his sports bag, hidden below the table. He was satisfied he now knew enough about Kyle Smith and he was also satisfied that, although he was keen to get out of this, if Smith was to be the last one, at least he deserved it. Hopefully he would be able to teach this guy a lesson and make him change his ways towards women in the future. Be a bit more respectful. Austin closed his eyes and leant back into his seat to try and get some rest for the remainder of the journey.

A little while later the train arrived at Leeds station and Austin made his way out towards the car park. He'd texted Strong from the train and the detective was already there waiting for him. Strong was driving a dark green, four door, saloon, which had been provided for him from the Leeds police car pool. Strong knew that some of his fellow detective inspectors would have been disappointed by the car, seeing it as not good enough for someone at their level, but Strong wasn't really a car person. He never had been, and whilst he liked a nice car, mostly he just thought of them as a machine that took you from one place to another. That was their main purpose, and as long as they did that with a reasonable degree of comfort and without breaking down, then that was good enough for DI Strong.

Austin got in the car and they drove back to the house which had been provided for Strong during his stint in Leeds. As they drove along Strong quizzed Austin about his meeting with Lucy, trying to find out why he had arranged it, and what he was going to do next. The detective's advice was still that he should have no further contact with Lucy. It was obvious from what she had done that first time, that she was going to try and hand him over to the police and Strong cautioned Austin that he might not always be able to warn him in time to allow him to make an escape.

'She didn't tell us the whole truth about meeting you this time,' DI Strong said. 'She told me that she thought it would be in a week or so and it was lucky I managed to call you, with you of course knowing you were going to meet her that same day. She also called my DS, Campbell, and if she hadn't got through to me first, he would probably have got to you before I could warn you. I can't guarantee that will be the same outcome if you try and see her again.'

Austin nodded. He was very aware of what had happened, he'd gone over it enough in his head, and he knew the risks, but when he'd thought about it afterwards, overall he felt that it had gone fairly well. He'd needed to see Lucy and she'd at least let him talk for a few minutes - and that was a start. She could easily have set a trap and arranged for the police to be waiting to arrest him as soon as he arrived. Of course he'd looked around the park before he approached Lucy and it seemed normal, but he wasn't to know for certain that there weren't undercover police in the park waiting for him.

He hadn't known what to expect from seeing Lucy, how she would react, but he was pleased that he'd managed to get at least some of his story across to her although he knew there was still a lot more to talk about. If there was ever going to be some sort of reconciliation for them, whatever that might mean, he knew it wasn't going to be easy and there would be difficult times along the way. Maybe too difficult for her, and that was still something to be found out. He had to keep going though, now that he'd taken that first step, he had to find out where it could go, and, in his mind, he knew he was definitely going to call her again. He really wanted to meet her again, she looked so beautiful, but he knew he'd have to be very careful. Strong had made his views very clear though, and Austin understood that, so he felt there was nothing to be gained from discussing it further with the policeman at this point and so he stayed silent, not responding to Strong's speech.

Strong interpreted Austin's reluctance to talk as a sign that he wasn't going to take his advice and that he'd probably try and contact Lucy again. That was the power of love, he mused, thinking what he would have done if he'd been in the same situation. He honestly didn't know. Austin and Lucy was definitely a risk, in Strong's mind a loose end, and something he'd need to keep an eye on. He didn't like loose ends, he liked to be in control. The detective made a mental note to contact Lucy and make sure she told him as soon as she received any contact from Austin so that he could manage the situation. Strong decided there was nothing more to be gained at this point so he moved the conversation onto the current matter in hand, Kyle Smith, asking Austin if he'd read the material and if there was anything else he needed. Austin said it was fine and he didn't foresee any problems in giving him a bit of a reprimand and hopefully putting him back on the right track when it came to women.

Strong nodded. He had faith in Austin's ability to do what he wanted and it was best that he didn't know too much detail or got involved in any way that could be traced back to him. They arrived back at the house and Strong showed Austin where he would be staying that night before they set straight off out again.

'I'll drop you off in the centre of town, let you wander around a bit, get your bearings, before you do your thing' Strong said to Austin as they left Strong's temporary Leeds accommodation.

The plan was that Austin would do his thing with Kyle Smith that evening, lay low at Strong's house afterwards, and then head back down South on an early train the next day. Quickly in and out with minimal fuss. Austin had seen that Kyle Smith usually went for a drink in the same pub after work and so he decided that he would try and get to him after he left it. Kyle always walked home on his own from the pub and there were a lot of conveniently, quiet side streets between the two locations.

They left the house and Austin got in the car, sliding into the passenger seat. He was wearing a dark brown jerkin, black jeans and he had a black baseball cap on his lap. He had thought about bringing a weapon, something to hit Smith with, but he had decided against it. He was hoping that a few strong words would do the trick, or, if need be, a bit of a slap. As DI Strong locked the house door and approached his car, another car drew to a halt by his driveway and the driver wound down his window.

'Hey Guv,' a man shouted from the car.

Strong looked and saw it was one of his Leeds team, DS Kerry, calling to him.

'What's up?' Strong called back as the man got out of the car and started walking towards him.

'I was just passing and saw you coming out. I wondered if I could have a quick word?' DS Kerry asked as he approached the back of Strong's car.

'Sure, can it wait? I'm just dropping a friend off and then heading into the station. I'll be there in twenty minutes. Shall we talk then?'

'Yeh, sure that's fine.' DS Kerry replied. 'Sorry I didn't realise you had someone with you,' he said bending down and nodding towards the car. 'See you at the station then,' he said and he turned, walked back to his car and drove off.

Strong dropped Austin off at the bus terminus near the main shopping precinct. The journey had been quiet, apart from Strong's police radio messages interrupting the car radio every now and again. There had been no further discussion on Austin's planned activity for that evening and Austin had got out of the car with a simple 'see you later.' Strong re-joined the flow of traffic and headed towards the police station. Austin was a very useful resource for him, carrying out jobs which were very difficult to successfully undertake through normal police processes. Over the years, the job had got more and more frustrating. There were too many rules nowadays. Too much red tape and forms to fill in before you could even do anything.

On top of that, there were police departments whose job it was to hope you made a mistake so they could catch you out and so justify their existence. Using Austin had helped him avoid all of that but he knew it couldn't continue like that for ever. He'd have to end it with Austin sometime and that might be quite soon. He could see Austin was getting fed up with it and was looking for a way out and Strong knew that he was the only one who could do that for him. Whatever that end might be. Strong had been very careful not to leave any trail that could incriminate him if Austin did get caught and tried to implicate Strong. He was confident that he'd be able to disprove any of that should Austin decide to do that. It was still a risk though and any accusation of wrongdoing was not good for a police officer, especially one at Strong's level. He'd had a clean career up till now and he wanted to keep it that way. Strong knew that the cleanest end to the situation with Austin would actually be the end of Austin. There would be no risk of any accusation then, but Strong hoped it wouldn't have to come to that. Despite what Austin had done, Strong still had a degree of sympathy for him, having gone through a similar loss and subsequent feeling of injustice himself. Strong knew there were alternative endings for this arrangement he had with Austin and, when the time came, he would have to decide which option was best.

Chapter 25

'Sandwiches, snacks, hot drinks,' a woman's voice called out just as Andy Austin was beginning to drop off to sleep.

He stretched out his legs and body as much as he could without disturbing the three other passengers who were sat around the same train table as him. There wasn't a lot of room, but he was fairly comfortable and he was tired, not really wanting to move much, or do anything in particular that needed more space. The man sitting across from him had opened his laptop as soon as he sat down and since then he appeared to have been writing a lot of emails, or maybe just one really long email. If Austin had wanted to be awkward he could have asked the man to move his computer back a bit, because technically he was encroaching on Austin's half of the table, but he didn't really care. Austin was on an early morning express train heading back down south and it was much busier than the outward journey had been, with a mix of business men and women and other people heading seemingly out early for a day trip to London or the South Coast.

The trolley lady reached his seat and Austin and his three adjacent passengers all ordered a variety of teas, coffees, sandwiches and snacks.

Luckily for all, the trolley seemed to be more fully stocked on this train and everyone got what they wanted. The trolley woman seemed much more pleasant too and Austin wondered if she'd still be like that later in the day after she's pushed her trolley up and down the train a dozen times. Austin sat back in his seat and slowly sipped his decaf coffee, looking out the window at the passing country-side as the train hurtled south. There were a lot of green fields, some trees, quite a few areas of what looked like flooding or at least standing water and not much else. Occasionally they'd speed through the station of a small town or village but always too quickly for Austin to be able to read the sign. He closed his eyes again and his mind began to drift back to the events of the previous evening.

After Strong had dropped him off in the town centre, he'd headed towards the Estate Agents office where Kyle Smith worked. Pretending to look at the various house details shown in the shop window, he was really looking past them at the layout inside. There were four desks, three of them occupied by young smartly-dressed individuals, one woman and two men. He immediately recognised Kyle Smith as one of the men sitting at a desk towards the rear. He was wearing a dark blue suit, white shirt and a red tie. He had a slight growth of stubble and his dark hair was gelled flat to his head, appearing shiny from the reflection of the ceiling light above him. Austin watched him closely as he began to type something on his keyboard. Happy that he knew where Kyle Smith was, he looked at his watch and walked across the street to a café to kill some time. Austin got a seat at a table by the window, ordered a coffee and kept an eye on the Estate Agents office immediately across the road.

Right on time, at five thirty pm, Kyle Smith and his two colleagues all left their workplace. The woman locked the door behind them and the three of them said brief goodbyes to each other before heading off in different directions. Austin was already standing outside the café and he watched as Kyle Smith headed off down the street in the direction of his usual place of refreshment. He followed him at a safe distance and sure enough Kyle went into the bar. Austin gave him a minute and then he entered the pub too. He walked towards the bar, looking around the place as he approached it. He saw Kyle Smith standing at the far end of the bar on his own, sipping a freshly poured pint of beer and apparently looking around to see if he knew any of the other customers. Or maybe just checking them out. The majority of them seemed to be people like him, stopping off for a drink after a day at the office, before they went home. Austin ordered a coke and stood at the bar, keeping a sight on his target. Kyle had approached a group of five girls, all similarly dressed in blouses and skirts, a typical office uniform. It looked like he knew them and he had begun chatting to one of the girls who was partially turned towards him. The other four girls were standing in a circle and suddenly they all began to laugh really loudly. The fifth girl turned back towards the group and joined in with the laughter, leaving Kyle standing behind her on his own. Austin saw Kyle lean in and say something to the girl, over her shoulder, but she appeared not to notice and carried on laughing with her friends. After a few seconds Kyle casually returned to where he had been standing at the bar and placed his pint back on the bar-top. Another two young girls entered the bar and Austin watched as Kyle looked towards them, giving a smile and stepping back from the bar to create a space. However the two girls appeared not to notice and instead they joined another group of men and women sitting at a nearby table. Kyle stepped back towards the bar and took another sip of his drink, whilst appearing to make a comment to the barmaid. A man stood up from the table where the two girls had just sat down, and went to the bar. He edged in beside Kyle and ordered some drinks. Kyle appeared to have a brief conversation with him, but Austin was too far away to hear what they were saying. The man returned to the table and, as he sat down, Austin noticed a couple of his friends look across at Kyle, before returning to their own conversations at the table.

The rest of the time in the bar was uneventful. Kyle gradually finished his drink and Austin kept pace with him, so they both finished at the same time. Kyle said something more to the barmaid before turning away and walking to the door. Austin gave him a few seconds and then followed his target outside. He kept a safe distance as they made their way along the street, gradually leaving the brightly lit commercial area and entering a more residential district. There was less light here, no shops, just street lights and Austin gradually increased his pace, cutting the distance between him and Kyle. A few minutes later, Kyle turned right down a narrow alleyway. There were no street lights and Austin turned into the same alleyway a few seconds after him. Kyle was unaware of Austin being behind him until he was only a few metres behind. He looked around and saw Austin, dressed in dark clothing and wearing a black baseball cap. He stopped and stood to the side to let Austin past, but Austin stopped too and stood facing him. They were both about the same build and height but Austin was definitely in control.

'I know about you, Kyle Smith,' Austin said quietly but with intent.

'What….what do you mean, who are you?' Kyle replied, feeling a little nervous at this stranger standing in front of him.

'I know what you do to women. You need to stop harassing them. You need to learn some respect. Do you get what I'm saying?' Austin said, staring hard at the man in front of him.

'I, emm, who are you?' Kyle replied, looking around to see if there was anyone else he could see, but there was no-one.

'I'll tell you who I am,' Austin replied as he grabbed Kyle's shirt collar with one hand and twisted it tightly under his chin. He leant forward so his face was up against the other man's. He could see the fear in Kyle's eyes. 'I'm the man who's going to come and get you if you don't start behaving yourself around women. And believe me you don't want that. If I have to come back, no woman will want to look at you again, not even your own mother. Do you understand?'

He gave Kyle's shirt a final twist and leant his face in even further until their noses touched, before releasing the pressure and standing back a pace.

'I said do you understand?' he said aggressively, keeping his eyes on Kyle's.

'Yes,' Kyle whispered nervously.

'What? I didn't hear you,' Austin growled back at him. 'What did you say?'

'I said, I understand,' Kyle said more clearly this time. Austin could see he was shaking.

'You better,' Austin snarled at him. 'This is your only warning. Next time it'll hurt.'

He released his hold on Kyle and stepped back. Kyle smoothed down his shirt front not sure who this man was or what was going to happen now.

'Now give me your phone,' Austin said, holding his hand out.

'What?' Kyle responded, still trying to understand what was happening here.

'Your phone, give me it. Now,' Austin said more aggressively.

Kyle fumbled in his jacket pocket and produced his phone, handing it over to Austin.

'Now, piss off,' Austin said, looking straight at him, 'and remember what I said. If I hear of you harassing any women again, I'll come and get you. And believe me you don't want that,' he snarled the last part. Leaning in close to Kyle and he could see the fear in Kyle's eyes.

Kyle nodded slightly before nervously turning and walking slowly away, further down the alleyway. He looked back over his shoulder as he did so a few times before he started to run and as Austin watched him go, he saw him trip over something on the ground, landing full length, face first, on the path. He quickly got up and rubbed himself down. He looked back at Austin once more and started running again until he reached the end of the path and disappeared out of Austin's sight. Austin laughed briefly to himself and turned back to where he had entered the alleyway, returning out onto the deserted street. He removed the sim card from Kyle's phone and put it in his pocket before placing the phone on the ground and stamping on it a few times until it broke into several pieces. He picked them up and deposited them in a nearby bin, pushing them down towards the bottom.

He made his way back to Strong's house and found the detective sitting in the lounge doing something on his laptop. Austin told him that the job had been done and he didn't think there would be any comeback on that. Strong thanked him but said he didn't want to know any of the details.

'It's best I know as little as possible,' he said.

After that brief conversation, Strong had returned to his laptop and Austin cut the sim card into several pieces before flushing them down the toilet and retiring to bed, where he'd slept soundly.

Suddenly, Austin was disturbed from his train journey nap as he heard the passenger opposite close his laptop and he felt aware of him moving from across the table. Austin opened his eyes and saw the man was standing up, reaching into the overhead shelf to retrieve a bag and coat. Austin looked at his watch and saw that they were due in to London in around five minutes, assuming the train was on time. He stretched his legs out under the table before pushing himself up into a more upright position. He'd only managed to have a brief conversation with Strong that morning about his desire to get back to a more normal lifestyle. He knew there were many reasons why that couldn't happen and so he was resigned to the likelihood that he would have to make this a cautious, ongoing conversation with Strong. At this point he just wanted Strong to agree that it was a possibility, however remote, so that they could start working out how he might get there. Although Strong hadn't said much, Austin was pleased that he hadn't written it off as being impossible and he knew that without Strong's help it would be. Another good point had been that, although Strong hadn't outright agreed to giving Austin a break from doing these jobs, he at least seemed to appreciate Austin's desire for a pause. Austin knew he would need Strong to be on his side and so he hadn't pushed him any further but he was optimistic that at least they'd started a conversation along the lines he was hoping for.

Chapter 26

'Have you seen this?' Sophie asked Emily, handing her the freebie newspaper that had dropped through their letterbox along with a load of junk mail. 'Look on the front page.'

Emily took the paper from her flatmate and unfolded it, spreading it out on her lap. Normally neither of them ever read any newspapers, they got all the information they wanted on-line or by watching Gogglebox on TV, but this time the front page had caught Sophie's eye as she'd picked it up from the doormat. Emily looked at it and the headline shouted out in large, bold print. "Local Estate Agent Assaulted". Alongside the headline there was a photo of Kyle Smith, looking battered and bruised. He had a black eye and what looked like cuts on his forehead and face. She quickly scanned through the story to see what had happened. There wasn't a lot of detail, maybe that's why the headline was so big, Emily thought. Apparently he'd been attacked after leaving The Bull's Head, a pub she had been in once or twice in the centre of town. According to Kyle, he'd been attacked from behind and hadn't had a chance to respond.

'Luckily, I managed to somehow fight back a bit and push him off, even though he was a big guy, otherwise who knows what he might have done,' Kyle was quoted as saying. He went on to say that the man had grabbed his phone and then ran off as he realised Kyle wasn't going to be as easy a victim as he'd first thought. The police had appealed for witnesses and said they were looking for a man, aged somewhere between twenty five and thirty five, but with no other description. Mmm, only a few million of them, Emily thought. She finished reading and looked up towards Sophie

'Oh my god! It's Kyle,' she exclaimed.

'I know, I can't…I wonder what happened?' Sophie replied hesitantly.

'Well it's obvious isn't it?' Emily replied.

'Is it?.. What?' Sophie asked, looking at her friend, open-mouthed, thinking the same but she hadn't told Emily about meeting with her dad, thinking it was best she didn't publicise it.

'Well, basically he's got what he deserved. The dad or brother or boyfriend of one of the other women he has no doubt been harassing, has obviously tracked him down and given him a good hiding. Can't say I blame them. If I told my dad or brother they'd both have been straight up here and done the same.'

'You think that's what's happened?' Sophie replied.

'One hundred percent,' Emily replied decisively, 'and it explains why he's stopped hassling me too. Someone's taught him a well-deserved lesson.'

'Yeh, but they also took his phone so I guess he doesn't have the number any more. You should get rid of that phone now,' Sophie replied.

Later that evening Sophie was sitting in her bedroom thinking. She'd been thinking all day since she'd seen the article in the local newspaper. She didn't know what to do. It seemed too much of a coincidence and her dad had always told her that he never believed in coincidences. There was always something else, he said. Some connection. So if that was true, did that mean there was a connection between her telling him about Emily's problem and Kyle Smith getting beat up? She'd been thinking of calling her dad all day long, but couldn't work out what to say. In the end, she'd decided there was no smart way to do this, she would just have to ask him outright and see what he said. She made sure her bedroom door was firmly shut, she didn't want Emily to overhear anything, and she sat down on her bed, picked up her phone and dialled her dad's number.

Strong was sitting in his rented police house, just finishing eating his takeaway pizza, an American Hot, when his phone rang. He glanced down at the phone and saw that it was his daughter Sophie calling which was usually a pleasant surprise. Most times, when his phone rang, it was someone having to give him some bad news usually due to a criminal activity, normally involving someone being badly injured. He'd been wondering if Sophie would call today and he picked it up and answered. After they'd exchanged a few pleasantries, he told her that it had just been agreed, that afternoon, that his job in Leeds was now complete and so he'd be moving back home in the next few days.

'Oh that's great,' Sophie said, 'well I don't mean it's great that you're leaving Leeds of course, but mum will be pleased that you're coming back home.'

'Yes, I hope so,' Strong replied, 'I haven't been able to tell her yet, I think she's got one of her classes on tonight, Yoga or Zumba or something?'

'Yes, Thursday night is Yoga,' Sophie replied. 'So did it all go to plan, what they asked you to do up here then?'

'Yes, seems to have. I had to write a report and I delivered it to the regional head this afternoon. He seems to have accepted my findings so there's nothing else for me to do here now, other than clear out my paperwork and get back home,' Strong replied, taking a bite from a section of pizza but it had gone cold and he threw the remainder of it back on his plate and pushed it to the side.

Sophie hadn't really been listening to what her dad had been saying. She was just using the conversation as a way to take up time before she could ask him what she really wanted to, the reason for her call.

'Oh dad?' she started, 'do you remember that guy who was hassling Emily, the estate agent? Remember I told you about him and you said you'd get one of your guys to have word with him, warn him off? Well,...did you do that?'

Strong had been expecting this. He knew what had happened. He'd seen the report in the local paper that morning and so he'd given Austin a call to get his take on it. Austin had explained that he hadn't hit Smith but he'd seen him fall over when he was running away and so assumed that's where he might have got his bruises and cuts from. Strong was satisfied with Austin's explanation, but knew he was going to have to convince his daughter that Smith's injuries weren't anything to do with him.

'Yes, I believe so. Why, has he been bothering you and Emily again?' Strong asked his daughter.

'No, not at all, he seems to have given up on Emily, which is good,' Sophie replied, 'but he was in the local paper today, apparently someone beat him up. Did you see it?'

'Really? No, I didn't see that,' Strong said, glancing automatically at the paper lying on the coffee table in front of him. 'Not surprising I guess, considering what he was doing, in my experience it usually catches up with you.'

'So you think it would be some other girl's boyfriend or someone like that who did it?' Sophie asked.

'Probably, but I've not been involved in it I'm afraid. I can ask around before I go, if you like, see if anyone knows anything?' Strong replied.

'So it definitely wasn't anything to do with me telling you about it? Sophie asked her dad directly.

'What, of course not, what do you mean?' Strong replied, feigning surprise, but knowing this was what Sophie had really been wanting to ask him, and part of him felt proud that she had. She had grown into a strong, young, independent woman. Just like her mum.

'Well, it's just..., well it seems a bit of a coincidence, doesn't it? I tell you about him, you say you'll sort it out and the following week he gets beaten up. You told me never to believe in coincidences,' Sophie said wondering whether she'd gone too far but knowing she'd needed to ask him.

'I don't normally believe in coincidences, but there are always exceptions, Sophie,' Strong replied, impressed that he'd taught her something. 'I certainly didn't beat the guy up.'

'No, I didn't mean you, of course not, but what about the guy you told to warn him off. What did he do? Maybe he went a bit too far, or something happened? Did you ask him?' Sophie asked.

'Yes of course,' Strong replied, 'he just had a word with him, it's all in the files. You don't seriously think I'd ask a policeman to beat someone up do you?' Strong laughed. 'Sometimes I wish I could, it'd make my job easier, but I'm afraid I wouldn't have a job if I did that,' Strong continued to laugh. 'You need to worry less, you're getting too much like your mum.'

'Haha, yes, I guess so,' Sophie replied, 'I guess I just wanted to make sure. It wouldn't be right, someone taking the law into their own hands like that, and I just....I don't know. You're right, maybe I worry too much. Listen I'd better go now, I'll speak to you soon when you're back home with mum. Love you.'

The call ended and Strong threw his phone onto the settee and walked through to the kitchen to deposit the remainder of his cold pizza into the bin. It would be good to get back home and have some proper food, he'd eaten too many takeaways over the last few weeks and he could sense his expanding waistline every time he put his trousers on. He was feeling slightly uneasy after the call with Sophie. He was confident that he'd convinced her and that she wouldn't bring it up again, but he realised he'd been getting too cocky, using Austin as his judge and jury whenever he felt he wanted to. He should never have had him up in Leeds, staying at his place for a night. That was risky. Even though it was very unlikely anyone would know it was Austin, it was a risk that he didn't really have to take. One that he shouldn't have taken. It had also been stupid of him to use Austin to help out Sophie's friend Emily. That was too close to home. Too personal and, as had been shown by Sophie's call, he had again put himself in an awkward position, one that he should never have been in. He had definitely got over confident with his use of Austin because he'd been doing such a good job, but if he continued like that, it would lead him into making mistakes. Mistakes which could have serious consequences for him.

He knew that Austin was angling for an end to their arrangement, or at least a break, and he decided there and then that maybe that wasn't a bad idea. He had taken a few chances lately and he knew DS Campbell had got close a couple of times. He needed to be careful, at least until things calmed down a bit again. Too many people were beginning to ask questions.

Sophie was still sitting on her bed, thinking. She wanted to believe that her dad had nothing to do with Kyle Smith being attacked and she thought that was probably the case. As he'd said, surely he wouldn't risk his police career just to teach some stupid young guy a lesson. He'd do it by the book, as he'd said he would. So why did she still have a nagging doubt about it? It was the "coincidences" thing. She couldn't get that out of her head. It seemed too much of a coincidence not to have some mileage in it. She should be able to trust her dad though and the more she thought about it, the more she realised she didn't really know him that well. No, that wasn't quite it, obviously she knew him, he was her dad and he'd always been there since she was born. She knew the 'home dad'. The kind, loving father he had always been to her. But there was another side to him she didn't know, the 'police dad.' She didn't really know what he was like as a policeman, outside his family life. He didn't really talk about it and she'd never really thought to ask him. His work was never discussed. As she thought about her childhood, she could recall a few occasions when it had just been her and her mum. Her dad not being able to make her school play, or perhaps a birthday party, when he'd been working on a case. It hadn't really bothered Sophie at the time, it was just what she was used to. Her dad was a policeman and that was an important job. But now, as she thought about it, she realised she didn't know very much at all about her 'police dad' and that was a big part of him. It was like only knowing half a person. So the question she still didn't know the answer to was - would her 'police dad' have arranged for Kyle Smith to be beaten up? And if he had, then it was partly her fault for telling him in the first place. But of course the equally plausible answer could also be that someone else, not connected with Sophie, Emily or her dad, had got their revenge on Kyle Smith. Maybe she should just believe her dad, and let sleeping dogs lie, with the hope that they never came across anyone like Kyle Smith again.

Chapter 27

Campbell had just left the Chief Constable's office. Strangely, considering how long he'd been a policeman, it was the first time he'd ever been there. It was an impressive office, there was no doubting that. Big and grand. Campbell reckoned it was bigger than his lounge at home and it certainly contained more expensive furniture. Up till now, DI Strong had always been the main liaison with the Chief, and Campbell had preferred it that way. He wasn't into all the political stuff that went on at that level, he just wanted to get on with the day job, doing his investigative work. Solving crimes. That was why he'd joined the force in the first place. That was what got him out of bed in the morning.

The Chief Constable, or more precisely, his PA, Maria, had invited Campbell to a meeting with the Chief in his office. That was a first, although with Campbell being an acting DI, he'd been half expecting it. As is often the case with these types of meetings, the Chief delivered a mixed message, some good, some not so good. Campbell had always been a bit cynical about review meetings. There always seemed to be an underlying theme of the boss telling his employee they were doing a good job, but there were also areas where they needed to improve. Wasn't that true of everyone? They reviewed the work Campbell had been doing over the period of Strong's transfer and on the whole the Chief had seemed very pleased with what they'd achieved. He had picked up on the Anniversary Killer though, and the fact that they hadn't been able to find him yet. Campbell conceded that but had pointed out that there had been no more murders and, backed up by a report he'd asked Doctor Collins to prepare, it was possible, perhaps probable, that Austin had now stopped the killings.

'Doctor Collins thinks the fact that he didn't kill anyone this year makes it much less likely that he will try anything again in the future,' Campbell had told the Chief, although the psychologist hadn't been able to explain why he seemed to have stopped.

It was obviously good that he hadn't killed anyone else, but both Campbell and the Chief Constable knew it would have been better if they'd caught him and brought him to justice for the two murders he had already committed the previous year. While he was still out there, there remained a risk, and the families involved could still not fully have their closure. Of course Campbell had kept quiet about the two times he'd almost caught Austin. There was no benefit to anyone in bringing that up. It would only have made him look less competent and he definitely didn't want that. Better to focus on the areas where he'd done well.

'So, on the whole, we think you have done a very good job on your first post as an acting DI,' the

Chief had said, 'and it'll certainly look good on your record going forward. Keep working hard Joe and I'm sure your rewards will come,' he had said, which Campbell took as being pretty non-committal on the Chief Constable's part, but experience had taught him not to analyse these things too deeply.

'Meantime, I'm sure you'll be pleased to know that DI Strong has completed his temporary role in Leeds and from tomorrow he will be returning to lead the Serious Crime Squad here again. I am sure he will want to thank you for holding the fort while he was away and I look forward to the two of you working together again as we move forward. You seem to make a good team and I am sure you can learn a lot from DI Strong which will help you as you continue to progress in your career.'

Campbell returned to his desk, relieved that he'd come out of the meeting relatively unscathed. Overall it had been fairly positive, and he was glad just to get back to his day job. He had mixed emotions about Strong coming back. He had enjoyed being in charge, being able to make his own decisions and get on with the job without needing approval from above. He knew he'd made a few mistakes along the way, but then didn't everyone? Wasn't that how you learned, by making mistakes? Maybe that was something to discuss with DI Strong at an appropriate time. He was a little disappointed that they hadn't found a permanent DI role for him, but on the whole, he had to concede that the Chief was probably right. He'd learned a few things in the acting DI role and the experience would definitely help him better understand the role should a future opportunity arise. Maybe it wasn't the right time just yet.

Aside from all that though, he was keen to see Strong again. He had always liked working with DI Strong. The chief was right, they did make a good team with different strengths. Strong was often the voice of reason when Campbell just wanted to go storming straight in. Maybe they would have already arrested Andy Austin if Strong had still been here. He wouldn't have let Campbell go in on his own at Austin's house and, in retrospect, that had definitely been a mistake. There were still a couple of niggling questions Campbell wanted to ask Strong about Austin though, things that he hadn't sorted out in his head, and he wanted to do it face to face so he could get Strong's immediate explanation.

DS Campbell got to work early the next morning, skipping his gym session for once, and found there was no-one in the main office. Usually it would be filled with a continuous buzz of noise, but today it was strangely quiet. There were no major cases on the go and it looked like everyone else was taking advantage of that and having a lie in, although he had to concede six thirty am was quite early, even for Campbell. Usually at this time of the day he would be in the gym doing an early morning workout before the day's work started. He found the exercise always made him more alert, as well as keeping him fit. He'd always done a lot of sport in his younger days, but as he progressed in the police force he found he had less time to commit to regular sporting activities and so the gym had become his main source of exercise.

He walked along the corridor to the vending machine to get a fix of caffeine and as he passed DI Strong's office, he noticed the light was on inside. He stopped and tapped on the door, opening it slowly and putting his head around the door to look inside. Strong was there, sitting at his desk, his reading glasses perched on his nose, looking down at a file of papers in front of him. He looked up, saw Campbell, and smiled widely.

'Joe, come in, it's good to see you.' The DI got up and walked round from behind his desk, meeting Campbell halfway across the room.

'Welcome back sir, all go well in Leeds I take it? and they shook hands.

'Have a seat, I was going to call you anyway,' Strong replied. 'I got in early to try and make a head start on what I'd missed while I was away, but let's have a catch up now, that'll help me a lot,' and he walked back to his own seat as Campbell sat down, as instructed, on the visitor's chair in front of Strong's desk.

Strong gave Campbell a potted version of his time in Leeds, leaving out the parts to do with Andy Austin, but giving him an overview of the review he had carried out and its main recommendations. He also said he'd had very good feedback from the Chief Constable on how Campbell had done while he was away.

'I spoke with the Chief yesterday and I think you've done yourself a lot of favours there,' Strong said. 'The next time a DI post comes up I'd say you'd have a good chance, I'll certainly support you for it and I think the Chief would be up for you to get it too. The only slight blip was when you knocked yourself out at that house. What happened there?' Strong asked.

Campbell had given a lot of thought about how he was going to cover this with Strong, but he now found himself slightly on the back foot with DI Strong bringing it up first. He guessed that Strong must really know why he was there, or at least some of it, because of his call for an ambulance, and so he decided that there was no point in trying to cover that up as Strong would see right through it. It would also show that Campbell was capable of lying to Strong. Campbell knew that would be a mistake, he needed to keep Strong on his side if he was going to get answers to the points that were niggling him, as well as being able to keep working with him again in the same way as they had before.

'Ah, well, It was Austin. I found out that he was living there and I thought, foolishly, that I could just take him, just like that. I saw him at the hospital and I followed him back to where he was living, thinking if I got him there, we'd also get a load of evidence too. I had him as well, and I would have got him if it hadn't been for the stupid doorstep,' Campbell said. 'I fell over, knocked myself out. Idiot, I know.

'But if you knew it was Austin, why didn't you get back up?' Strong asked. 'Made sure you had enough resource to get him properly. You could have called me?'

'I know. I should have. I know,' Campbell replied, leaning forward and looking down at his feet. 'The thing was, it happened so quickly and I guess I just got caught up in it, I didn't want to lose him. I saw him get in his car in the hospital car park and so I followed him to the house. When he went in, I thought I'd just follow him in there and grab him, get him cuffed then call for back up before he had time to react. I know I shouldn't have, but it was like, all too quick. I didn't think anything could go wrong.'

'Did you tell anyone else it was Austin you'd seen?' Strong asked him.

'No, I didn't see the point, to be honest. It was all embarrassing enough and I knew Austin would have cleared out when I was lying in hospital. I did get a couple of the guys to look through the place but it was clean, like no-one had ever lived there. No-one really asked me about it, until you did now. One of the benefits of being the DI, I guess,' he replied smiling timidly at his boss. 'Can we just keep this between the two of us?'

'Of course we can, no sense in anyone else knowing, it's not going to help us catch Austin,' Strong replied.

'Thanks,' Campbell nodded. 'One thing I wanted to ask though,' Campbell continued. 'How come it was you that called the emergency services? How did you know I was there?' he asked looking directly at his boss as he spoke.

Strong didn't flinch, he'd been expecting this question and he was ready for it. He knew

Campbell was a thorough detective and would have listened to the recording of his emergency call.

'I got a call in, the caller didn't say who he was but I guess it could have been Austin. Must have been I suppose. He just gave your name and the address where you were. Said to call an ambulance because you were unconscious. I called one, but not knowing the whole story and still being in Leeds, I didn't want to drop you in it so I didn't tell anyone else. When I found out that you had been there on your own and you'd made no mention of Austin, I wanted to wait till I saw you to see why,' Strong explained.

'I see,' Campbell replied. He was thinking through everything Strong had just said. Did it fit? Did it make sense? I guess it could, he thought. Strong had certainly been always very supportive, very loyal to Campbell. He could have easily dropped Campbell in it, if he wanted to. He could have made a big fuss about Campbell losing a great opportunity to catch the Anniversary Killer. It would have ruined Campbell's chances of becoming a DI, certainly in the near future.

'Yeh, I guess that makes sense,' Campbell said. 'Thanks, I really messed up.'

'While we're on it,' Campbell continued, 'I should also say that before that, I found out an address for Austin, but it turned out to be a false one. He wasn't there when I went to check. Never had been.'

'Where was that?' Strong asked.

'Connolly Street,' Campbell replied.

'What, the one I went to?' Strong asked, looking confused.

'You went there? When?' Campbell asked back, looking equally baffled.

'Yeh, just before I went off to Leeds. I'm sure I told you, didn't I?' Strong replied looking earnestly at his detective sergeant. 'It was a false lead, there was just a woman with some kids. It was pretty obvious he'd never been there.'

Campbell was thinking. He definitely couldn't remember Strong saying that, but then why would he lie? Maybe the bump he'd got on his head had affected his memory? He couldn't be sure.

Strong could see Campbell thinking, trying to work it out, and decided to give him an out.

'Do you know, maybe I didn't tell you,' Strong started. 'There was so much going on with my move to Leeds and it was just a chance thing, something one of my informants told me. I didn't think it was going to be right, but I thought I'd take a quick look as I was passing. I think Austin's way too smart to get caught like that. Maybe in my mind I just wrote it off as a wasted journey. Not worth reporting. I honestly can't remember. Sorry. Anyway it looks like you finding him at least managed to scare him off, even though you didn't manage to catch him. We're well past the anniversary date now and he hasn't done anything else so I'd say congratulations Joe, it looks like you've stopped him. I saw a summary of Doctor Collins' report too which would seem to back you up.'

'Yeh, that was useful,' Campbell replied. 'I guess you're right. Still, it would have been good to have caught him and put him behind bars though. But at least he seems to have done all he's going to do, although we don't really know why he's stopped, but I suppose it's a good secondary outcome.'

'Yeh, definitely, you never know a hundred percent with killers, there's no logic, and I'm sure he'll pop up again at some time and we'll get him then,' Strong replied smiling. 'He won't be able to stay hidden for ever. He was lucky this time.'

'Maybe he'll get back in touch with his ex, Lucy Morris,' Campbell said to his boss.

'Yeh, that's a possible,' Strong replied. 'We need to catch up on that, them meeting in the park and so on. I didn't have time to talk to you about it at the time, but it sounds like he still has some feelings for her and so I guess there's a chance he'll try and see her again. Hopefully she'll be able to give us more notice this time.'

'Yeh, I'm not convinced she told us everything, I'm not sure what, but I just had a gut feeling she was keeping something back from me,' Campbell replied.

One Year Later

Chapter 28

Lucy put the phone down and sat back in her settee. It had been a while since she'd spoken with anyone from the police and so it was both a surprise, and a little un-nerving, to get the call from detective inspector Strong. It was a bit out of the blue. He told her he was just checking in with her to make sure that everything was alright. In answer to his follow up question, which she guessed was the real reason for his call, she told him that she hadn't heard anything from Andy Austin again, not since she'd met him in the park that day, last year. DI Strong told Lucy that they didn't have anything new to report on him either, but again asked her to please contact him personally if he did get in touch. The Anniversary Killer case was still open and they were obviously keen to get him, but there had been no sightings of Austin and Strong had told her that he thought it was probable that Austin had left the country again. At the moment, the detective said the Andy Austin file was on the back burner, but if anything changed they'd let her know. Strong explained that they believed that he'd recovered from his PTSD and so he was no longer a threat to anyone at this point, but of course he should still be brought to justice for the crimes he committed. Unfortunately there were also many other serious crimes they needed to work on as a higher priority at this point. Lucy had wanted to ask the detective about Austin's tumour but she couldn't remember if he knew about it, and she was frightened she'd give away too much, and lead Strong to suspect that she had been in touch with him again.

Which of course she had been. Quite a few times now. She'd lost count. A few weeks after that first meeting in the park, Andy had called her again. Lucy had been cautious at first, still not knowing what she wanted to do. Or what she should do. Should she report him to the police again or give him a bit more time, give him the benefit of the doubt? Not that there really was any doubt – he'd definitely murdered two innocent people. There was no doubt about that. But maybe there was a reason, something that explained his "out of character" behaviour?

Lucy was still worried that she wasn't doing the right thing, but gradually, over time, as they spoke more and more, it seemed to get easier. Andy had taken his time and patiently explained everything to her, about how his illness had affected him. The tumour and the PTSD. Lucy hadn't just taken his word for it though, she'd also done her own research about his condition on the internet. It certainly seemed to be plausible. She'd found lots of stuff on PTSD and, more specifically, a couple of medical papers on a condition called post traumatic embitterment syndrome or PTED. Although there wasn't a lot on PTED, it seemed to fit the bill. From what Lucy had read, PTED was some sort of pathological reaction following a major traumatic event. It seems that the casualty, Andy in this case, would develop an obsession on getting revenge for some perceived wrong he'd suffered. The more Lucy thought about it she could see how it could equate to what happened with Andy. His family had been killed and he developed this PTED which meant he needed to get, what he saw was, justice. She still couldn't fully believe that could drive someone like Andy to actually murder someone, not the man that she had known, the man she had lived with and loved deeply, but there didn't seem to be any other explanation. She wondered if his tumour perhaps had an accelerating effect on the condition, although there was nothing to suggest that in any of the papers she'd read.

At first it had just been phone calls between the two of them. Lucy had been very wary about meeting him again at that point, knowing how it had affected her emotionally that first time. She didn't know how she would handle that the next time. It also gave her an excuse not to consider contacting the police about him. As long as it was just a phone call, she couldn't really set him up like she'd tried to do that first time. But after a few months of delicate phone calls, she agreed to meet him in a local café for a coffee. It wasn't one she usually went to, she didn't want to bump into anyone she knew in case they saw her with him. She remembered being very nervous that day. She'd arrived early at the café but her hands were shaking so much she could hardly lift her cup to take a drink. Andy had turned up a few minutes later and looked exactly just as he had that first time. In contrast to Lucy, he didn't seem at all nervous, although she knew he might be like the proverbial duck, paddling furiously underwater. The conversation had been difficult at first. A bit stop-start, with regular pauses and periods of silence where neither of them knew what to say. It was definitely an awkward situation and they were both frightened of the truth, of exposing too much too soon.

Lucy remembered she couldn't stop herself being accusatory with him at points at that first meeting, but he was very patient. She appreciated that he had taken a big risk meeting her again, especially after the last time when she'd called the police. She could have easily done that again but Lucy had decided to give him some time, without completely ruling out the possibility of involving the police if she felt he wasn't being truthful. The truth – that was a slippery thing, hard to know when you had got to it. There was still a niggle in her brain telling her she should do the right thing, but she'd convinced herself that she needed to know more before she could determine what that "right thing" was. It wasn't that straightforward.

She assumed that Andy must trust her a bit more now, trust that she hadn't involved the police. Unless he'd already cased out the café, and found out where the back door was in case he needed to make a quick escape. Maybe he'd get spooked by someone coming in and make a bolt for it. She thought it best not to ask him. But Lucy hadn't called the police this time, she wanted to give him a chance. A second chance. Didn't everyone deserve that? Even a double murderer?

After that first meeting, they'd started getting together more regularly, but always in a public place – various cafes and, if the weather was good, sometimes a park. Over time the conversation had got easier and Lucy found herself getting more relaxed in Andy's company and looking forward to seeing him each time they met. There were times when she felt they were almost back to where they were before all this happened and she sometimes hoped she could just wake up one day and find it had all been a bad dream. But of course that never happened, unless you were in a big American TV soap opera.

Despite the progress, Lucy knew they were still a long way from being anywhere near how they'd been a couple of years before. Although they were getting on well, it wasn't just about the two of them. They couldn't exist in isolation. There were a lot of other people in Lucy's life and the only one Lucy had told about him so far was her best friend Jane. She trusted her and valued Jane's advice. After a few calls with Andy, Lucy had realised that she was getting more deeply involved in something she didn't really understand, and she was on her own. She needed to get someone else's advice, someone who knew her but wasn't emotionally involved and could see the woods from the trees. Lucy realised she was getting lost in the woods.

Although she'd told Jane about the first meeting a year before, she hadn't confided in her about the subsequent calls and meetings, not sure if she should. She was worried about what Jane might say or do and she didn't want anyone else making decisions for her. However when it came to the point where she needed to discuss it with someone, to get a different perspective, Jane was the obvious choice.

Her friend had been a bit shocked at first, although she'd never met Andy and so only knew him as the man on the run, the man the police wanted for murder. The man that had conned her best friend Lucy. Jane's initial reaction was to protect her friend and she was worried that he was worming his way back into her friend's life, only to end up hurting her again. But after a few long discussions, over several bottles of wine, she began to understand Lucy's point of view and agreed to support her in whatever she chose to do.

'But if he ends up hurting you again in any way, I'll cut his balls off and throw them in the rubbish,' she said. And she looked like she meant it.

It had really helped Lucy to have Jane as a confidante and, knowing she wasn't just doing this on her own anymore, she became more relaxed in her meetings with Andy. They'd even been to the cinema and out for a meal a couple of times. There were still some major hurdles to overcome though. Her mum and dad, she wasn't sure how she could tell them, or how they would take it. And the biggest hurdle of all, maybe too big, the little baby. CJ. Although not quite as little now, it was amazing how quickly he was growing and some of his little mannerisms, some of the ways he looked sometimes, reminded her of his father, Andy. She'd put off telling him that she had a baby, that *they*, had a baby, and the longer it went on, the harder it seemed to get to own up to him. She didn't know how she was going to do it. But if they kept seeing each other then she knew she'd have to, but what then? How would he take it? Jane hadn't been much help with this one, telling her jokingly that she should wrap little CJ up and present him to Andy as a birthday or Christmas gift. She couldn't do that of course, it was too serious. She'd dug herself a hole and didn't know how to get out of it. Well, she did really, but she hadn't been brave enough to do it yet.

Andy had asked about coming round to the flat, her flat, the flat they'd used to share together but she'd said no, and he hadn't pressed her on it. But maybe now was the time to do that. She'd have to do it sometime and the longer she left it, the harder it was going to be. She decided she'd have to do it on their next call, invite him around so she could introduce him to the baby. His son.

As it turned out she didn't have to wait too long, as he called her that same afternoon. Their interactions were getting more frequent now, and more friendly too, and there wasn't a day where they didn't have some kind of communication, a text, a WhatsApp message or a call.

'I know you'd like to come round to the flat but that's been quite difficult for me,' she said, 'I've been worried about the memories it will bring back when you and I lived here together. But I know it's something I can't keep putting off forever, so why don't we set a date to do it?'

'Really?' Andy replied, 'Wow that would be great, I'd love to, and you know if you feel a bit strange about it I can always leave, or we can go out to the park or for a coffee or something.'

'Yes, okay, but I'm sure I'll be fine. Things have moved on and well. I might have a little surprise for you too,' Lucy couldn't stop herself from teasing him.

'Ooh, what kind of surprise, chocolate donuts with the coffee?' he replied laughing, 'you know how I love my choccy donuts.'

'No, a better surprise that that, but I'm not saying any more, you'll have to wait and see. How about next Wednesday afternoon, would that be okay?' Lucy asked.

'Yeh, sure, that sounds great. I can definitely make that,' Andy replied.

After they'd finished their call, Lucy sat thinking, wondering if she'd done the right thing. But she had to do it sometime. How would he take it she wondered, the fact that he had a son? Across town, Andy sat in his flat with a big grin on his face, wondering what could be a better surprise than eating chocolate donuts with the girl he loved.

Chapter 29

DI Campbell and DS Kerry were in the main Leeds meeting room, doing a review of all the outstanding cases. Campbell had been in Leeds for the last six weeks, after having been promoted to the role of detective inspector and been given his first posting at Leeds CID. He'd been put forward for the job by DI Strong and had also had the support of his Chief Constable, who apparently went through the police training college at the same time as the Chief Constable of the Yorkshire police. Campbell didn't want to think too much about that though, preferring to believe that he had proved himself, through the rigorous selection process, to be the best man for the job. The process had certainly been long and difficult, with many interviews and a variety of psychological tests. Thankfully he seemed to have completed it all successfully and was delighted when Strong told him he'd got the position.

The only downside had been that he'd been going through the selection process at the same time that his wife had been coming to the end of her pregnancy and, although he'd managed to make it to the birth of their daughter, he knew he hadn't been as involved in the lead up to that as much as he could have been, or as much as his wife thought he should have been.

'Why don't you just admit it? Your job is more important to you than me or our baby,' had been a commonly uttered phrase in the Campbell household.

When Campbell had been offered the position in Leeds, his wife had been adamant that she didn't want to move there with the baby. There were numerous reasons.

'She's too young. I haven't got her settled into a routine. I don't know anyone in Leeds. What if I need help? You'll be working all hours. You don't know how long you'll be there.'

Campbell had wanted them to move as a family, but he knew he would be working long hours, establishing himself in the new role, and so they agreed on a compromise that he would come home as much as he could at weekends and, when everything was right, in a few months say, she would move up to Leeds with the baby so they could all be together again. Unfortunately, Campbell quickly realised that there was more work to do than he'd anticipated, and he ended up having to work most weekends too. In fact he'd only managed to make it home twice in those first six weeks, and even then only for one day. The rest of the contact had to be via facetime on their mobile phones. It wasn't ideal, in fact that was putting it lightly as far as his wife Femi was concerned, but Campbell hoped that once he'd got settled in, things would get easier and they'd be able to spend more time together as a family.

'What about this one, this estate agent, Kyle Smith? Did we ever get any leads on that one?' Campbell asked as he flicked through the file in front of him.

'No, nothing. Nobody on the street seemed to know anything about it. It was all strangely quiet afterwards. Usually we hear someone talking about it, but nothing. He was a local estate agent, had a bit of a reputation as a player, but never been in any trouble himself. Might just have been a random attack or he'd upset somebody sometime. Maybe he couldn't sell their house?' DS Kerry laughed. 'I remember it though, it was when DI Strong was up here doing his review and I think we were all hoping we'd get a quick result, show us in a good light, but nothing, and nothing like it since either. Seems like it was a one-off.'

'Mm…Did Strong say anything about it?' Campbell asked as he continued reading.

'Not really, I think he was getting towards the end of his time here and wasn't really directly involved. I remember the day it happened though, because earlier that same day I was driving past his house and saw him getting into the car with another guy and I stopped to talk to him,' Kerry replied.

Campbell had finished reading the file, but something had caught his interest, something that Kerry had said.

'Oh right, who was he with, another of the Leeds team?' Campbell asked.

'No, I don't think it was anyone I'd seen before, although I only saw him from behind. He was a younger guy, short blond hair and I think he might have had a beard. I think the DI said he was a friend or something,' DS Kerry replied. 'Why you asking?'

'Oh, no reason,' Campbell replied. 'I didn't know Strong had any friends in Leeds. In fact I didn't know he had any friends outside of the police force!' He laughed at his own joke, Kerry joining in with him.

Maybe there were a lot of things I didn't know about Strong, Campbell thought. But he's always looked out for me. He knew he wouldn't have been here today, a detective inspector in Leeds CID, without Strong's guiding hand and maybe more. But something was niggling him, it had been for some time now.

'Do you know if there is any CCTV at the house DI Strong was staying in?' Campbell asked his DS.

'I'm not sure, I could get one of the guys to check it out. It's a house we use every now and again if we need to put someone up, police or a witness or someone,' Kerry replied.

'Okay, if you could, not urgent, but I'd just like to see if I know the guy Strong was with. I guess it could have been one of my previous team from down South.' Campbell replied, wondering why he was doing this, and where it might lead him. A little voice inside his head was telling him to leave it alone, but he couldn't, he was a detective.

Later that day, Campbell was sitting alone in his office when there was a knock on the door. That still surprised him a bit, he wasn't quite used to having his own office. It had its pros and cons. Not being in the main office with the rest of his team meant that he missed out on the general chat between them, some of which might be important, without them realising it at the time. There had been a few occasions in the past where the general office discussion had led to the team putting two and two together and coming up with a common link which had helped them secure a conviction. Campbell missed that now, but he also liked the fact that he had his own space, his own quiet place, where he could just think without being disturbed by the general office hubbub.

'Come in,' he called and the door opened and DS Kerry stepped into the room.

'You got a minute?' he asked DI Campbell.

'Sure, grab a seat,' Campbell replied, nodding towards one of the chairs in front of his desk.

'Just an update on the CCTV at the safe house,' Kerry replied, 'not very conclusive though.'

'Oh, why's that?' Campbell asked, raising his eyebrows.

'Well it seems the CCTV wasn't on when DI Strong was in the house but it's not clear why. No-one seems to know if it's usually switched on or off or whether DI Strong could have even turned it off himself.'

'Oh, whats the usual position with it?' Campbell asked.

'Well, it seems to depend on who you ask. Some say on, some say off. Maybe DI Strong wanted it off to give himself some privacy, or maybe he had a fancy woman while he was here,' DS Kerry laughed.

'Mmm, okay, thanks anyway, no worries, I just wondered,' Campbell replied, still not sure what that meant, who the mystery man was, but also partly relieved that he'd checked it out as much as he could and there was nothing further he could do. Best let sleeping dogs lie.

Chapter 30

DI Strong had managed to get a rare weekend off from work and he had resolved to spend some well-earned time with his wife, Catherine. They hadn't actually seen each other that much over the last year. When he'd been posted to Leeds, it had been a case of working long days to get himself established in the post and get the review done as quickly as he could, so he'd just thrown himself into it without really thinking about anything else. He knew his wife was used to it and she would cope well enough without him. She was a very independent and capable woman. When he returned to his normal role back in the Serious Crime Unit, he'd had to spend time catching up on everything that had happened while he'd been away. He realised now though that this had been an unusually long period and that it could be to the detriment of his marital relationship, although his wife did seem to understand, and in fact had largely carved out a social life of her own, without it appeared, too much of a problem. He often didn't know what she was doing on any given day. There seemed to be so many clubs she was a member of – book clubs, Zumba, Yoga, art as well as having a wide circle of girlfriends who she seemed to drink endless cups of coffee with.

This weekend was the first time for a while that Strong had been able to take a break. He'd decided to surprise her, and so had told her on the Friday night, just as they were getting ready for bed.

'Oh, by the way, I'm not working at all this weekend. I have the whole time off and I'm going to stick to it, no phone calls, no emails, so you've got me for two whole days,' he said smiling at her, 'I thought maybe we could get a few things from the garden centre, then maybe have a nice, long pub lunch at The Horse and Groom?'

'Really? That sounds good, it has been a while since we've had a bit of time together. The only thing
is I have the hairdresser in the morning, but I should be back about one. I'm supposed to be meeting Julie after that for a coffee but I could move that to next week so we can do something in the afternoon,' she replied, before giving him a goodnight kiss.

So the next morning, Strong found himself sitting alone in the kitchen with a mug of coffee, the local newspaper spread out on the work surface in front of him. There wasn't much going on locally. The front page headline was about a teenage girl who had collected money for charity by camping in her garden for two weeks. Strong was inclined to think that was really a holiday, he'd often camped in the garden when he was a young boy, but maybe things had changed now. With that being the main headline, he didn't have great expectations for the rest of the paper and so it proved. He gave up when he came to a page full of obituaries. He'd seen enough death in his police career without having to read about it on his weekend off.

His wife had left for her hairdresser's appointment about half an hour earlier, and he knew from previous experience that she would be away for at least two to three hours. It was something he'd never fully understood, why did it take five times as long to do her hair, compared with when he got his cut? Ten or fifteen minutes did him, a quick trim and out again.

Despite his wife being out and Strong left on his own, he was determined not to do any work. He hadn't touched his phone, but the truth was he was already getting bored. There wasn't anything needing done around the house, not that he ever did that much anyway. Apart from his long working hours, DIY wasn't one of his strengths and Catherine seemed to have a man for every job they required, as well as being able to adequately manage everything else around the house without him needing to interfere. Sometimes he felt like a lodger.

After a few minutes more sitting around, he gave in and picked up his phone and listened to his voicemail. He had five messages, all of which he'd listened to before, but had left as being non-urgent. Three of the messages were from one of his regular informers, Red Ricky. He'd left them at various times over the last few weeks, saying he had some good information for Strong. Something he'd be interested in. Strong had not had the time to call him back, but now he was back down South he knew exactly where he would find him. On a Saturday, as well as most other days, Red Ricky was always in The White Horse pub. It had been his regular haunt for as long as Strong had known him, which was at least twenty years. Strong had first come across Richard Jamieson when he'd arrested him for obstruction after he, and fifteen others, had occupied the electronics factory building they worked in, after it was announced that it was closing. Apparently it was cheaper to make the electrical components somewhere in the Far East. Red Ricky had been one of the organisers of the sit-in and that, along with his association with the trade union movement, had earned him the name which everyone now knew him by. Strong looked at the clock on the kitchen wall, made a quick mental calculation, and decided he might as well go and find him. He'd have time to do that and still be back before his wife returned from the hairdressers and it would be better than just sitting around here doing nothing.

There were only two other cars in the pub car park when Strong turned in. Not like the old days. Twenty years ago the car park would have been full on a Saturday lunchtime. The pub would have been full too. Full of men, all drinking pints of beer and talking about football. But not any more. Society had changed, and there were too many other things to do now. Too many family responsibilities and men were now expected to play their equal part. So, rather than being in the pub on a Saturday lunchtime, the men were now more likely to be found in a shopping centre, or at some kids activity centre. Times had changed from when Sophie was a young child. Strong parked his car and entered the pub. It was an old fashioned bar, there weren't that many like this any more. It had a long counter and at the far end there was a darts board and a fruit machine. There were a number of brown leather stools against the bar, in various states of repair, most with tears and stains but still adequate for sitting on if you weren't too fussy. Between the bar and the window, there were half a dozen small, square wooden tables with matching wooden chairs scattered around them. Strong noticed Red Ricky sitting at one of the tables and he raised his half empty glass towards the policeman, indicating he was ready for another drink. Strong went to the bar and a minute later joined his long time informant at the table.

'There you go,' Strong said, handing the pint of ale to Red Ricky.

Ricky pushed his empty glass to one side and picked up the new glass, taking a long slow drink, before placing it back on the table in front of him.

'Ah, they still do the best pint of ale in here, you know,' he said to Strong, his top lip lined with white froth. 'You not having one?' he asked Strong.

'No, afraid not, it's a bit of a flying visit. Got family duties this afternoon, so I can't stay long. I got your message though, what did you want to tell me?' Strong asked.

Ricky took another slow drink of his pint, before again putting it down on the table and looking directly at Strong. Strong noticed that the glass was now only half full.

'Well,' Ricky started, 'It's emm, well, there was a lad in here, two weeks back, sitting at the bar bemoaning his luck. He'd had a few too many and I somehow got chatting to him. As you do. I think we were the only ones in at that point. I think he'd had a few too many and got to the stage where he wanted to talk to somebody and I just happened to be there I guess. People seem to do that with me, funny that. Maybe I missed my calling and should have been a priest. Anyway he kept going on about something that had happened a few years back. Something bad. He said it had ruined his life, but he wouldn't say what. Said he couldn't tell anyone, not even his mum. To be honest I was getting a bit bored by then and was thinking of heading off home, but he insisted on buying me another pint and I thought it would be rude not to take it. So I stayed. He was getting drunker by the minute and at one point I thought he was going to start crying, but he held it together, good lad.'

Strong glanced at the clock on the wall over Ricky's shoulder, thinking he'd better get going soon otherwise he'd miss his wife coming home and he wanted to be there to at least spend some time with her on his big weekend off. Ricky noticed Strong's eyes move and turned around to see what he was looking at.

'Ah, sorry,' he said, 'I'm rambling a bit aren't I?' and he took another gulp of his pint, this time almost finishing it, before looking at Strong and smiling.

Strong took the hint and went to the bar, returning with a second pint for Red Ricky.

'There you go,' Strong said, sliding the glass across to where Ricky's empty glass now stood. 'So you were saying, this guy, what did he do?'

'Yeh, right, thanks,' Ricky nodded, picking up his pint and looking at it appreciatively. 'So eventually it starts to come out, he needed to get it off his chest I guess. Apparently he'd had some sort of road accident, a while back. He'd knocked a couple of people over one night, on his way home, hadn't seen them he said, but he didn't stop.'

Strong felt a shiver run down his spine.

'Where was this? When did it happen? Did he say?' Strong asked quickly, leaning forward over the table, staring intently at Red Ricky.

'Yep, he said it was somewhere over by Newton Forest, he didn't say exactly where, said it was a dark road and they'd just appeared out of nowhere, he couldn't avoid them. And he said it was eighteen years ago,' Ricky replied.

'Shit….SHIT. You know what that means, don't you?' Strong replied.

'Yep, looks like it was your mum and dad. He said he didn't know what had happened at the time, said he wasn't looking, but he'd seen it in the local paper in the newsagents the next week and guessed it must have been them,' Ricky replied. 'He said he'd felt guilty, but he was scared, and as the days went by after it happened and no-one came for him, he'd just kept quiet. He said he thinks his mum might have an inkling, she knows something happened, but she's never said anything and he's never told anyone until he told me.'

'Yeh, the bastard might have felt guilty, but he didn't own up to it did he? He took my mum and dad. Ended their lives and then just got on with his,' Strong said determinedly, both fists clenched.

'Yep, well, you just don't know, I guess,' Ricky replied not wishing to upset Strong any further.

'What was his name?' Strong asked, looking directly across the table at Red Ricky.

Ricky smiled. 'Well that was the funny thing. He said it was Dylan and I couldn't stop myself thinking of Dylan from the Magic Roundabout. Do you remember the big, hippy rabbit with the big floppy ears and…'

'Dylan what?' Strong interrupted him.

'Oh, ….emm…, Dylan Hughes, he said' Red Ricky replied.

'Thanks,' Strong said, standing up. 'Thanks for telling me. I have to go now,' and he turned and left the pub, leaving Red Ricky sitting on his own with his pint of ale, wondering what Strong would do with the information he'd just given him.

Chapter 31

Strong spent the rest of his free weekend with his wife and it had gone very well. A nice weekend. They'd got a few things from the garden centre, without spending too much money, which could be easily done, and enjoyed the rest of Saturday in their garden, planting and rearranging things and just generally chatting. It was nice to just do something normal for once. The next day they'd managed to get a table at one of their favourite pubs, The Horse and Groom, and had a long, relaxing Sunday lunch in the pub dining room. After polishing off a roast followed by a stodgy pudding, they'd returned home and watched a film on the TV, before they both snoozed off on the sofa, early in the evening. Strong had managed to put his meeting with Red Ricky to the back of his mind, despite the enormity of the information he'd given him.

It was now Monday morning though and Strong's brain had returned back to its usual police mode. He'd got up early and was already in his office by seven thirty. He waited until just after eight then made a call from his secret mobile. It was answered by Andy Austin on the third ring. He'd just returned from his morning run and, knowing it was Strong calling him, he guessed it wasn't something he particularly wanted to hear. He was right.

Strong had known Austin wouldn't be keen to do another "job" for him but, in Strong's eyes, this was by far and away the most important one he would ever ask him to do, and he knew he had a few aces up his sleeve he could use to persuade Austin to do it. He decided to be honest about the reason for his call from the start and so, after a few opening pleasantries, he told Austin that the target was the man who had run down his parents.

'Remember I told you about it when we met after your court case,' Strong said. 'Someone ran them over and didn't stop, just left them lying there in the road. No CCTV in those days and we never managed to find out who the driver was. But now we have. The trouble is, it was so long ago there's no way we'll be able to prove anything, no evidence, and so he'll get off scot free, unless we hand out our own justice. It's much the same as what happened with you, which is why I sympathised with you and helped you get revenge for your family in the first place. I just need your help now to do the same for me. One last job,' he added, playing his first ace.

Austin was still reluctant, saying he understood it was really important for Strong, but didn't know if he could do it. He said he didn't know if he had it in him anymore. Since he'd had the tumour removed, he told Strong he'd felt completely different. He no longer had that need for revenge or justice, and he had lost the aggressive streak that had enabled him to become a killer. He didn't think he could do it anymore. He just wanted to get on with a normal life, as much as he could. That was his one wish.

Strong told him he understood and promised him that this would definitely be the last job he asked him to do. Strong said he understood Austin's desire to return to some sort of normality, but he also knew that Austin wouldn't have any chance of getting there without some further help from the detective.

'If you do this one last thing for me, then I'll help you, as much as I can, to return to a normal life. I promise,' he said, starting to play his second ace. 'We struck a deal a while back and as far as I'm concerned this last job will be the end of it.'

'What do you mean?' Austin asked, knowing that he would need Strong's help if he were to achieve any kind of freedom, and keen to hear what the detective had in mind. He knew they were now in some sort of weird negotiating phase, with the stakes being one man's life and another man's chance at a second life.

Strong went on to tell him that he would effectively shut down the Anniversary Killer file. It was already on the back burner and Strong would now arrange for it to be moved out of the police's current workload and into a category they referred to as historic, unsolved cases. After that it would be unlikely that anyone would ever look at it again, and it would just remain on the system as an unresolved case. These things happen, Strong told him, it's pretty standard, the police don't secure a conviction every time and it is generally thought in the unit that the Anniversary Killer won't strike again. The families were thought to be safe and of course Strong and Austin knew that to be the case. It would just be written into the statistics as an unresolved case and everyone would forget about it.

'Okay,' Austin said, 'that would be helpful, thank you, but it still leaves me on my own, always looking over my shoulder in case something happens, a minor traffic offence or something like that and then I'd be done. Presumably they'd match my fingerprints or DNA or something? What can you do to help me return to a more normal life, without that danger?' Austin asked, seeing that this was his one opportunity to get as much as he could from DI Strong in return for helping him one last time.

'That is a possibility, but probably a lot less likely than you think. What you see on TV detective programmes doesn't reflect the reality of the inefficient systems and processes we have to use in our daily police work. That's why a lot of these guys get off. But, putting that aside, what would you see as a more normal life then, what do you want to do?' Strong asked him.

'Okay, ideally, and I know there are a lot of hurdles to this, but ideally I'd like to get back with Lucy and have as much of a life with her as is possible,' Austin replied, putting his cards on the table.

'And what does she think of that?' Strong asked, interested to hear what Austin would tell him. He suspected there had been further contact between the two of them, despite Lucy's denial of that to him when he'd spoken to her. He knew there had been a strong bond between the two of them and, despite what had happened, he could tell that it hadn't been fully broken. Of course, there was also the son and Strong didn't know if Austin knew about that yet.

'Well we haven't really discussed it yet, but we are meeting up fairly regularly and, slowly, we're making progress, I think. We meet in cafes or go for a walk sometimes, just the two of us. It's getting better, but there's not much more we can do without me putting her in danger, or hurting her again, if I'm caught. I'm guessing your man Campbell would have me arrested if he saw me with her, and there's always the chance that might happen.'

'Yes, well he's been posted to another region at the moment but your point is correct. There are some things we can do that would lessen the risk though. You're already used to changing your identity, so that would be a first. You could also move somewhere else, where no-one knew you as Andy Austin, you could go abroad but I don't think you'd necessarily have to. The UK is a big enough place and it's pretty easy to find somewhere to live where no-one would know about your past. I could help you with all of that, I've got some good knowledge of how best to do that through stuff we do with witness protection. It'd be a similar idea. Of course Lucy would have to make some major changes too, although the police wouldn't be watching her, but it would obviously still impact her. She wouldn't be able to tell anyone who you were without her risking them turning you into the police. But assuming Lucy wants to do it, it's definitely do-able.'

The two men went on to discuss how it might work in further detail, covering the various options and risks of each before they found themselves going round in circles with Austin still not sure. He was desperate to try and get back to a normal life and he knew he couldn't do that without Strong's help but he didn't know if he had it in him to kill another human being. Now that he was recovered from his PTSD, he wouldn't have any excuse and, if there had been any doubt before, he would now definitely be a murderer, a hired assassin. He didn't know if he could live with that and of course he wouldn't be able to tell Lucy. It would have to be a secret he'd have to keep from her for the rest of his life and that didn't sit well with him. Lucy had already made it clear to him that "no secrets, no lies" was a pre-requisite to them even meeting up for a coffee. Would it be fair to her if they became a couple with him always having this awful secret that had allowed it to happen? He didn't know if he could do that to her.

'I need some time to think about this,' he told Strong, 'I'll call you back later.'

'Okay, but remember what we've said,' the detective replied. 'This is your one chance for you to get a life with Lucy. If you don't do it, you'll always be on your own, on the run. One day you'll make a mistake and get caught. Then you'll spend the rest of your life in prison, which believe me is not something you'd want to do.'

After the call ended Austin sat thinking. Mulling things around in his mind. What if we did this, or that? Trying to come up with alternatives. But he couldn't find any. He was trapped. Strong held all the aces and he knew it. The only way he was going to get out of the situation he was in was to agree to Strong's ask and get as much help from Strong as he needed to move forward with Lucy.

An hour after the first call, Austin phoned DI Strong back and told him he would do it.

Chapter 32

'You look very nice,' Strong said looking admiringly at his wife, as she stood in front of the bedroom mirror. Catherine had definitely aged well, Strong thought. Like a fine wine. Even though she was now forty eight years old, she still had the same beauty that had first attracted him all those years ago when he'd first seen her with her friends in the Metro shopping centre. Anyway, why shouldn't she, forty eight wasn't that old was it?

Strong's thoughts wandered back to that first time they'd met. He had been a young policeman, just starting out on his career, and she was just about to start her training to become a nurse. Police Constable Strong had been sitting in the passenger seat of a panda car alongside his colleague, PC Adamson. A call had come through on the police radio that someone had been caught shoplifting in HMV and, as they were just outside the shopping centre, they took it. The store security guard had caught a teenage boy, trying to hide a couple of CDs down the front of his jeans. Not an uncommon situation. What was it with teenagers and shoplifting? Was it a rite of passage all teenagers had to go through? Strong remembered feeling a bit sorry for the boy, he'd looked like he was going to throw up when he saw the police arriving.

Catherine and her friends had also been in the record shop when the boy had been apprehended and Strong had to interview them as witnesses to what had happened. He'd immediately noticed Catherine. She stood out from her friends, slim with long blond hair, wearing a white t-shirt, denim dungarees and black and white baseball boots. Strong immediately liked her style, she seemed somehow different. After Strong had asked her what she'd seen, which wasn't actually very much as she'd not been looking at the boy when he'd picked up the CDs, he wrote down his name and number and told her to give him a call if she remembered anything else. He hoped she would. There seemed to be a connection of sorts. On his way out he looked back and saw her give him a knowing smile, one that only he would notice. The next day, when he arrived at his desk, there was a message from the duty sergeant saying she had called and left her number. He phoned her back and, after a bit of hesitation, he asked her out for a drink. And that was that. Thirty years later they were still together.

Like all relationships, it had changed over the years. They didn't go out together as much now as they had done when they were younger and there were other things they didn't do so much of too. Although they were still very much in love, it had gradually developed into a different type of relationship where they both spent a lot of time doing their own things. Strong's work had always taken up a lot of his time and as he had progressed through the ranks, he found he had more calls on his time outside of normal working hours. There always seemed to be some sort of local community or social event where his presence as a senior representative of the police was expected. He'd tried to limit these to a couple a week but it was hard to turn any of them down. They all had some sort of pull, especially the charitable ones. Usually he would go to these events on his own, in his official capacity as a senior police officer. However, tonight's occasion was different. Tonight, the two of them were going to the retirement party for one of the longer serving members of Strong's Serious Crime team, Dave Martin. It was one of the few times the Strongs had been out together in the evening since he'd come back from Leeds. With this one being an informal, social occasion, partners had been invited along too, which made a welcome change for Strong and Catherine. When he told her about it, she seemed pleasantly surprised.

'Oooh, a night out where we are actually together and you don't have to make a speech or shake everyone's hand,' she said smiling at Strong. 'It'll be nice to see some of your work colleagues again, I haven't seen Joe Campbell and his wife for ages. Did you say she'd had a baby?'

'Yes, I believe so. A little girl I think, or was it a boy? Campbell hasn't said much. We don't really talk about those sort of things,' he laughed. 'But no, he won't be there anyway. He's got a DI post in Leeds now, doing very well, I hear.'

'What? You didn't tell me that! But you should talk about personal stuff with the people who work for you, you know. I've told you before. If you're running a team, you should know what's important to the people in it. Everyone's different. They all have their own issues, their own dreams,' his wife lectured him. 'You need to know that to get the best from them.'

'I know, I know, you're right. I'll try harder I promise,' Strong replied, holding up his hands. She had told him the same thing many times before and he knew she was right. Probably. It just wasn't the police way.

Strong was pleased how things had worked out for Campbell. Sure, he had helped him get the detective inspector post in Leeds, following his own time there and the contacts he'd made, but he probably would have reached that level on his own, without Strong's help at some point. Maybe.

Campbell's posting was good for Strong too. Although he liked working with Campbell, he didn't like deceiving him about what he had done with Andy Austin. There was also the fact that Campbell was a good detective and Strong knew there were a few things that had happened which didn't quite seem right, raising Campbell's suspicions slightly. The visits to Austin's addresses, Strong calling the ambulance. Strong would have been the same had he been in Campbell's position. Thankfully, Strong had been able to come up with reasonable explanations for these events which, combined with Campbell's loyalty to, and his trust for, Strong meant that Campbell didn't seem to have taken his suspicions any further. Now that Campbell was in Leeds and Austin no longer a danger, Strong was hopeful that the whole Austin situation would fade in Campbell's mind. He would have enough other crimes to worry about in establishing himself in his first detective inspector post in Leeds. The two detectives still kept in touch but Strong had deliberately reduced the frequency of their interactions over the last few months to help Campbell forget about his previous role and switch his focus to his new DI post.

It was Friday evening and the retirement party was being held in a pub near to the police station, called The Drop Inn, although the pub was more commonly called Coppers, due to the fact that, more often than not, most of the customers in there were policemen and policewomen because of its proximity to their place of work. It had always been that way since the area had been regenerated around forty years ago including the building of the, then, new police station.

Strong and his wife arrived by taxi and after Strong paid the driver off with a generous tip, the two of them entered the bar. The retirement party was being held in a private function room towards the rear of the building and Strong led the way there. He'd been in this room many times before, almost always on some police related event. The couple entered the room and were immediately hit by a wall of noise. The place was already pretty full, with people standing around in groups chatting and drinking. Strong recognised the majority of the guests and knew most by name. He quickly picked out Dave Martin who was standing in a small group of four or five people at the bar on the far side of the function room. He guided his wife across the floor towards the group, nodding at several other guests as he passed them by. When he reached the group, they parted slightly to allow him and his wife in and Dave Martin turned to face him smiling. They shook hands and Strong introduced his wife before turning to the bar and ordering drinks for the two of them. It was a free bar, partly funded through police funds and Strong turned back to the group with two glasses of white wine, some variety of Pinot Grigio, and handed one of the glasses to his wife.

From what Strong knew, Dave Martin had been in the police since he'd left school. A real lifer. He was a grafter, not the sharpest tool in the box but a pretty reliable guy nonetheless. Someone you could give a laborious task to get on with and although he wouldn't be the quickest, he'd be thorough enough. Strong remembered once, working on a serious assault case, he'd asked Martin to check out the victim's mobile phone records. It was just a standard thing they would always do and Strong didn't expect anything to come out of it but Martin had found a link between the victim and his assailant which had been crucial to them being able to secure a conviction. Martin had been a hero that day and you never forget those days. He'd worked his way up to sergeant level, mainly due to just the length of time he'd been in the police force, and he was never going to get any higher than that. But that didn't matter. He had played his part and you needed people like Dave Martin in your team. Not everyone could be a hero all of the time and Martin had done as well as he could. Strong knew that he'd got a good pay off and he should be comfortable on his retirement pension as a reward for all the time he'd spent working.

As Strong moved amongst the various groups of guests, he found himself separated from Catherine who was doing her own bit of socialising. Strong knew she'd be perfectly happy doing that, she loved meeting new people and just getting to know them a little. "Everyone has an interesting story to tell," she'd often tell her husband. "You just need to spend a bit of time with them to find out what it is. Believe me, it can be really rewarding."

Catherine was getting a top up drink at the bar when another woman approached the bar and stood beside her. It wasn't anyone Catherine had met before, she was quite small and slim and smartly-dressed, probably somewhere in her mid-forties Catherine estimated.

'Hi, I'm Marsha Hughes, I work for your husband,' the woman said smiling at her. Catherine noticed that the woman was blushing slightly, maybe the effects of the alcohol. She was trying to remember if Strong had mentioned this lady before but she couldn't recall hearing him talking about her. Strong and Marsha, series 3 episode 3, the one where Strong's wife came into the story. That would complicate any potential relationship between the two main characters. There had been a few hints, but nothing obvious. Keep them guessing.

'Oh, yes, Mo's spoken a lot about you. It's good to finally meet you,' she lied and noticed the woman's blush getting stronger.

'Oh, really?' Marsha replied, surprised that Strong had even mentioned her to his wife. Maybe he spoke to her about all his colleagues? She wondered what he'd said about her. Hopefully good things.

'Can I get you a drink, what would you like?' Marsha asked her boss's wife

'Oh, thanks, that's very kind,' Catherine replied, although she knew it was a free bar, at least she'd offered! 'I'll just have another pinot grigio please, just put it in there,' she said to the young girl behind the bar and the two women took their drinks and retired to a nearby table to rest their feet and continue their conversation.

DI Strong and his wife had left the party around ten o'clock and were now back home sitting in their lounge. Strong knew that most of the others at the party wouldn't want the boss there all night, so he had quietly said his goodbyes to Dave Martin and left the pub to allow the others to get up to whatever they wanted to, without feeling that the boss was watching them. Strong knew that it was good for them to let their hair down every now and again and he didn't want to stop them doing that. Working for the police was often a highly pressurised job and they needed the opportunity to work off some of that steam. Besides that, Strong also felt a bit too old for late parties with lots of drinking nowadays. Those days were in the past.

'I saw you talking with Marsha earlier. What was she saying?' Strong asked as he picked up the TV remote to check the latest news.

'Oh, just this and that. She seemed nice, a bit serious. She told me her life story!' Catherine replied.

'Haha, that's typical you,' he replied, flicking through the news stories. 'She's been working in my team for, I guess, fifteen years now and I hardly know anything about her. How do you do it?'

'Emm, well maybe I just listen. You should try it sometime instead of living in your own world. There are other people out there too you know. All with their own lives to live and their stories to tell,' Catherine replied.

'Oh, yes….what was Marsha's story then?' Strong asked, finishing reading the last news story and putting the TV remote back down on the coffee table.

'Well it was mostly family stuff. All about her husband and son mainly. You know her husband died a long time ago, not long after her son was born and she's had to bring him up on her own since then?'

'Yes, I'd heard about that a while back but she hasn't said anything to me about it. She doesn't say much to me, but she's a good worker,' Strong replied.

'Mmm.. maybe you should ask her sometime,' Catherine replied. 'It seems her son's been a bit of a handful over the years but she says he seems to have settled down a bit and he's got his own place and a job now.'

'Oh that's good,' Strong replied as he walked to the kitchen to get a glass of water.

'Yes, funny when she said his name I couldn't help thinking of The Magic Roundabout. You know Dylan, the rabbit who played guitar, do you remember?' Catherine asked her husband.

'Dylan? That's her son's name?' Strong replied as he came back into the lounge. 'Dylan,' he repeated, trying to think what Marsha's surname was, 'that's an unusual name.'

He had a funny feeling.

'Did Marsha say what her second name was? I've forgotten. I'm getting old,' he laughed. 'Did she mention it to you?'

'I can't remember,' Catherine replied, standing up and yawning. 'Ooh, excuse me, I think I'm going to go to bed now. Are you coming up?'

'Yes, I'll be there in a minute, just got to check something first,' Strong replied, reaching for his mobile.

He picked up his phone and quickly scrolled through his contacts until he came to the one called Marsha. But that was all it said. Just Marsha. No surname. He got up and walked through to his study. Sitting down at his desk he switched his laptop on and waited till it fired up. He entered his password and immediately logged onto his email. He scrolled down his inbox until he came to the email that had been sent out with the details of Dave Martin's retirement party. He clicked on it and it opened up. He looked at who it had been sent to, carefully scanning the names until he came to the one he was looking for. Marsha. He stared at the screen for what seemed like a long time and then sat back in his seat.

'Shit,' he said, sitting forward again and looking at the screen to make sure there was no mistake.

'Marsha Hughes,' he said aloud.

He looked at his watch and then picked up his briefcase, opening it and taking out the small mobile phone from the inside pocket. He quickly switched it on and dialled a number. It rang a few times and then went to voicemail. He didn't want to leave a message, something that could be potentially traced back to him, but this was an emergency.

'Change of plan. Tonight's job is aborted. Do not do it. I repeat, tonight's job is off. Call me when you get this to confirm.'

He texted the same message to the same number and then sat back in his seat thinking. It had to be the same man, it was such an unusual name. There couldn't be two people called Dylan Hughes surely? He should have looked more into his background. He had been too keen to get his revenge, he hadn't looked deeply enough into who Dylan Hughes actually was. Why would he, he had killed Strong's parents that was all that mattered to him. But now he'd found out that he was actually Marsha's son, that changed things. Marsha was his most loyal and trusted colleague and he couldn't organise her son's killing just like that. He needed some time to think. But he needed to call Austin off to give him that time. He looked at his mobile phone, willing it to ring or ping that he had a message, but it just sat there blankly. Strong knew that Austin was planning to do the deed that night, but he didn't know where. He'd provided Austin with details of Dylan's regular movements but he couldn't remember what he usually did on a Friday night, or even the address of his flat. He glanced at his watch again. He needed to do something. He needed to stop it. He picked up his normal mobile and called a number. After a few seconds a woman's voice answered,

'Hello,' she said, 'everything okay guv?'

'Yes, sorry to call you Marsha but do you know where your son Dylan is tonight?' Strong asked.

'Dylan? Yes, he's at home. I just spoke to him. Why? Is everything okay?' Marsha asked. This was an unexpected turn in the script. Even she hadn't seen that coming. Maybe they were in series four of Strong and Marsha already? Things seemed to be moving on, first there was Strong's wife, now Marsha's son. What did that mean, maybe it was a good thing, the series was developing. More characters were coming into it.

'Yes, yes, nothing to worry about. I just need his address. Have you got it handy?' Strong asked.

'Sure, it's Flat five, Dartnell House in Holmesly, just off the High Street. Why do you want it?' Marsha asked, feeling a bit concerned at this unexpected late night request from her boss.

'Thanks, I know it,' he said as he picked up his car keys and walked quickly towards the front door. 'Don't worry, all's okay, I'll explain on Monday,' he said as he got into his car. 'Can you give him a call and tell him I'm coming to see him.

He's not in any trouble but tell him to lock his doors and not to let anyone in until I get there.'

'What's going on sir?' Marsha asked anxiously. 'Is Dylan in trouble?' She was hoping Strong and Marsha wasn't taking a surprising, unpleasant turn. She preferred it when it was just the two of them solving cases. Catching the bad guys. Did they really need her son, or Strong's wife involved? Maybe the ratings had been going down? The public could be so fickle.

'No, just do as I say,' Strong replied. 'I have to go now, I'll explain on Monday, but nothing to worry about,' Strong replied, hoping that was true, and he ended the call and reversed out of his driveway, turning quickly and heading towards the address Marsha had given him, hoping he was going to get there in time.

He drove his car quickly, but carefully, conscious that he was probably over the alcohol limit, and within a few minutes he turned into Holmesly High Street and immediately saw the three blocks of flats about half way down the road. He knew this area well, it wasn't the nicest of places and he'd had to arrest quite a few of its residents over the time he had been a policeman. The three blocks of flats had been built in the seventies in an effort to regenerate the area, but they now looked like they were in need of regeneration themselves. He turned into the car park and pulled up outside the entrance to Dartnell House. There was a fenced in basketball court off to his right but everything was quiet, there was no-one around. Or at least no-one that he could see. He hoped he had got here in time.

There still hadn't been any response from Austin on the small mobile phone which was now lying on his passenger seat. He got out the car and entered the block of flats. There was an old, faded diagram inside the doorway and he saw that Flat five was on the first floor. He quickly skipped up the stairs and was soon stood outside a blue door with a roughly painted number five on it, alongside a silver letterbox. He was about to knock when he heard a slight sound. Someone was coming up the stairs. He moved closer to the wall, edging out of the light. It was a man, dressed in dark clothing and wearing a black baseball cap, As he came towards Strong, the detective inspector recognised him as Andy Austin. He felt relieved, he'd made it in time. He stepped forward into the light and Austin stopped, a look of surprise on his face, as he saw Strong standing there directly in front of him.

'What are you doing here?' he asked.

'I tried to call you. Tonight's off. Change of plan. I just need to have a quick word with him. I don't need you to do anything. Just go home and I'll give you a call in a few days,' Strong said.

Austin turned around and walked back the way he had just come. He wasn't sure what was going on but he didn't ask Strong for any explanation. He was just glad that it seemed he wasn't going to have to kill Dylan Hughes. He subconsciously felt the kitchen knife in the pocket of his anorak. The knife that a few minutes earlier was destined to become a murder weapon. He wondered what Strong was up to. Maybe he was going to kill Dylan himself, maybe this one was too personal for him? But he doubted it. It wasn't Strong's style, he had always been very careful to stay in control while ensuring that he couldn't be tied to any of the murders and other attacks that Austin had carried out. Whatever the reason, Austin didn't really care. He just felt a huge sense of relief that he had been stopped and a hope that this period of his life would now, finally, be over.

Chapter 33

There was a light knock on Strong's office door before it opened slowly and Marsha entered the room. She looked as Marsha always looked, smart, professional looking, but Strong knew she would be worrying about the events of Friday evening and that he would have to do a good job to convince her that all was well. Marsha had been a great help to him over the years and he didn't want anything to spoil the arrangement they had. She sat down on the chair without speaking and he could see that she was looking pale and not her usual self. She had her hands tightly interlocked on her lap and she was looking tense.

'Morning sir,' she said hesitantly, 'I emm, I just wanted to ask you about Friday night. I, emm, wasn't really sure what was going on. What happened exactly?' This must be the start of a new episode of Strong and Marsha.

'Of course, Marsha, I guessed you'd be a bit worried and my apologies if I upset you at all, calling you like that,' Strong replied.

'No, no, you didn't upset me sir, it was just, well…, just a bit of a surprise to be honest and I just wondered what it was all about, is Dylan in some sort of trouble?' Marsha replied, locking and unlocking her hands as she spoke. She hadn't seen this twist coming in the story and she didn't like it.

'Yes, I understand and I should have handled it better, I didn't really think it through properly and I thought it would be easier and quicker to get your son's address from you. I should have just got it from the system, but....' Strong hesitated. 'Anyway, no, he's not in any trouble, it was nothing really. Not much anyhow. It was just one of my informants had left me a message saying that your son had upset someone, someone we knew, and I just needed to sort things out that was all. It's all done now, so case closed as they say,' Strong said, laughing and trying to make light of the matter.

'So Dylan's not in any kind of trouble then?' Marsha asked again, wondering why he had been involved at all. Just a bit part to add some flavour to her character? She hoped it was nothing more than that.

'No, no, he's perfectly fine. It was just one of these pieces of info I get from time to time. I know a lot of people and when I heard your son's name mentioned, I just wanted to make sure all was okay. It's all finished with now, he won't get any trouble, just a little misunderstanding,' Strong replied, smiling reassuringly.

'Oh thank you sir. I was so worried. Dylan's been a bit of a handful in the past, I'd be the first to admit it, but just lately he seemed to have got himself back on track. Got his own place and a decent job. I was hoping....well you know,' Marsha replied.

'Yes, well if you're okay, I'd better get on with things. The chief wants to see me later and I need to prepare,' Strong replied, glad that he'd managed to cover things off with Marsha.

'Yes, of course sir. Thank you again sir,' Marsha replied and she left Strong's office and returned to her desk.

She sat down, feeling mostly reassured. Not absolutely, but DI Strong's explanation of what had happened seemed reasonable, if a bit unusual. At least it wasn't anything to do with Marsha's real fear. But she worried that might be destined for a future episode, series seven, episode five. Or maybe they'd run it as a prequel, Strong and Marsha – The Beginning. That seemed to be the current trend. That would be when it all came out. She'd look a lot younger then.

Marsha could still remember that night eighteen years ago as if it had been yesterday. She'd been in bed, not able to get to sleep, waiting for Dylan to come home. He was at an awkward age, although she couldn't remember any age that hadn't been awkward. Maybe when he had been a baby. He'd just turned eighteen and Marsha had bought him a car, a second-hand Ford. She'd used all of her savings to buy it, her planned spa break would have to wait. She'd recently started an administration job in the new police station but she was still on a low salary grade and every penny had to be carefully watched. She didn't want Dylan to miss out on anything though, so would often put off treating herself if Dylan wanted something. The car had done a few miles, but the man in the garage said it was in good condition for its age, and Dylan was delighted to get it. He hated relying on his mum or friends to drive him around everywhere and the car had given him a new life, a new sense of freedom. Marsha was happy about that but it also brought her another worry. Now she didn't know where he was half the time and she always seemed to imagine the worst. On top of that, she knew he didn't take any notice of the drink/driving laws and she also suspected that he was dabbling in soft drugs. She'd noticed a funny smell in his room and suspected it was probably cannabis – although she had no idea what that really smelled like. It wasn't something she'd ever come across. When she'd tried to question Dylan about it, he just laughed her off and said he was eighteen now and could do what he wanted. It was at times like these that she wished his father was still alive to help her teach him some discipline. It was hard telling a big strong man, as Dylan now was, what he should be doing. Although he'd never threatened her, she knew that physically she was no match for him.

Marsha heard him come in and she looked at her bedside clock. It was eleven thirty, Friday night. That was fairly early for Dylan nowadays and she could hear him moving about downstairs. She decided to go down and see if he was all right. She found him in the kitchen, sitting on a chair, bent over with his head in his hands, shaking.

'Dylan, what is it? What's wrong?' she asked him, concerned.

He looked up, surprised, as if he hadn't heard her entering the room. His face was white and his eyes were big. He looked at his mother, but didn't say anything. He seemed to be in some sort of trance. Marsha walked across to her son and held him by the shoulders, looking directly into his face.

'What is it Dylan, what's happened?' she asked him again.

Dylan looked at her, but really looking through her, and she could see he was thinking about what he was going to say. Finally, he spoke,

'Nothing, I just had a bit of a fright driving home. It shook me up a bit, that's all. I'll be all right in a minute or two,' he said.

'What happened?' Marsha repeated.

'Nothing, I think I might have hit something with the car....an animal, ...maybe a dog or a deer or something. I just felt a bump as I came round the corner but it was too dark and I couldn't see anything,' Dylan replied.

'Did you not stop to look?' Marsha asked him, still holding his shoulders.

'No, I didn't think and well.....I'd had a couple of drinks. Not many though,' he added quickly. 'I looked in the mirror but didn't see anything. It probably just ran away.'

'Dylan, I need you to tell me exactly what happened. You were driving home, then what?' Marsha said surprising herself by how firm she sounded.

'I told you, I was driving along, it was dark, I went round a corner. I reached across to turn the radio up and then I felt a bump or maybe two bumps. I don't know, mum,' Dylan replied to his mum and she could see tears welling up in his eyes.

'So you think there were two ….bumps?' Marsha asked him.

'I think so, maybe a bang and then a bump, I don't know mum, he said, tears now beginning to roll down his face.

'Okay, I'm sure it will be fine. Why don't you just get yourself off to bed,' she said and she steered him out of the kitchen to the bottom of the stairs and watched as he went up to his room.

She knew there was no point in her pressurising him further tonight, deciding it was best to leave it until the morning. As soon as he closed his bedroom door, Marsha went back to the kitchen and got a torch from one of the drawers. The one where she kept batteries, bulbs, a couple of screwdrivers, things you might need once in a while. She then picked up her coat from the hallway, slipped it on, and went outside. She shone the torch on Dylan's car and walked all the way around it, not sure what she was looking for but thinking it might be the right thing to do. She couldn't do nothing, she had to do something. She noticed a crack in the passenger side headlight. Had that been there before? It could have been she thought but she didn't know. She would ask him in the morning. She then noticed something poking out of the radiator grill, a little bit of grey something. She bent down to get a closer look at it, shining the torch from one side to avoid the reflection back from the metal grille. It looked like a piece of material and she reached forward and gently eased it out with her thumb and forefinger. She shone the torch on it again. It was a small scrap of material, a few centimetres, maybe from a coat or a pair of trousers. Marsha had a strange feeling, and she felt herself shiver. She put the scrap of material in her coat pocket and carefully examined the remainder of the car. There were a few small dents and scratches, but nothing you wouldn't expect in a second hand car owned by a teenager. She looked carefully for any red marks, but thankfully couldn't see any. Marsha returned to the house and had another close look at the piece of material she'd found in the radiator grill, convincing herself it could have come from anywhere and could have been there for a long time. She put it in the kitchen bin and went upstairs to bed.

But she couldn't get to sleep, and after a few minutes she got up and went back downstairs. She went to the kitchen and retrieved the material scrap from the kitchen bin. She placed it in a small bowl, lit a match and set it alight. She wasn't sure why she was doing that, but she just thought it might be safer to burn it. It burned quickly and she threw the ashes into the downstairs toilet and flushed it twice, checking that it had all gone.

The next day was Saturday. Dylan had stayed in his room for most of the morning, which wasn't unusual for the weekend, and Marsha knew from experience it was best not to disturb him. When he finally did appear, just before mid-day, she gently tried to find out more about what might have happened the previous evening. She stayed calm, careful not to accuse him, or infer he'd done anything wrong, but, despite that approach, she didn't get anything more from him. He seemed to be being honest and genuine, not knowing any more about what might have happened and Marsha believed him. He was her son, how could she not believe him? What sort of mother would that make her?

Everything had carried on as normal for the next few days, the incident beginning to fade from Marsha's mind. Marsha went to work as usual and found she was really enjoying her new job working with the police. Dylan was doing a course at the local technical college on car mechanics. He didn't talk much about the course, but Marsha really hoped that he was enjoying it and would see it through to the end. He'd tried a few other things previously before giving up, but he seemed to have made a few new friends on this course so Marsha was optimistic that might encourage him to complete it. After that, she thought he might get a job in a local garage, there certainly seemed to be a lot of them around.

Everything changed on the Friday.

Marsha came home from work, looking forward to a relaxing weekend. A movie that evening then a bit of gardening on the Saturday before meeting one of her friends for a catch up coffee in town. She knew Dylan would have his own plans for the next two evenings but she might try and see if she could get him to have lunch with her on Sunday. She'd tempt him with a roast, that might do it. When he was younger they always used to have Sunday roasts together, just the two of them after his father had passed away.

As she opened her front door, she could feel, and hear, the morning mail and other freebies sliding across the hall carpet. She bent down to pick it all up, flicking through the envelopes as she closed the door behind her. Mostly junk mail, one that was probably a bank statement. The local newspaper. Nothing interesting. Was there ever? When she was younger the morning post had been exciting. Something to look forward to. She'd rush downstairs when she heard it popping through the letterbox. Often there would be a letter or a postcard, something to read. Something for her. At some point, when she was at primary school, her class had linked up with a school in Canada and they'd all got allocated pen-pals. Marsha's was called Alice and she seemed to have an amazing life which Marsha was very envious of. She made living in Canada sound like heaven. Her family always seemed to be doing something, going on trips, camping weekends and meeting grizzly bears! Marsha's life in the UK seemed so dull in comparison, maybe the odd squirrel in the garden, but never a bear! Marsha always looked forward to getting Alice's letters and she would spend hours in her bedroom, reading them over and over, imagining she was there, imagining she was Alice. They wrote to each other regularly for a year or so before the timescales between letters got longer. and the letters got shorter. There were only so many grizzly bears to talk about in Canada.

Marsha put the mail down on the kitchen worktop and the free local newspaper fell open. She caught sight of the paper headline. It seemed to be shouting out to her.

"Local Couple Killed in Hit and Run."

Marsha felt a shiver run down her spine and she gripped the kitchen worktop to steady herself. She pulled the paper towards her and read the headline again, frightened to read any more. But she made herself do it. She read the story three times to make sure. It had happened on the Friday night, the night Dylan had come home thinking he'd hit a dog or something. It had happened on a quiet road Dylan would probably have taken on his way home. Out of the main town, with no streetlights. It had been an elderly couple (two bumps), a Mr and Mrs Strong, both had been found dead at the scene around midnight. There were no witnesses and the police were appealing for anyone with any information.

Marsha folded the paper up and took it upstairs to her bedroom, placing it in her work bag. She didn't say anything about it to Dylan, as far as he knew he'd hit a dog and, sad as that was, he'd already moved on. On the Monday morning she went into work and, first thing, shredded the local paper. Out of sight out of mind. Not really, but she wanted rid of it.

Nothing more came of it, although Marsha couldn't erase it completely from her mind, as time went by there were days when it nagged at her less often. Dylan seemed to be getting on well. He'd finished his car mechanics course and although he didn't get a job from that, he had got a position in a local warehouse and was doing well. Marsha threw herself into her own job and a couple of years later (series one, episode three) she applied for a researcher/admin position with the Serious Crime Squad. It sounded really interesting and she was delighted when they told her she'd got it. A month or so after she started there was a team meeting and that was when she first met Mo Strong. He was a detective constable at the time and when he introduced himself to her with a firm handshake, she hoped he didn't feel her trembling. It was when he'd said his name. Strong. That was such an unusual name and Marsha immediately feared that there might be some connection to that awful night a few years ago. Back at her desk she did a bit of a trawl around the internet, but it wasn't as developed at that time and so she didn't find anything more that could link DC Strong to the accident. She felt partly relieved, but still concerned, and she knew she needed to find out for certain for her own peace of mind.

She found out later that day when she was getting herself a coffee from the kitchen. There might not have been the internet back then, but there was Dorothy. Dorothy had been in the Serious Crime team for many years and she'd also taken a coffee break. Dorothy was a very friendly person, liked to chat, some would say gossip, but she had helped Marsha settle in to her new role. She'd always been ready to show Marsha how to do something, or answer one of her many questions when needed. Marsha had really appreciated Dorothy's help in making the transition to her new role so much easier.

'Hi Marsha, how's it going?' Dorothy asked her as they waited for their drinks to brew.

'Good, really good in fact. I met a few more of the team today, at the meeting earlier, they all seem nice,' Marsha replied.

'Yes, some nicer than others though,' Dorothy whispered conspiratorially and laughed.

'Oh. I met DC Strong. He seemed nice,' Marsha replied.

'Oh yes, he's one of the better ones. Really nice guy. Married though.' Dorothy responded, laughing again at her own comment. 'He's destined for greater things I think, he'll be a detective sergeant before long and then more after that. He deserves it though.'

'Why do you say that?' Marsha asked her colleague.

'Oh, he's just a good policeman I guess and knows how to play the system. Gets on with everybody. Of course you'll have heard what happened to him a few years back?' Dorothy asked, lowering her voice slightly.

'No, what was that,' Marsha asked, beginning to worry about what her colleague was about to say.

'His parents were killed in a hit and run. The driver didn't stop and there were no witnesses. They didn't find anything, poor DC Strong, it almost finished him, but he seems to be okay now. Are you alright, you look a bit pale?' Dorothy said, noticing her colleague gripping tightly onto the kitchen top.

'What?...Yes, yes… I'm, I'm…fine. Just a bit, just need a coffee,' Marsha replied and focused on staying still despite feeling like she was going to collapse.

After hearing that, Marsha tried to avoid DC Strong as much as she possibly could. She was in some sort of state of shock and she even thought about leaving, but she was loving her job so much she decided to stay and just try to keep out of DC Strong's way as much as possible. She couldn't shake the feeling of guilt though.

Then one time she had to do a piece of research for him, on a case he was working on, and at the end he told her he was really pleased with what she had done. He seemed such a nice, genuine man. Marsha began to wonder if it was fate that had thrown them together, giving her a chance to do some good for him as some sort of recompense for what had happened to his parents. Over the subsequent years, more and more he'd asked her for help, often in secret, telling her it was best if only they knew. Strong and Marsha, the series was born. Marsha enjoyed working for him and she also knew how to keep a secret.

Chapter 34

DI Strong was driving home from work. It had just gone seven o clock and it had been a busy day. When was it ever not? Meetings, meetings and more meetings. It was summer though and the sun was still shining in the beautiful, blue sky. He was looking forward to sitting in the garden with a cold drink for an hour or so, just relaxing on his own. It was a Wednesday evening and his wife would be out at her art class. She'd taken it up a few weeks ago, saying that she'd always enjoyed art at school and she wanted to try and recapture some of that enjoyment again. Strong hadn't seen any of her work yet, she told him they were just covering some of the basics at the moment, but building up to an end of term watercolour painting. He would have to wait for that.

As he drove along, his mind started to wander back to something he'd been thinking a lot about over the last few weeks and months. Loose ends. When he'd first met Andy Austin and came up with the plan of using him to deliver justice where the system wouldn't let him, he thought he was being very clever. And to some degree it had worked well, although not exactly how he'd wanted it to, but maybe he'd expected too much. Maybe he'd also got a bit careless too. Not in incriminating himself, but more in not realising that as time went by it was inevitable that more and more people would become involved. People he had no control over. Loose ends. All of them with a little bit of detail or a little bit of involvement in some way. All of whom could maybe put two and two together and come up with something. Something that implicated him. Loose ends, it was a risk. Austin was the biggest, he knew a lot, but there were others too. How much had Austin told his girlfriend Lucy? What would she do if she knew? And there was Campbell, his trusted right hand man. More than once Strong had to cover his tracks with a plausible explanation, but he knew some were more plausible than others. Campbell was a good detective and Strong knew he would still have some doubts, some niggles in his mind, about DI Strong. And there were others. Too many loose ends. Marsha, Dylan, Ricky… even his own daughter Sophie and her flatmate Emily. How much had they talked about what happened to the estate agent in Leeds? He'd met Emily a couple of times before when Sophie had brought her home and he knew she liked to talk. How many people had she told that her mate's policeman dad had gotten someone beaten up? The list could be endless.

And Dylan. What to do with him? He couldn't just let him get away with killing his mum and dad and leaving them lying in the road like rubbish. He needed to be punished. But he was Marsha's son. Marsha his trusted confidante. The woman who had helped him so much in the past, without question. How could he do anything that would hurt her? She'd be devastated. At one point he'd considered using Dylan in the same way he'd used Austin. Getting him to clean the streets of scum. But when he met Dylan that night he knew immediately he wouldn't be able to do what Strong asked of him. He wasn't someone who could deliberately kill another person. He'd made a mistake, a big one, but that was it. Still, something had to be done.

Too many loose ends. Although there didn't seem to be any immediate threat to Strong, he knew that could change at any time, and if one doubt emerged it could easily snowball and gather more and more along the way. Maybe Lucy would persuade Austin that if they had a future together then there could be no more lies. The whole truth and nothing but. Would Austin do that and implicate him? The truth was he didn't know. Austin had deceived him at the start, killing two innocent people and although he now seemed more reliable, Strong knew that he couldn't fully trust him. If Lucy did get involved, love was a powerful weapon. Yes, too many loose ends and too much unknown risk out there, biding its time, waiting to strike.

As he turned into his driveway and pulled to a stop in front of the garage, Strong knew that he'd let this whole thing run for too long and it was only a matter of time before he'd have to do something about it. Before it was too late.

Chapter 35

Lucy was excited. And nervous. Today was the day little CJ was going to meet his father for the first time. She didn't know how Andy would react, but in her heart she thought it would go well. Despite what he'd done in the past, she knew he was really a good man and the last few months of them meeting, slowly getting to know each other again, had reminded her of that. In particular, over the last few weeks, he'd seemed really positive, just like the man she'd first known and fallen in love with. Something had happened, Lucy was sure, but she didn't know what. Maybe things were just getting back to normal and Lucy found it easier to think that might be the case. Forget about what had happened before and just move on. Of course it wasn't going to be as easy as that, but they were definitely headed in the right direction and everyone deserved a second chance didn't they? Why not her and Andy? If it went well today then she might suggest they take a walk to the park. It was supposed to be a nice sunny day and they could push little CJ on the swings. CJ loved the swing, squealing as it got higher and giggling away as it came back down again. Always a big, wide smile on his face. He seemed such a happy baby. After that they could all get some ice cream and sit on the grass. Just like all the other families.

A few miles away, in his own place, Andy Austin looked in the bathroom mirror and smoothed back his hair. He smiled and then laughed at himself, a little embarrassed. But the truth was he couldn't stop smiling. Today was going to be another step in the right direction, meeting Lucy in her own flat, the flat where they had once lived together. That was definitely another tick in the box. Since DI Strong had called off his "final job", he had only spoken with him once. He hadn't told Austin why he had stopped him killing Dylan Hughes, but he didn't really care. He was just glad that he had. Even better than that, he had told Andy that their arrangement was now complete, over, no more, and that, as promised, he would close down the police file and help him set up a new life with Lucy, if that was what they both wanted. Austin hadn't discussed it with Lucy yet, but meeting her in the flat today, felt like the right time to bring it up and start the conversation. He knew he would have to take it gently with her, a bit at a time, and it would probably take some time to get things moving, Lucy would need to be sure it's what she wanted to do and Andy knew she would have a few misgivings and lots of questions. At least Andy could be wholly honest with her now, not having any more secrets he had to keep from her. He could tell her everything and not have to live under a shadow of lying to her this time.

He picked up a bottle of red wine and put it in a green carrier bag before leaving his flat and heading towards the station. He was going to see Lucy in her flat, what used to be their flat, and she was probably going to have chocolate donuts for him! Could life get any better? He was so happy, he couldn't stop smiling.

Jack Wilson was driving along the High Street in his new car. Well, a new car to him anyway. It was actually a second hand, low mileage, one careful previous lady owner, fully serviced, Volkswagen Golf. Black and quite sporty looking. He was pleased with it. It was great to be driving again after his year's ban for the accident. Somehow it felt right, a man needed his car. He felt back in control again.

Things had definitely moved on for Jack since the accident, despite not being able to drive for the whole year, he'd managed to bag himself a beautiful new girlfriend, Rachel. He'd seen her around a few times, she was a friend of a friend, and one night they'd found themselves in the same club and got chatting. They swapped numbers at the end of the night and it had escalated from there. They now saw each other two or three times a week and spent most weekends together. They had even been talking about getting a flat together, which Jack was very keen to do, if only just to escape the family home. He felt a bit guilty about that though, his mum and dad were still grieving the death of their son, his brother, Pete. Jack still missed him greatly too, but he couldn't live like that for ever. It had been more than a year now. He needed to move on and live his own life. Maybe that would be with Rachel, who knew?

As he turned into Oatlands Avenue, the street was deserted apart from a man walking along the pavement on the opposite side of the road, with what looked like a bottle of wine in a green carrier bag. A bit early for that Jack thought. As he got closer to the man he recognised who it was. Suddenly he was transported back over a year in time to the day of the accident. But now they were both on their own, Jack in his car and Austin on the street. Nobody else. Jack noticed that Austin was looking happy with himself. He looked in his driving mirror and saw the street was still empty. As he got closer to Austin he suddenly accelerated and pulled the steering wheel sharply to his right, mounting the pavement and hitting Andy Austin straight on, their eyes momentarily locking. Austin had no time to react and the carrier bag flew out of his hand, into the air and landed on the road, red wine seeping out and running into a roadside drain. Jack pulled the wheel back to the left and re-joined the road, looking in his mirror as he did so. What he saw was an empty street. Empty except for a discarded carrier bag and a lifeless body.

Acknowledgements

There are a few people I'd like to thank for helping and encouraging me to write this latest book. As always these things are a team effort and their support has been invaluable. Firstly my family and friends, especially my wife and daughter, Gill and Megan, for just letting me get on with it - and supplying teas and coffees….along with the occasional biscuit as I sat upstairs, alone in the study.

I'd also like to thank my regular team of first readers who have all helped with the final draft – (Wee) Jean Farrell, Jim Anderson, Angela Wilson, Gill Anderson and Jackie Stanley. Thanks to all of you for your extremely helpful input, suggestions and just picking me up on the bits I'd missed.

Now that it's all done, it's time to start writing the next book….

Loose Ends – Due for release in December 2021

The third book in the DI Strong series. Following on from The Deal, find out what happens next.

Other books by Ian Anderson:

Jack's Lottery Plan

This is the funny and moving story of Jack Burns. One day he finds out that a friend has secretly won the lottery and he embarks on a clandestine plan to get a share. But his plan goes hopelessly wrong impacting Jack and his friends in ways he would never have imagined.

Jack's Big Surprise

Jack Burns is planning a surprise proposal for his girlfriend Hannah. But as is usually the way with Jack, his plan doesn't quite go the way he was hoping it would. Instead he finds himself hopelessly involved in a series of hilariously funny, and sometimes, unfortunate incidents. This is the sequel to Jack's Lottery Plan and finds Jack just as chaotic as he always is.

The Anniversary

In the first book of the DI Strong crime thriller series, Andy Austin's family are killed in a road accident. With a sense of injustice, he becomes obsessed on seeking revenge. He befriends DI Strong and uses him to help carry out his plan. As the police get closer to catching him it becomes clear that not everyone is without a guilty secret.

For more information, please visit my website at:
www.ianandersonhome.wixsite.com/ianandersonauthor

Or find me on Facebook at:
www.facebook.com/IanAndersonAuthor

Printed in Great Britain
by Amazon